Stone HEARTS

AMBER KELLY

ISBN: 978-1-7336899-3-9

Cover Design: Sommer Stein, Perfect Pear Creative Covers
Cover Image: Michaela Mangum, Michaela Mangum Photography
Editor: Jovana Shirley, Unforeseen Editing, www.unforeseenediting.com
Proofreader: Judy Zweifel, Judy's Proofreading
Formatter: Champagne Book Design

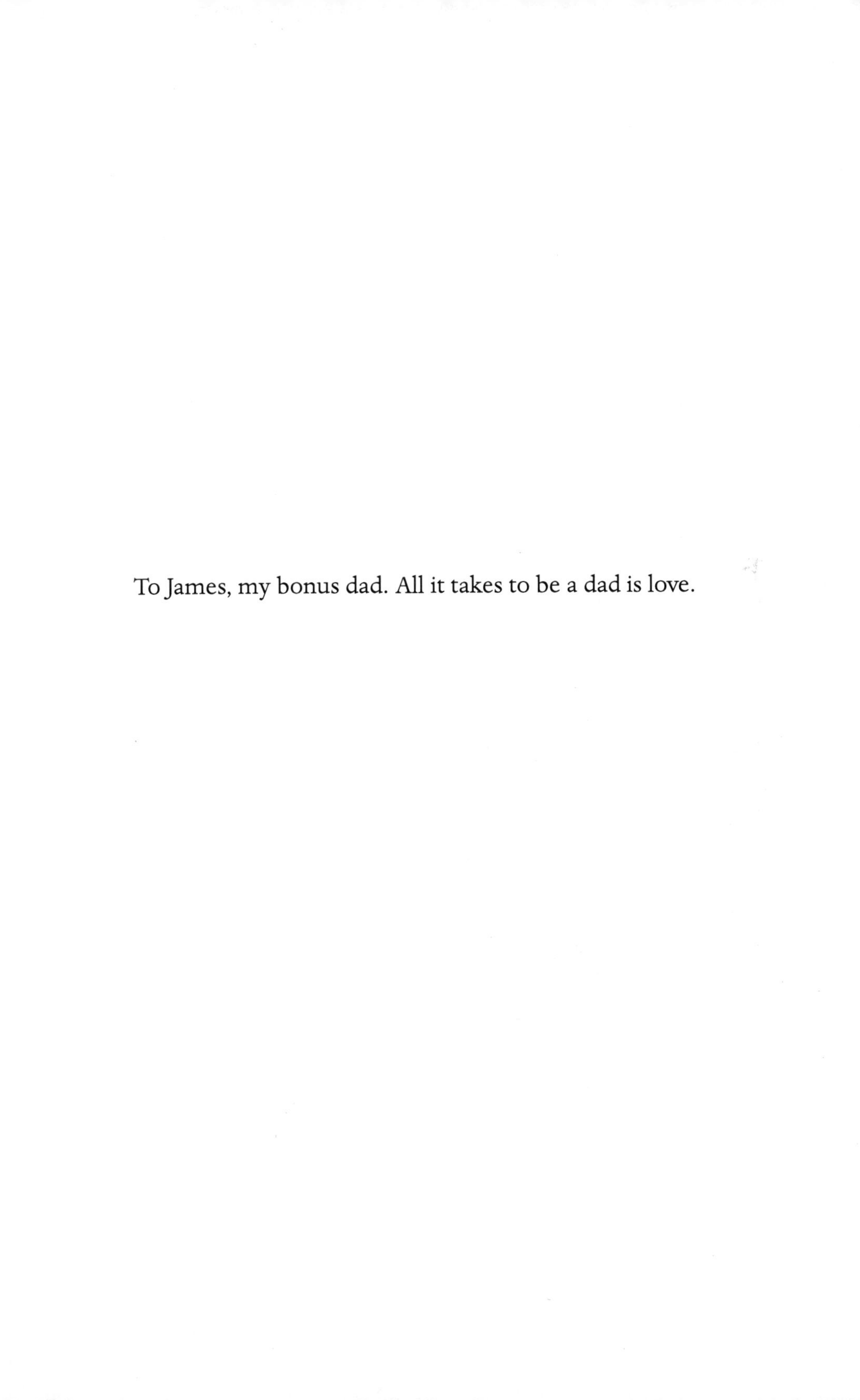

To James, my bonus dad. All it takes to be a dad is love.

Stone HEARTS

Prologue

DALLAS
Six Years Ago

SWEET JESUS, THIS LITTLE MONSTER IS RIPPING HIS WAY OUT OF ME. I've never felt pain like this before. When he finally makes it, he's getting his first time-out for trying to take all his momma's insides with him as he exits my body.

"Breathe, Dallas," Momma coaxes.

I tightly squeeze her hand as another contraction hits me like a freight train. The pain shoots down my spine and explodes in my pelvis.

"I *am* breathing, Momma," I scream.

"No, you're not, sweetheart," she says gently.

I cut my eyes to her and bite through gritted teeth. "Yes. I. Am."

"Whoa, I think her head spun around on that one. Did you hear that demon inside her?"

I whip my head around to my stupid brother, Payne, who has his iPhone pointed directly at me.

Why in the hell did I agree to have him in the room while I expelled a human torture device from my vagina?

"You shut the hell up and remember to stay north of the Mason–Dixon Line with that thing, asshole," I spew in his direction.

He just grins at me.

"Payne, dear, I think we might have to switch."

Momma is gently trying to tug her hand from my death grip. Her expression is one of intense pain, and the tips of her fingers are starting to turn purple. I let go as the contraction eases, and she hurries back from my bedside.

"Sure thing, Momma. I can handle it," Payne says as he hands the phone off to our mother. He plops down in the seat beside me and raises his right arm to me in an arm-wrestling challenge.

The doctor looks up from between my legs and pipes in, "He's crowning."

"Well, it's about time. I thought he had decided to stay in there until college," I spit out just as another contraction starts to ripple through me.

I grab hold of Payne's hand and nearly stand up in the bed. He starts trying to play thumb war with me, and I reach over and grab his thumb with my other hand and bend it back as hard as I can.

"Shit!" he yells. "I think you broke my thumb. That hurt like hell."

"Oh, really? Is a head the size of a bowling ball trying to break its way out of your pee hole? No? Then, suck it up, pansy-ass!"

"Children. Let's be nice. We don't want the baby watching his birth video and hearing you two cursing and fighting," Momma interjects.

"Give me one more big push, Dallas," the doctor commands before I can release my wrath on my mother.

Payne stands and grabs my hand harder. "Come on, sis. You've got this. Little man is almost here. One, two, three …" he counts as I bear down as hard as I can and push with all the strength I have left.

"He's out," the nurse excitedly announces just as I hear the first soft cry ring through the room.

"Oh my goodness, he's perfect!" Momma cries as I try to muster the energy to raise my head and look at him.

Before I have a chance, the doctor asks if anyone wants to cut the cord. I look up at Payne, and he is pale as a ghost.

Momma lays her hand on my shoulder and steps around to the doctor. "I do," she says tearfully.

A few seconds later, a gooey, bald bright red mess of screaming baby is laid on my chest.

His eyes are closed, and he is unhappy.

"Hey now, mister," I coo at him as I bring my hand to his face. "What's all that racket about? I'm the one who had her hoo-ha ripped in half, not you."

His eyes pop open as he starts to settle, and his little head moves to bring his face closer to my voice.

"There you are," I whisper. "You must be the one who's been playing soccer with my bladder the last three months, huh? You've already bought yourself extra chores until you're twenty-one, buddy."

He grunts at me and blinks his eyes shut.

"Already ignoring me, I see."

One eye opens back up, and what looks like a faint smile but is more than likely gas passes over him.

"Playing opossum. Mommy is onto you, Beau Stovall." I cradle him in my arms and plant a kiss on his forehead before nestling him under my chin. "It's you and me, kiddo. We're in this together from here on out. I will love you and protect you with my last breath. Oh, baby boy, we're going to have great adventures, you and me."

I hear a sniffle and look to Momma, who is staring affectionately at the two of us.

I hope that I'm able to be half the mother to him as she has been to me.

One

DALLAS
Present

"OKAY, THERE WE GO." I STEP BACK TO TAKE A LOOK AT my work.

Beau stands in front of me in his homemade Fly Guy costume for Book Character Day at school. The getup consists of white-and-black bug eyes made of small Styrofoam plates, construction paper adhered to a headband, and cardboard wings attached to a set of Daddy's old suspenders, paired with a brown turtleneck and cords.

He patiently waits, grinning, as I make my assessment, and he is undeniably the cutest little snaggle-toothed bug I have ever seen.

"Perfect!" I squeal as he beams at me.

I gather his lunch box and shoes as he runs to his room to grab his backpack.

"How am I going to get my coat on and get in the truck with my wings?" he asks as he runs back into the living room.

"You'll have to remove the suspenders and ask Mrs. Perry to help you put them back on when you get to your classroom."

He snaps them off and carefully tucks them under his arm. Once we are in the truck, I start our daily routine.

"What day is today, Beau?"

"The best day ever!" he replies.

"Why is it the best day ever?"

"Because we woke up this morning," he answers.

"What are we gonna do today?" I ask.

"We are going to be kind and give everyone our brightest smile."

"What aren't we gonna do?"

"Let anyone steal our shine."

"How much do I love you?"

"All the way up to the moon and back."

"That's right, baby," I confirm and put my right hand in the air for a high five, which he immediately returns.

God, I love this kid.

When I turn the key, the engine makes a horrible grinding noise, and then it rumbles before it stops.

Oh no, please don't do this right now.

I try again. The lights on the dashboard start flashing dimly, and the engine makes a clicking sound but doesn't turn over at all.

I groan, close my eyes, and lightly bang my head against the steering wheel.

A few minutes later, two little arms come around my neck from behind and squeeze.

"It's gonna be okay, Mommy."

I take a deep breath and turn my head to look at his earnest face. His round glasses have slipped down on his nose, and his big brown eyes are fixed on me. I remind myself that this tiny human takes his emotional cues from me, and I don't have the luxury of breaking down. So, I smile at him.

"You're right; it's going to be okay. In fact, I think this old truck just gave me extra time with my favorite boy in the whole wide world this morning."

He beams at me and sits back down as I fish my cell out of the bag. Momma already left for the bakery today, and Payne and Daddy left at the crack of dawn to meet the crop-dusting plane. I could call Sophie, but it would take her a while to get here, and I don't want Beau to be that late on Book Character Day. He'd be devastated if he missed the group class photo. So, I press Myer's name saved in my favorites in my phone and pray he isn't out on the ranch where he can't answer.

"Hey, Dal." His deep, rich voice comes over the line, and I release a relieved breath.

"Hey, Myer. I hate to call this early. I know you're probably busy with the calves, but my truck has crapped out on me again, and I need help getting Beau to school. Momma's at the bakery, and Daddy and Payne are having the fields dusted today."

"Pop can handle things for an hour or so. I'll swing by and pick you guys up in ten."

Myer Wilson is my brother, Payne's best friend. His family owns Stoney Ridge Ranch, which backs up to my family's farm and orchard.

"Thanks, Myer," I say as I collapse in relief.

"No problem. See you soon."

He disconnects, and I turn to Beau.

"Looks like you and I get to have a slice of Nana's apple cake before school."

"Yay! It really is the best day ever, Mommy," he exclaims before he opens his door, hops out, and runs to the porch of our home.

It's a modest home. My daddy and Uncle Jimbo turned one of the old grain silos behind my parents' farmhouse into a one-bedroom loft home for my son and me when my ex-husband was sent to prison on felony drug charges while I was pregnant with Beau. He has the bedroom, and I sleep in the loft that overlooks the open living room and kitchen. It's not big, but it's not tiny either. It fits us just right, and we love it.

I follow Beau inside, help him pop his wings back on so I can snap a few pictures and then I slice us each a piece of cake and pour us a glass of milk. He regales me with made-up stories of Fly Guy's coming adventures of the day while we wait for Myer to arrive.

The knock comes just as we finish up.

"It's open," I call as I rinse our plates.

Myer swings it open, and his blue eyes sweep the room. When

they land on Beau, he fakes a start. "Whoa, you scared me there for a minute. Are you a monster?"

"No, silly. I'm Fly Guy. I'm not scary at all. I'm a good friend," Beau informs him.

"Well, it's nice to meet you, Fly Guy. I heard you need a ride to school, but that can't be right. You have wings so you can fly yourself there."

Beau giggles. "They aren't real. See?" He turns around to show Myer the wings stapled to the suspenders. Then, he turns back around and lifts the big eyes off of his head. "It's me, Myer, Beau Stovall. I'm just pretending to be Fly Guy."

"Well, look at that. It is Beau Stovall. That's a good costume. You sure had me fooled."

"I tricked him, Mommy. I bet I'll win the first-place prize!" Beau says excitedly.

"In that case, we'd better get you to school right away," I say in answer.

He nods his head and races past Myer and out the open door.

"Thank you for rescuing me. Again," I offer as I grab my keys and purse from the kitchen island and follow.

"Not a big deal, Dal," he replies warmly as I ease past him.

He shuts the door and takes my keys from my hand to lock the dead bolt behind us as I wrangle my buzzing fly into the backseat of his white Silverado.

A few beats later, he climbs behind the steering wheel in the extended cab and passes me my keys.

"Go ahead and take your truck key off that ring. I'll drop you off at Rustic Peak, and I'll come back and have a look under the hood after lunch today."

Rustic Peak Ranch belongs to my best friend, Sophie's family, and I work there part-time, helping her keep the ranch's books.

"You don't mind?" I ask as I gladly hand over the key.

"Nope. Hopefully, it's something Payne and I can fix ourselves this time. If not, I'll hitch it to my truck, and we'll haul it over to Jackie's garage this evening."

Ugh, just what I need. Another repair bill.

"Don't start worrying now. It could be nothing," he says, reading the look of concern on my face.

"Yeah, Mommy. Don't let that truck steal your shine," Beau chimes in from the backseat.

"I don't think it's possible to steal your momma's shine, little man," Myer replies while looking at Beau in the rearview mirror.

A warm feeling pours over me, and I decide they're right. Me worrying about what's wrong with that old horse of a truck isn't going to change a single thing, so I might as well have myself a fabulous Monday. I'll figure out how to pay for the repairs once I know what they are.

I take my sunglasses from my purse and slide them on, and then I roll the window down and let the cool spring air waft through my hair as I plant a big old smile on my face.

Two

DALLAS

"Hey. Sorry I'm late," I apologize as I plop into one of the chairs at the kitchen table at Sophie's family's house.

Sophie and Braxton, her fiancé, live in a loft apartment above the big barn for the time being. He's currently building their new home about half a mile behind said barn. He hopes to have it finished, so they'll be able to move in after their wedding, which is scheduled for the second weekend in June. That's just over three months from now. I don't know how he is going to accomplish such a feat with branding season coming up fast and the wedding date even quicker, but Braxton Young is as stubborn as they come. If anyone can pull it off, he can.

Doreen, Sophie's aunt and kind of the matriarch of the Lancaster family, sets a cup of coffee in front of me. "It's fine. Sophie has been on the phone with Charlotte most of the morning anyway. She's flying in this weekend to see the ranch and meet everyone ahead of the engagement party. Then, Vivian will come in sometime next week for the festivities. She's bringing all the bridesmaid dresses with her for the fittings, and Elle's friend, Sonia's mom will be doing the alterations."

Thank goodness.

Vivian, Sophie's mom, was not a fan of the idea of trusting our dresses to a local seamstress, but flying to New York for fittings and adjustments was just not in the cards—or the budget—for Elle or me. Vivian finally gave in but not on the wedding gown itself. Poor Sophie will have to make at least two more trips to New York before the wedding—which is precisely why Vivian insisted the dress be kept in New York. She is still butt hurt that Sophie decided to stay in Poplar Falls with her dad and Braxton instead of returning to the city.

"Awesome. I can't wait to meet my citified doppelganger," I say as I sip the coffee I need so badly.

Sophie has told me on more than one occasion that Charlotte, her New York best friend, and I are like peas in a pod.

"I'm sure if Sophie loves her, we'll all love her. Sophie has excellent taste in friends," Aunt Doreen assures me with a wink just as the back door swings open, and Sophie walks in.

"Coffee. Yes, I need coffee," she whines as she slides into the chair beside me.

"Looks like your day has started as spectacularly as mine," I surmise.

She groans into the mug Doreen just set in front of her. "My mother is driving me crazy over this wedding. I swear it's like I have to wrestle her over every little detail."

"It's your wedding, Sophie. You need to be happy, not your mother. You're going to have to put your foot down," Ria, Sophie's other aunt, adds as she walks in, carrying a basket of vegetables she must have just cut from her garden.

"I know. That's what I was doing on the phone with her for the last hour. She wants to fly some five-star chef and his staff down on Stanhope's company jet to cater the reception. That's ridiculous, right? All Braxton wants is a pig pickin' catered by Walker's uncle. I mean, we are getting married on a ranch in spring. His groomsmen are wearing jeans and cowboy boots with their dress shirts and vests. I don't need a Michelin star chef serving caviar. No one will eat that here."

"What do you want?" I interrupt her rant to ask.

She stops and looks at me. "I want to walk down the aisle in a pretty dress, meet Braxton at the end and promise to love him for the rest of my life. Then, I want to eat, drink, dance, and celebrate with our friends and family under twinkling stars. I don't care if the food cost twenty-five dollars a plate or a hundred twenty-five dollars a plate. I don't care if the champagne is twenty dollars a bottle or two hundred dollars a bottle. As long as everyone enjoys it and enjoys themselves, that's all I care about," she says in answer.

"Then, there you have it. Pig pickin' it is. Walker's uncle is a master at roasting hogs, and you cannot beat his aunt's sweet potato casserole and pasta salad. Let Viv spring for the highfalutin bubbly if it will make her feel better. Brax won't be drinking that anyway. Walker and the boys will make sure there's plenty of iced-down beer and moonshine," I offer.

"She'll hate that, but I think it's a great compromise," she admits.

"Yeah, well, she got over the boys wearing jeans and boots. If she can survive that epic meltdown, then this one should be a breeze," I remind her.

"And you gave in on having that fancy designer do all the girls' dresses and having all the flowers flown in. Which I still don't understand. You're having farmhouse flower arrangements and centerpieces brought in from New York City instead of getting them from the local florist right down the road, who grows her flowers on her farm," Aunt Ria declares, shaking her head.

"I know, but I had to give her something," Sophie grumbles.

"I swear, if I ever get married again, we are going down to the courthouse and getting it over with. None of this madness," I share.

"You are not!" Sophie exclaims.

"Why not?" I ask.

"Because I missed your first wedding. I won't miss this one too. And what about Beau? Don't you want him there?" she asks incredulously.

"Jeez, you could come too. I'd need a witness. Besides, it's never going to happen anyway. Unless Keanu Reeves himself shows up and sweeps me off my feet, I'm pretty sure I'm done with the whole marriage thing," I assure her.

"What? Are you serious? Dallas, you're only thirty-two years old. You have a lot of life left to live. Don't you want to fall in love again?" Aunt Doreen asks.

I look up, and all three of them are staring at me.

"Not really." I shrug. "Beau is the only man I need in my life."

"That's nonsense and too much responsibility to put on that baby," Aunt Ria says as she places a hand on my shoulder.

"That's true. Your someone is out there too, Dallas. Don't go giving up on love because of that no-good ex-husband of yours. You and Beau deserve better, and God has better out there for you both," Aunt Doreen continues.

They're sweet, and I know they mean well, but I'm not sure I believe someone else could love me or if I even want that anymore. I'd be happy with a friend with benefits to knock the cobwebs off my bedpost every now and again, but I'm not interested in anything more than that. It's hard enough, just keeping my and Beau's needs met. The last thing I want to have to worry about is a man's need for time and attention.

I don't say any of that out loud though. I just smile sweetly and agree. No one wins an argument with the Lancaster sisters. No one.

Three

DALLAS

Once Sophie and I finish with our workday, she drives me to the school to pick Beau up. His face lights up when he sees her truck waiting in the pickup line as his class files out.

He runs toward us with his white wings flapping behind him.

"Hi, Miss Sophie," he greets as he wraps his arms around her legs and squeezes tight.

"Hey there. Don't you make the handsomest little bug?" she says as she squats down to his eye-level and tugs at his suspenders.

"I didn't win first prize, but I did get third." He holds up the yellow ribbon for us to admire.

"Who won first place?" I ask, a little miffed that my creation only garnered a third-place win.

"Logan. She was Mary Poppins, and she looked just like the lady on the movies," he explains as I bend down and help him remove his wings.

"I guess that deserved first place, then, huh?" I ask, trying to gauge his level of disappointment.

"It sure did," he agrees as he plucks the eyeballs from his head and hands them off to me.

"Brock got second, and he was Ron from *Harry Potter*. His mommy bought it for him for Christmas at the park in Florida. Mrs. Perry said mine was the best homemade costume though, so we all three got ice cream at lunch," he declares proudly while holding up three fingers and grinning big.

"That's pretty awesome," Sophie congratulates him, and he agrees enthusiastically.

He is such a great kid. He doesn't get offended easily, and he is always happy for other people when something good happens for them. I don't know how I got so lucky to end up as this human being's mother, but I'm grateful.

I buckle him in the backseat and toss his backpack beside him.

Then, I shut the door and mumble to Sophie over the roof, "They aren't even old enough to read Harry Potter yet. They were supposed to dress as characters from their favorite books. Brock's momma is a cheater!"

She wholeheartedly agrees.

Beau was robbed.

When we pull up outside of our home, the hood of my truck is up, and Payne and Myer are elbows deep in my engine.

Hopefully, this means a trip to the garage won't be necessary.

Sophie parks, and we all hop out and head to the boys.

"What's the damage?" I ask as we approach.

Myer's head pops up. "Alternator is bad. I called and had Payne and your dad pick one up from down at the parts store on their way home. Once we get it on and charge the battery, you should be good to go," he says as he wipes a bead of sweat from his face and leaves a streak of grease across his nose and cheek.

"How much was the part?" I ask my brother, who is loosening a bolt with a ratchet.

Thank goodness these boys grew up tinkering with tractor and truck engines.

"It was about a hundred dollars. Dad charged it to the farm's account," Payne answers.

"Great. He can add it to the outrageous sum I already owe him and Mom," I state as Beau pulls an old milk crate up beside Myer and climbs up to look under the hood.

"Beau, be careful. Don't get in Myer's and Uncle Payne's way," I scold.

"He's fine. We need an extra helper anyway, don't we, Payne?" Myer asks as he looks down at Beau's excited face.

"We sure do. Think you can hold on to this for me while I remove this bad part?" Payne asks as he hands the ratchet over to Beau.

"Yep. I got it," Beau says proudly as his uncle removes the bad alternator and chucks it to the side.

Sophie walks up beside me. "Look at his face. He sure loves helping the boys work, doesn't he?" she asks as we both watch Beau beam with pride as he holds the tool.

Myer and Payne are both patient and explain every step to him as he eagerly watches and listens.

"Yeah, he definitely has a little rancher in him," I agree.

I thank her for the ride, and she heads home to Braxton while I go inside and start cooking. The least I can do is feed the two and a half men out there, spending their evening working on my old truck.

"Thanks for supper. It was delicious," Myer says as he brings his plate over to the sink, where I'm running the water to do the dishes.

"You're welcome. It's the least I could do since you spent most of your day helping me," I reply without meeting his eyes.

He gently elbows me in the side. "You know I don't mind," he says earnestly.

I look up at his handsome face and giggle. The smudge of grease is still there, so I wet a dish towel, add a little dish soap, and turn to him.

"What?" he asks as I stand on my tiptoes and reach up.

"You have grease on your nose. Hold still," I command as I start to gingerly swipe at his face with my cloth.

He places his hands on either side of my waist to steady me, closes his eyes, and bows his head closer to me, so I can reach him easier.

I notice the way his long eyelashes fan out on his cheeks and the smattering of dark stubble that frames his strong jaw. He has a nice face—a really nice face. I involuntarily trace his jaw with my fingertip as I admire it.

His breath stutters for a brief moment, and his fingers grip tighter on my hips.

His eyes open, and they meet mine for a split second before a throat clears. We both turn to see Payne holding Beau wrapped in a towel.

I step back and drop the cloth into the sink before walking to them with my arms open. "Thanks for giving him a bath for me," I say as I take my sleepy boy into my arms.

"Are we going to have a sleepover?" he asks as I start to walk him toward his room.

"Not tonight, baby. It's a school night, and Uncle Payne and Myer have to get home and get some sleep because they have to be up early for work tomorrow."

"But they can sleep in my room," he offers as a big yawn escapes.

"Maybe this weekend, buddy," Payne calls over my shoulder.

"Promise?" Beau asks as we reach his door.

He knows that we don't make promises in this house unless we intend to keep them.

I turn and raise an eyebrow at my brother. He walked right into that one.

"Yeah, I promise."

He won't be able to get out of that, which means that I'll get a night to myself. It's perfect timing, too, with Sophie's friend Charlotte coming into town this weekend. I won't have to ask Momma to babysit or pay Sonia.

"Tell Uncle Payne and Myer good night."

"Good night. Don't let the bedbugs bite," he singsongs as he waves at them, and I carry him to his bed.

We recite his bedtime prayers, but he is fast asleep before I retrieve the book from his shelf to read his bedtime story, so I tuck him in tight and kiss his forehead. I pull his door almost shut, and I tiptoe back into the living room.

Then, I whisper to Myer, who is standing by the door, "You heading out?"

"Yeah, Payne just took off, but I wanted to make sure you locked up when I left," he whispers back.

I look over to the kitchen, and the dishes are on the drying rack, the table has been wiped down, and everything is put away.

"Thank you again, Myer. I don't know what we would have done without you today," I say as I wrap my arms around his middle and squeeze.

"Anytime, Dal," he answers as he lays a kiss on the top of my head.

Then, he walks out on the porch, and I shut the door.

I sigh. It's been a long day. I want to take a hot shower, get in my pajamas, and watch some trashy reality TV for a while.

"Locks!" I hear the command yelled from the driveway.

I quickly turn the dead bolt and slide the chain in place.

I don't know why he's so demanding. I live on my family's twenty-acre farm, practically in my parents' backyard, and Payne's house is so close that I could throw a rock and hit it. It's not like we're in any danger out here.

Still, that warm feeling slides over me again because he stayed to make sure we were secure before he headed home. We sure are blessed to have a friend like him.

Four

DALLAS

"Order's up, Dallas," Andy bellows as he bangs on the silver bell in the window.

"Yell or bell, Andy. This place is twelve hundred square feet. Choose one," I call out to him as I wipe down the cracked red pleather seat of one of the recently emptied booths.

I quickly rinse my hands, and then I load the hot plates on a tray and deliver them to the waiting table as the door chime rings to let us know another customer has entered the diner.

"Here you go, Joe. Be careful; these plates are extra steamy today. I can't have my favorite customer getting blistered."

I wink at the kind, elderly gentleman who comes in every single morning for scrambled eggs, jelly toast, and coffee and always leaves a tip equal to the bill.

I grab two menus and head over to the table where the new arrivals have just seated themselves.

"Welcome to Faye's," I greet as I place menus in front of them. "You guys must be new in town," I add as I turn over their coffee cups.

"Is it that obvious?" the good-looking, dark-haired stranger answers in a sexy-as-hell baritone.

"Not really. I just know all the comings and goings here in Poplar Falls, and I never forget a face, especially a handsome one. You guys just passing through?" I flirt as I retrieve a carafe, raise it in question, and begin to fill their mugs when they both nod.

He moves his green eyes from the menu, and a dimple peeks out on one side as his mouth lifts in a bashful grin. Then, he extends his arm. "Brandt Haralson," he offers as I take his hand.

"Dallas Stovall. So, you're our new vet," I say as the name registers.

He sits back and crosses his arms over his chest. "You really do know all, huh?" he asks with a raised eyebrow.

"Sure do. Plus, I work in the office over at Rustic Peak Ranch, and my parents and brother own Hendersons' Farm and Apple Orchard. This is just my side hustle."

I sit down beside him, and he does a surprised scoot across the bench.

"Dr. Sherrill retiring is big news around here. Your name has been on everyone's curious lips since he announced it last year. We weren't expecting you until the end of summer though," I continue.

"My house in Oregon sold quicker than I expected, so we decided to head this way and look at properties. Dr. Sherrill offered his guesthouse while we choose, and I offered to help with the branding season. Figured it was a good way to get out and meet everyone and get acquainted with the town before I take over the practice," he explains.

"Good call. People will be more accepting of you if Doc brings you around and introduces you."

"I take it, I have big shoes to fill?" he asks.

"Yeah, he's well-loved, but don't worry; we're a very welcoming town once we get to know you. Might work you to the bone, but we'll feed you and treat you kind. And just who is this beauty you have here?" I look to the older woman seated across from us.

"I'm sorry. How rude of me. This is my mother, Elaine," he introduces.

"It's nice to meet you, Momma Haralson," I say with a smile.

"The pleasure is mine," she offers in return.

I stand as I hear Andy's bell go off again.

"I'll give you two a chance to decide. Everything is good, except for that egg-white veggie scramble thingy Faye added last week. Yuck.

But you can't go wrong with the home fries, and the pies are made by hand and to die for. A secret family recipe. Dessert's on me, by the way," I say as I walk off.

"Dessert? At breakfast?" I hear Mrs. Haralson whisper to Brandt.

"Yes, ma'am. It's never too early for pie!" I call back over my shoulder, and I hear a rich laugh ring out around me.

After my shift, I drive out to the house to deliver sandwiches to Daddy and Payne before picking Beau up from school.

It's my favorite time of year. The weather is just starting to warm up from the blistering winter freeze, so you can open your windows and let the fresh air in, but the nights are still cold enough to require a fire to keep you cozy.

As I pull up to the farm's gate, I'm greeted by the scent of hollyhocks blowing on the breeze. All of Momma's flowers are starting to spring up in a stunning array of colors, and the trees are beginning to prick back to life. Early spring in the Colorado Mountains is hard to beat.

I find Daddy and Payne in the backyard, tinkering with an old lawnmower.

Daddy retired from the day-to-day running of the farm and orchard last year after his knee replacement surgery. His heart still very much wants him to be out there, working in the fields full-time, but his body has had enough. It hasn't been easy for him. Marvin Henderson is not a man comfortable with idle hands. So, he sleeps in a little more than he used to and then spends his days piddling around and tending to Momma's flowers. He rides the orchard and fields on the Gator with Payne sometimes. He still feeds the livestock and, much to our dismay, saddles and rides his horse from time to time.

Payne and I used to fuss at him for it, but Momma sat us down one afternoon and told us that if we put him out to pasture, he will wither away. Men like Daddy are not built to sit and drink tea and watch grass grow. They need to be useful. So, Payne lets him come and go as he pleases and do what he feels up to doing, and he accommodates and respects Daddy's input and help.

"Hey, Daddy," I greet as I walk up with the bags of food.

"Hey, baby. Did you have a good shift today?"

"All right. It wasn't too busy, but I made decent tips. Speaking of which"—I pull the bills folded together from my back pocket—"this should cover the cost of the alternator."

I hand the cash out to him, and he eyes it for a minute and then focuses back on the mower chain he is cleaning.

"Keep it. You can pay me back later."

I walk over to him and stuff the money into the front pocket of his flannel shirt. I kiss him on the cheek. "No, Daddy. I appreciate it, but you can't keep me up forever. I really did make decent tips today."

He sighs but doesn't argue with me.

"Come on, Dad. Let's get cleaned up. I'm starving," Payne says as he tosses a wrench into the toolbox at his feet.

"I'll grab some glasses and tea and set you guys up on the front porch," I offer as I head in the direction of the house.

A few minutes later, they join me and tear into the sandwiches I had Andy make them.

"I met our new vet today," I inform them.

"Yeah? He's early. We weren't expecting him in town for months," Daddy notes.

"Yep, he and his momma are here, house-hunting, and he's going to help Doc during the brandings this year."

"What was your impression of him?" Payne asks with his mouth full.

I shrug. "Hard to judge his medical skills from his breakfast order, but he seems nice enough, and he is a handsome devil." I waggle my eyebrows at them.

"Great. The last thing I need is you dating and dumping the only vet in town," Payne mumbles.

"Who said anything about dating him? I said he was attractive; that's all. I like my men a little rougher around the edges," I inform him, insulted by his assumption that I would throw myself at any new man who waltzed into town.

"Maybe that's the problem, baby girl. Your track record hasn't been stellar. Perhaps you should give a different kind of fella a chance," Daddy chimes in from his perch on the porch swing.

"A chance to what exactly?" I ask him.

"A chance to heal that broken place inside you."

Maybe I don't want it to heal. Perhaps I want it to stay as raw as it has been the past six years as a reminder to never let myself be so blinded by love again that I can't see what's happening right under my nose. I have more than myself to consider now. Every choice I make affects Beau, and I will never let my bad decisions touch him.

Five

DALLAS

"WHY DO YOU GET TO DRIVE?" I ASK AS I WALK OVER TO the four-wheeler.

"Because it's my four-wheeler. Well, it's Braxton's, and what's his is mine." Sophie grins over her shoulder at me as I climb on the back and wrap my arms around her.

"I'm not sure I trust your skills out in the woods. I should have brought Beau's helmet with me," I mumble as she starts the machine.

"Oh, quit being a baby," she says poking fun at me.

"A baby? You do realize you were the girl who didn't know how to drive a freaking car six months ago, right?" I remind her.

"But I do now," she yells as she presses the gas, and we shoot off into the trees.

"Jeez, I think you left my stomach back there. Slow down, speed racer," I demand as we fly onto the path.

She ignores me and keeps the crazy speed as I watch my life flash before my eyes.

"I've created a monster," I admit as I accept my fate and hold on tight.

We make it to our destination in one piece—*thank you, Lord*—and she parks in the pack of trucks.

I look up at the impressive progress that has been made on the house. The last time I was here, it was just a foundation, chimney, and framework. Now, the walls have been sheet-rocked, and there's the beginning of a roof.

"Wow, Brax is not playing around," I muse as we make our way to the ramp that serves as the makeshift entryway.

"I know. He's working himself and the boys to death. He's up at the crack of dawn, and then he works the ranch all day. Once he's done, he heads straight here and works until there is no daylight left. Somehow, he talked Payne, Myer, Walker, and Silas into pitching in too," she explains as we walk through hanging plastic, careful not to trip on any of the equipment lying around.

"It looks good though," I praise as I check out the work they have done.

"It does. He wants to do as much as he can with his own hands before we have to get a crew in here to finish off the electrical and plumbing. Plus, I want to hire out the outside stone and shingle work and the floors and interior painting as well. He's fighting me on it, but if we don't, I fear I won't have a groom in three months. He'll have wasted away. I've had to force him to come home and eat and sleep at night," she says as she shakes her head and calls out to them.

"In here, Princess," Braxton answers, and we follow the sound of his voice.

We find them in what will be the living room. They are on scaffolding and adding rocks to what will be the face of a large fireplace that will cover one wall.

"Wow, that looks so good!" she squeals.

Braxton smiles a rare, pleased smile at her reaction. "It's turning out better than I thought, and once we get the mantel stained, it'll look even better."

"I love it," she proclaims, and it's easy to see why she does. It's gorgeous.

I walk over to what will be huge bay windows that overlook the gap and down onto the river. "This is a great view," I tell her.

"Yeah, the deck will be built next week. It'll be nice to be able to sit out there and sketch while he's in here, working."

Sophie owns a successful jewelry design business with her friend

Charlotte in addition to running the office of Rustic Peak. If you can't find her, she's more than likely snuck off somewhere with a sketchpad.

"I'm so happy for you," I say as I turn to face her. "Raising a family here is going to be a dream come true."

"I know, right? If you had told me this time last year that I would be getting married and building a house in the woods on a mountain in Colorado today, I would have laughed in your face."

"I reckon that's what Momma means when she says, 'If you want to hear God laugh, just tell him your plans,' " I muse.

"Isn't that the truth?" she agrees.

We walk back over to the men.

"All right, fellas, it's time to call it a day. Aunt Doreen sent us to gather you for supper, and she made us promise not to come back without the lot of you. So, wrap this up. And one of you is giving me a ride back to the house because I'm not getting back on that four-wheeler with Mario Andretti over here." I sling my thumb over in Sophie's direction.

Braxton raises his eyebrow to her in question.

"Tattletale," she says as she sticks her tongue out at me.

"I got you, Dal," Myer offers from the scaffolding platform.

I glance up to see him bent over, watching us with an amused look on his face.

"My hero," I say, accepting his kindness.

"Oh, stop being so dramatic. I'm not that bad." Sophie elbows me in the side.

"Woman, I saw my life flash before my eyes. My poor, short life. You could have made Beau an orphan. Do you want that on your conscience when you meet your maker?"

She rolls her eyes at me as we hear Braxton chime in, "I'm getting you a helmet for that thing. And if you don't slow down, I'll put a plate on it, so it'll only go ten miles an hour."

She gasps and turns to me. "See what you did? Snitch."

When we all make it back to the house, Doreen and Ria have the table set and a feast waiting. Jefferson, Sophie's dad, and his wife, Madeline, are seated at one end of the table with Pop, Sophie's granddaddy. Elle, Braxton's little sister, is sitting next to them.

We all file in, and Doreen starts making a fuss of getting everything out of the oven. Emmett, Jefferson's best friend and Doreen's sweetheart, comes in from the back porch, carrying a few extra chairs with Beau on his heels.

"Look, Mommy," Beau says as he holds up a jar with a small green frog in it.

"What's that?" I ask with a cringe.

"It's Fritz, my new best friend," he says proudly.

"Fritz the frog. Awesome," I say as I look to Emmett, who grins at me.

"Why don't we leave Fritz on the porch while we eat?" Aunt Doreen suggests.

"Can we put something in his jar to play with, so he won't get bored and try to escape?" he asks her.

"Um, well, let's see what we have." She looks around the kitchen at a loss.

Emmett plucks a wine cork from the counter and hands it to Beau. "Here's something he can climb on. I'll take him outside. You go wash up for supper," he says as he takes the jar from Beau's hand, and Aunt Doreen leads him to the bathroom to wash his hands.

"What the hell do I feed a bullfrog?" I ask the table at large.

All of the guys have taken a seat and started to load their plates.

"Crickets or grasshoppers. Some will eat worms if they're fresh," Walker helpfully answers.

"Gross," I say as I cover my eyes.

"What's the matter, Dal? You aren't afraid of worms or crickets. I've watched you bait a hook with both," Myer taunts me.

"Yeah, but the fish don't live in my house, and I don't have to actually feed them and watch them eat," I say, scrunching my nose. "I prefer my house animal-free."

They all laugh.

"Get used to it. You have a boy. He is going to come home with all sorts of critters," Jefferson pipes in.

I sit down and place my head in my hands.

"I'll take him to get a tank and freeze-dried crickets tomorrow, and I'll teach him how to feed and take care of Fritz himself," Myer offers from beside me.

I look up at him. "Really? Thank you."

I sigh in relief.

"You're welcome," he whispers.

Six

DALLAS

After dinner, I wrangle a sleepy Beau into the truck and head home.

I park in front of our house and move around the truck to carry him in. He fell fast asleep about ten minutes into our drive home.

I get Beau loose and grab Fritz's jar from the backseat. I start for the porch when I notice my front door is ajar. I freeze in confusion for a moment, and then alarm hits me.

Beau rouses in my arms at the sudden stop. "What's wrong, Mommy?" he asks, confused.

"Probably nothing, baby, but let's hop back in the truck," I whisper as I quickly walk back to the truck.

I set him on the passenger seat and close the door. Then, I run around to the driver's side. I get in, lock the doors, and put the key in the ignition. Daddy and Momma are at a church choir meeting, so I fish my phone out of my purse and call Payne.

"Come on, Payne. Pick up," I say to myself.

He answers on the third ring. "Hey, sis. What's up?"

"Beau and I just got home, and my door is standing open," I say with a little more panic in my voice than I intended.

I look over to Beau, who is closely watching me with his brow scrunched in concern.

"It's okay, buddy," I say to him as I run my fingers through his hair and try to soothe him.

"I'm on my way," Payne says before the line clicks off.

"Mommy, are you okay?" Beau asks, fear lacing his voice.

"Yeah, baby. Mommy probably just forgot to shut the door this morning, but Uncle Payne is going to come and make sure before we go in," I say to reassure him.

He looks back at the porch with trepidation. He's a smart kiddo, and he knows the likelihood of me forgetting to shut and lock our door is slim to none.

A few minutes later, Myer's truck pulls in behind us, and Payne and Myer jump out. Payne heads to the house as Myer walks to us, and I roll down my window.

"You guys all right?" he asks as he looks into the truck and does a once-over of both me and Beau.

"We're fine. I'm probably just overreacting. I don't know how the door got open," I tell him, relieved and feeling a little silly now that they have arrived. "What are you doing here anyway?" I ask.

"I was at Payne's, just dropping him off when you called."

I look back at the door, waiting for my brother to emerge. He finally peeks his head out about five minutes later. He holds his hand up for us to stay put, and he walks around to the back of the house.

When he comes back around, he's carrying a five-gallon green bucket, and he walks up beside Myer.

"Everything is clear inside. It doesn't look like anything was taken, and it doesn't appear your lock was jimmied or your door forced open, but the kitchen window was wide open, and this bucket was under it," he says as he holds the bucket up.

"I had the window slightly open over the weekend, letting the fresh air in," I tell him.

"Did you leave it open, even when you left?" he asks.

I don't think much about leaving the kitchen window open because it's pretty high up.

"I can't remember. I do leave it cracked sometimes when the weather is nice," I admit.

"Why would anyone go to the trouble of climbing in a window and not take anything?" Myer asks.

"Beats me. Unless it was some kids messing around or someone broke in, something spooked them, and they ran off before they could grab anything." Payne shrugs.

I remember Beau having that bucket in the front yard yesterday.

"Beau, were you playing with that bucket?" I ask my son.

He leans over and looks out as Payne holds it up. "Yes, it was my barrel when I was playing rodeo," he says.

I take a relieved breath.

"He probably dragged it back beside the house," I tell them.

"Are you sure you shut and locked the door?" Myer asks me.

I think I did.

"I can't be sure. We were running a little late this morning, and we were in a hurry. So, it's possible I didn't," I say, still unsure how I could leave my door open and not notice. I have never done it before. "I'm sorry, guys. I guess I had you run out here for no reason," I admit, embarrassed that I panicked over nothing and feeling pretty bad that I freaked Beau out.

"That's okay. I'd rather you call me to make sure than walk in on an intruder," Payne says as he opens my door for me.

I exit, and Beau scoots over the seat of the truck. Myer reaches in and plucks him out.

"What's an intruder?" he asks.

"It's an uninvited guest," Myer answers.

"Are they bad guys?"

"Sometimes," Myer says carefully.

Beau hugs his neck tighter, and Myer gives me an apologetic look over his shoulder.

I walk over and place my hand on Beau's back. "It's okay, baby. It wasn't an intruder. Mommy just didn't shut the door this morning; that's all. There's nothing to be scared of," I say as he turns and leaps from Myer's arms into mine.

"Can I sleep in your room tonight?" he asks as we walk inside.

"Sure, but just tonight, buddy," I tell him as I set him on his feet. "Go brush your teeth and change into your pajamas, and then you can crawl into my bed."

He takes off toward his room.

"I'm sorry," Myer apologizes.

"For what?" I ask.

"For telling him intruders are bad guys, but he needs to know in case there ever is a break-in. I wasn't trying to scare him," he explains.

"It's okay. I would've told him the truth too. I try not to lie to him about important stuff."

I look over at the kitchen window above the sink, which is still wide open. I know I only opened it a couple of inches. *Could the wind have blown it up?* I walk over and firmly shut and lock it. A feeling of unease still clings to me.

"If you're sure you guys are okay, we'll take off," Payne says on a yawn.

They worked hard today, and I know they are both exhausted.

"Yes, get out of here. We're fine," I say as I shoo them toward the door.

Payne kisses me on the cheek and walks out on the porch.

"I'll be here around eight in the morning to pick Beau up," Myer reminds me as he follows.

"I'll have him ready when you get here. Thanks again, guys," I call after them. Then, I shut the door and turn the dead bolt.

I turn back and look around the house. Nothing is out of place.

Beau comes out of his room in his PJs, pulling his blanket behind him. He climbs the stairs to my bed, and I turn the lights out and follow.

Seven

MYER

I knock on Dallas's door and wait. I promised to pick Beau up first thing this morning and take him into town to get his frog supplies.

The door swings open, and there Beau stands, still in his pajamas.

"Good morning, little man," I greet him as I walk in.

"Mommy didn't wake me up!" he whisper-shouts.

"Where is she?" I ask as I look around the room.

"She's still sleeping," he says quietly as he points up toward the loft. "Let's go wake her up," he suggests as he giggles.

He takes my hand and pulls me toward the narrow steps that lead up to the open loft where she sleeps.

"I don't want to scare her, buddy. Maybe you should go tell her I'm down here," I say as I pull myself loose.

"Okay, be right back. Don't leave," he says as he trots up the steps.

I can hear him as he climbs up and starts rousing her.

"Mommy. Wake up, sleepyhead. It's morning time," he says sweetly.

She mumbles something incoherent.

"Mommy, wake up! Myer is here to get me, and I need to get dressed," he informs her a little more loudly.

A few seconds later, her head pops over the railing. "Oh God, I'm so sorry, Myer. I overslept. We'll be down in a minute," she says as I look up and see her pull a pair of shorts up her legs and under her sleep shirt.

Damn, I'll be thinking about those bare legs the rest of the day.

They both come racing down the stairs, and they're a sight. Her red hair is a mess of unruly curls, and her face is makeup-free. Beau's blond hair is sticking up in all directions, and his glasses are crooked on his nose. I swear I could wake up to this sight every morning.

"I can't believe I didn't hear my alarm go off. I meant to have him fed and ready when you got here. I'm supposed to be at Sophie's in half an hour to head to Denver," she says frantically.

"It's all right. We'll stop at Faye's, and I'll feed him breakfast," I assure her.

"You're the best. Are you sure you don't mind keeping him today? Charlotte's flight lands at eleven thirty, and then we'll probably stop for lunch before we head back. It might be three o'clock or later before we make it back to Poplar Falls."

"I don't mind at all. We'll have fun, won't we, Beau?" I ask.

"Yes!" he shouts.

"Go on upstairs and get ready. I'll get him dressed," I offer.

"Thank you. I owe you for this," she says as she throws her arms around my neck.

I pull her in close. She feels good.

"I'll hold you to that," I say as I bury my nose in her hair.

"Come on." Beau tugs me loose from her and leads me to his room.

Once I have him dressed, we get into my truck with Fritz in tow and head to town. After eating, we walk the block to the pet store where we get Fritz a nice, roomy aquarium, heating pad, some gravel, and a few plants along with a water mister for the tank. Mr. Belcher, the shop's owner, gives us a few care instructions and sells us pellets for food as an alternative to crickets, which I'm sure will please Dallas.

We take everything back to my house and set it up. Fritz seems very happy to be out of his jar and immediately hides in the shade of the plants. I sure hope this frog doesn't die in a day or two. Beau would be heartbroken.

"Myer, are you a superhero like Batman?" Beau asks the peculiar question while I make us peanut butter and jelly sandwiches for lunch.

I'm not much of a cook. I can make sausage gravy and scramble an egg, but that's about it.

"Why do you ask?"

"Mommy called you and Uncle Payne when she was scared of bad guys last night," he says as if the question made perfect sense.

"No. We're not superheroes; we're just regular men," I tell him.

"Batman is a regular man. He just has a cool suit, and he's strong and smart like you and Uncle Payne. Like I'm gonna be when I get big," he schools me.

"So, you wanna be a superhero, huh?" I ask as I hand him his plate.

"Yep, I wanna be just like Batman!" he says as he throws his arm in the air like he's about to take off in flight.

I bend over the counter and look him in the eye. "I think you already are a superhero. Look at those muscles," I say as I point to his little bicep.

"I can't be a superhero now. I'm just a little boy. But when I grow up, I'll be big and strong, and then I can save Mommy and Nana from the bad guys," he informs me, and I can see the serious determination on his face.

The incident last night must have really shaken him up.

"Tell you what. Until you get bigger, I'll help protect Mommy and Nana," I offer.

"You will?"

"I sure will. Anytime they need me or you need me, I'll be there."

"How will you know if we need help? Batman sees the Bat-Signal in the sky," he asks.

I think for a moment.

"I guess we're gonna need our own Bat-Signal," I suggest.

His eyes light up. "Like what?" he asks.

I scratch my head, and my eyes dart around the cabin and land on the lucky horseshoe nailed above the door. "How about a horse instead of a bat?"

"How will you see it?"

"You text it to me. If you're ever in trouble and need me, you text me a horse, and I'll be there as fast as Batman."

"I don't have a phone, silly." He giggles.

"Your momma does. My number is saved in her phone." I pull my phone from my pocket and show him how to find the contacts list. "If you guys are scared or need me, you or your momma just press my name in her favorite's list and message me like this the letter *H*. Do you know that letter?"

"Yes, Mrs. Perry taught us our ABCs."

He points to the *H* on the keypad.

"There you have it. I get an *H*, and I'll know what to do. You got it?"

"Got it!" he shouts. Then, he takes a big bite of his sandwich and grins, jelly covering his hands and mouth.

Man, I love this kid.

Eight

DALLAS

We're waiting by baggage claim when Sophie spots her friend.

"Oh my God. What is she wearing?" Sophie asks in horror.

I turn to see what she's talking about, and it's not hard to find. There stands a five-and-a-half-feet-tall blonde pixie in the most ridiculous outfit I have ever seen.

"You're kidding me, right? *That* is what you consider the New York version of me?" I ask as I gape at the vision.

"Um, she isn't usually quite this extra," she mumbles as we both stare in disbelief.

The girl spots us and dashes toward Sophie with her arms open wide. She drops her bags to the floor and lets out a high-pitched squeal as she wraps Sophie in a tight hug.

"Hey, Char. I'm so happy you're finally here," Sophie says as she backs up and gets a closer inspection of the girl's outfit. "This is my friend Dallas."

Charlotte turns to me and envelops me in her arms. "It's so nice to finally meet you, Dallas. Sophie talks about you all the time," she greets.

"It's nice to meet you too, but what's with the getup?" I ask.

"What?" she says in confusion as she looks down at herself. "Jeff over at Western Spirit said it was the perfect bougie cowgirl attire."

"I don't think there is such a thing as bougie cowgirl," Sophie softly breaks to her.

"You don't like it? I think it's awesome."

She does a little turn. She is wearing jeans with rhinestone-embellished back pockets, a black velvet duster that comes to mid-thigh with leather fringe hanging from the arms, and a matching black velvet bedazzled cowgirl hat.

"You look like a rodeo clown," Sophie says as she wrinkles her nose.

"Really? Is that a bad thing?" she asks with a frown.

"It's not good. The word *clown* is your first clue," Sophie answers.

"Damn, Jeff owes me. This outfit cost a fortune. He assured me that it would catch the eye of a cowboy," she complains with a pout.

"It'll catch their eye all right," Sophie adds with a nod.

"Come on," I offer as I loop my arm in hers and lead her toward the exit. "I'm sure I can find something for you in my closet that's country and just trashy enough to say *I'm on the prowl* without saying *I hope Woody and Buzz walk through the swinging saloon doors and buy me a drink.*"

I hear Sophie's laughter as she follows us out.

"We'll have three mimosas to start," I say as the waitress sets glasses of water in front of us.

We decided to stop in the city for brunch before heading back to Poplar Falls.

"Got it. I'll get your drinks and give you a minute to look over the menu," she says before heading to the bar.

"I'm so glad you're here," Sophie says as she squeezes Charlotte, who is sitting next to her and across from me at our booth, which is close to the entry.

Charlotte accepts her hug and then looks her up and down. "You sound different, and you look different," she observes.

"Different how?" Sophie asks in confusion.

"I don't know. I can't put my finger on it, but it's like you're glowing or something." She shrugs.

"Maybe it's all the fresh air and sunshine I've been getting," Sophie offers with a smile.

"It's all the sex," I deadpan as I pick up the menu and peruse the selections.

Charlotte looks from me back to Sophie, wrinkles her forehead like she is assessing her, and then agrees, "You're probably both right. She didn't get either back home."

The waitress returns with our mimosas just as two chatty figures enter the restaurant.

One stops and does a double take before speaking, "Dallas? Is that you?"

I look up to see Karen Wright. She and her husband were friends Travis and I used to spend quite a bit of time with when we lived here in Denver.

"Oh my God, it is you. I can't believe it," she squeals.

"Karen, hi," I say as I stand and give her a quick hug.

"It's so good to see you," she coos. "I've missed you terribly."

Funny, I haven't heard a peep from her or any of our other so-called friends since I left.

"How have you been?" she asks with fake concern dripping from her words.

"Great," I chirp as I lift my glass to my lips and bat my lashes at her.

"I'm so sorry about the house. Steve went to the auction when the government sold it off. We bid on a few of your nicer pieces of furniture, and I told him to offer the most he could to help you with your unfortunate situation," she declares for the entire restaurant to hear.

"And what situation was that?" I ask.

"You know …" She covers her mouth and loudly whispers, "Restitution."

I shake my head. "Not my situation, Karen. Never was."

"Oh, I know it wasn't. Travis was such a snake. I knew something was off with him all along. Intuition," she says as she pats my shoulder, placating.

"Is that right?" I ask.

"Yes. And for him to leave you in the predicament he did? None of us could blame you for running off to take care of that …" she says in a fake whisper out of the side of her mouth.

"Take care of what?" I ask innocently as I look up at her.

"You know," she says as she widens her eyes and rubs her stomach.

I start to see red, and Sophie can tell I am about to blow.

"Hi, I'm Dallas's best friend, Sophie, and this is our friend Charlotte," Sophie says as she reaches her hand out.

Karen takes it and gives her a quick shake. "Nice to meet you girls," she says on a smile.

"What exactly do you mean, take care of that?" I ask over the exchange.

Her head snaps back to me. "You know, get rid of it. You did get rid of it, didn't you?" She looks confused.

"Why would I get rid of a perfectly innocent baby?"

"Because of its genes, obviously. It was half Travis after all. Besides, who would want to raise a child all by themselves, much less one with a convict as a father?" she says on a nervous laugh. "Right?"

"Right," I bite out.

"Uh-oh," Sophie mutters under her breath.

"Well, Karen, I have met your mother and father, and they are lovely," I say as her smile widens. "So, suffice to say, the catty-bitch gene you carry is not genetic. I guess there is hope for my sweet boy after all."

Her smile falls, and she is puzzled by my honeyed tone for a moment until my words finally sink in. She starts to sputter and search for what I assume is an insincere apology when I wave her off.

"Run along; you're ruining our pleasant brunch vibe."

She huffs and then turns, scurrying off to her waiting friend.

"Shall we order? I'm starving," I ask my friends.

Sophie's hand reaches across the table and takes mine. I'm still slightly shaking with fury.

I look up, and her steady gaze hits me. I calm and squeeze her hand.

"Yes, let's eat. Whew, that was intense. I thought you were going to get up and punch her in the face. I love Colorado already," Charlotte says as she hands me my glass.

"You good?" Sophie asks.

"I'm fine. They can all go to hell, everyone in this town I ever considered a friend. Not once in the last six years did any of them pick up a phone and call to check on me or to see if the baby or I needed anything. They were all too concerned with their reputations and worried about what their husbands were up to. They had good reason to be. I bet half their men were either in business with Travis or a customer of his."

Charlotte lifts her glass in a toast, and we follow suit.

"Screw 'em!"

We clink.

I look over as Karen and her friend exit the restaurant without getting a table. How dare they put any label on Beau. He's not a mistake. He's a blessing. He saved me. Gave me something to pick myself up and fight for. There's not a trace of Travis Stovall in his kind little soul.

Nine

DALLAS

After dropping Sophie and Charlotte back at Rustic Peak, I head to Myer's cabin to relieve him.

I pull in, and he and Beau are down at the corral near the barn. Beau is sitting on the fence, and Myer is in the corral with a young light-brown horse. He has a rope in his hand, and he is walking the horse.

"Mommy," Beau shouts as he spots me making my way down the hill, and Myer turns.

"Hey, baby," I call as I approach.

"What are you two up to?" I ask as I scoop him up from the fence.

"Myer is gonna teach me how to ride a horse. He said we couldn't ride today because we had to get your permission first, but if you say yes, we can ride Thumper!" he explains excitedly.

"Thumper?" I ask as I look to Myer.

"Yeah, he's an older stallion we have. He's very docile and easy to ride. A great horse to learn on," he assures me.

"You think he's old enough?" I ask as I look down at my boy in my arms. He looks so tiny.

"Pop had me on one as soon as I took my first steps. I think the younger he learns to ride, respect, and care for the animal, the better."

"Please, Mommy. I will listen real good," he begs. His big brown eyes are filled with excitement and hope.

As much as the thought of him on a horse scares me, I know that Myer would be a great teacher and take excellent care with him.

I give in. "Okay. I was thinking about starting him with lessons with Madeline. Let's let him get a few classes in with her first to learn the basics, but you can take over after that, if you want."

"Yay!" Beau squeals and wiggles from my arms. "She said yes, Myer!" he informs him unnecessarily.

"I heard," Myer answers as he grins over at my son.

"Come and get me," Beau says as he raises his arms into the air.

I laugh. "Baby, you can't start today. It's getting late, and we have taken up enough of Myer's day."

"Nah, we had fun, didn't we, little man?" Myer brushes off my statement.

"Yeah, we got a house for Fritz and ate PBJs," Beau starts to prattle off their day as Myer exits the corral.

"It certainly sounds like you two had a big day," I confirm. "But I have to get you home and packed because you and Uncle Payne are having a sleepover, remember?"

"Oh, yeah. Yay!" He takes off running for Myer's front door, all thoughts of riding a horse gone.

"Thank you for the offer. You sure you want to take it on? He will be all over you to take him riding every time he sees you," I say as Myer falls into step beside me.

"I'm sure. I remember the excitement of my old man teaching me. I'll get him fitted to a saddle and get it on order."

I stop and look at him. "Can you wait until the end of the month? Madeline has saddles for kids at her place that he can use for now, but I can take a few extra shifts at Faye's—" I start.

He interrupts me, "Dal, I got the saddle."

"No, really. I can have it by—"

He stops me again. "I want to buy it. Not for you. For Beau. A gift to him from me. Your first saddle is a big deal. My granddaddy bought mine. I'll never forget that day or the first time he put me in it," he says, his voice full of nostalgia.

"I thought you learned to ride when you were a toddler?" I call him out.

"I did, but I didn't get a saddle of my own until I was big enough to ride alone."

"Oh," I say, uneasy about letting him spend that kind of money on us.

He takes me by my shoulders. "Dallas, it'll be an honor for me to teach him and an honor to get it for him. Please?"

I decide to give in because it probably would mean a lot to Beau.

"All right, but you just bought yourself a bunch of home-cooked meals at my table," I agree.

"Sounds like a sweet deal for me," he says as he follows me to the cabin.

Sophie and Charlotte meet us at my house after supper. Beau answers the door.

"Well, aren't you the handsomest little thing I have ever seen!" Charlotte declares.

Beau looks up at her and grins. "I'm not a thing. I'm a little boy."

She reaches down and ruffles his hair as she agrees, "You sure are."

He throws his arms around Sophie's legs in a hug as she introduces them, "Beau, this is my friend from New York. Her name is Charlotte."

"Hi, Miss Charlotte. Your hair looks like mine," he says as he points up at her.

I look over to see that her platinum pixie cut with a bit of a pouf on top does indeed look like his.

"It sure does. Thank goodness you're a knockout. I can live with that," she says with a wink.

He giggles.

"You want to see Fritz?" he asks.

"Sure," Charlotte answers, and he runs off toward his bedroom.

"You have to get your stuff together. Pop-Pop is going to be here to get you and take you to Uncle Payne's soon," I call after him.

Sophie and Charlotte walk on in and take a seat at my island.

"I love your place," Charlotte remarks as she looks around. "It's cool as shit. Did you build it this way, or was it actually used as a silo?"

"It used to be. We converted it a few years ago. My momma and I saw it done on some HGTV show not long after Beau was born. We needed a place of our own, and she didn't want her first grandbaby too far away, so we wrangled my daddy and uncle into renovating this old grain silo that Daddy wasn't using anymore. Took them forever to get it done, but that's because they're both perfectionists. We moved in right after Beau turned three years old. I pay them a small monthly rent to pay back all the cost."

"It's fantastic. Do you sleep up there?" she asks as she peers up at the loft.

"Yep."

She wrinkles her nose. "I guess you don't get much privacy, huh?"

"Haven't needed much, but I think, as Beau gets older, it might become a little bit of an issue. I'll figure it out when the time comes," I admit just as he runs back into the room with his hands held together.

He walks up to Charlotte and opens his hands wide. Fritz croaks loudly and hops out of his hold and up onto the island as Charlotte lets out a scream and jumps from the stool.

Chaos ensues as I lunge for the critter, and Sophie tries to catch him as he leaps out of my reach. Beau starts jumping around, calling the frog's name and yelling at us not to hurt him.

The front door swings open, and Daddy walks in just as Fritz hops from the counter to the floor and scurries under the table. Beau gets on his hands and knees and crawls after him as Charlotte continues to squeal.

Finally, Daddy and Beau corner him and scoop him up.

"Jeez, I thought Fritz was a stuffed animal or something," Charlotte says breathlessly.

"Beau, you can't get him out of his tank like that. He'll get lost in the house, and we'll never find him. Then, Mommy will have to go live with Nana and Pop-Pop," I scold. "Now, tell Miss Charlotte you are sorry you scared the bejesus out of her."

"I'm sorry, Miss Charlotte," he says with his face down.

"It's okay," she says as she pats his head. "I wasn't expecting him. I'm not really afraid of frogs. I have kissed a bunch of them."

He looks up at her and twists his little nose. "Ew, you shouldn't do that. You'll get warts on your tongue," he informs her.

"Or somewhere else if she's not careful," I say under my breath as I glance at Sophie.

We all laugh.

Ten

DALLAS

Sophie and Charlotte are sprawled across my bed as I raid my walk-in closet for outfit options.

Payne took Beau and Fritz camping in his backyard for the night, so us girls are heading out to Fast Breaks for a few drinks.

"Here we go," I say as I pull the dress from the back.

It's a cream spaghetti-strapped A-line dress with a lace overlay.

I hold it up for the two of them to see, and Charlotte's eyes light up.

"It will look great with your boots," I tell her.

It will. She brought a pair of dark brown distressed cowgirl boots with her. It's the only decent thing that clown at the Western store in New York sold her.

"You think it will fit me?" she asks as she reverently assesses it.

"Try it on," I say as I hand it off to her.

She flings her shirt over her head and drops her jeans to the floor. Then, she takes the dress, unzips the back, and slides into it. It's the perfect fit.

"That looks amazing," Sophie states.

"And expensive. Are you sure you don't mind loaning it to me?" Charlotte asks as she walks over to the full-length mirror and turns to see the back.

"I'm sure. Travis bought it for me to wear to an auto show banquet. I only wore it the one time, and I never plan to wear it again. Have fun, and don't worry about ruining it," I say, giving her permission.

"You think?" she asks as she throws her arms wide and slowly turns for us.

"Yes. You look like a smoking-hot cowgirl," Sophie approves.

"Yay! I might even wear it to your engagement party," she squeals.

"Ugh, I need to get something to wear to that shindig," I complain.

Sophie's mother insists on an engagement party even though the wedding itself is only three months away. It seems like a waste of money to me, but Sophie wants to make Vivian happy, and she enjoys nothing more than throwing a party.

"You can wear anything in your closet," Sophie informs me.

"Yeah, right. Your mom would die if I showed up in jeans and a tee. Besides, I'm sure you'll be wearing something stunning. I'll go shopping and at least get a nice dress."

"What about this?" Charlotte asks as she pulls the clear dress bag down from the hook on the back of my closet door.

I take it from her and unzip it. It's a soft light-brown leather dress. It's strapless and formfitting, and it has turquoise accents.

"Wow, that's gorgeous," Sophie says as she walks over and runs her hand over it.

"Yeah," I agree. "I bought it in Denver years ago, paid way too much for it, and just haven't had an occasion to wear it."

"There's no time like the present," Charlotte says behind us.

I hold the dress up in front of me in the mirror beside my bed. It does look amazing with my light-strawberry-colored hair and tan skin.

What the hell?

I shrug. "Looks like we're all dressing up tonight."

After Sophie and I throw our dresses on, we all pile in my truck and head to the bar. Braxton and his friends are meeting us there later.

We walk into Fast Breaks, and Elle and Sonia wave us over to a table near the pool tables.

"Hey, you made it," Elle says as she hugs Sophie.

"Hi, Elle. This is Charlotte. Charlotte, this is Braxton's sister, Elowyn," Sophie introduces the two.

"It's great to meet you. Wow, you look amazing. I love that dress!" Elle praises.

"Right? Isn't it hot? Dallas loaned it to me," Charlotte says as she slides into the stool beside Elle.

April, our server, takes our order as she places a shot glass in front of each of the five of us.

"What's this?" I ask as I pick the glass up and sniff it.

"Apple Jack shots. The fellas at the bar sent them over," April informs.

"Which *fellas*?" Charlotte asks, putting extra emphasis on the word *fellas*, as she turns around in her seat and searches the faces at the bar.

"The ones at the far-right end."

I look up to see Russ Eastman and one of his friends. Russ tips his drink in my direction and smiles.

"Friend of yours?" Charlotte asks as she turns back around.

"Sort of," I reply as I take the shot and down it.

"They dated," Sophie chimes in.

"We didn't date. We went on a date. One date," I correct her.

"What happened there?" Elle asks.

I shrug. "Nothing really. I like him well enough, but every time he called to ask me out, it was either a school night, so I needed to be home or Beau was sick or my babysitter fell through. Finally, he just stopped calling."

"Hmm, what a jerk," Elle says as she pushes the shot away.

"Nah, Russ is nice. He really is. Dating isn't that easy when you have a six-year-old. I won't introduce a man to Beau—at least not unless it's serious. I don't want to bring people in and out of his life and confuse him. So, scheduling time together to get to know each other beyond a quick hook-up isn't easy."

"When the right man comes along, it won't be a hardship to work around your schedule," Sophie declares.

"Yeah," I say as I roll my eyes and take Elle's shot.

April brings our drinks and an order of chips and salsa, and we dig in.

By the end of our second round, Charlotte has talked me into teaching her how to two-step. We're out on the dance floor, fumbling over the steps, when the door opens, and Braxton, Walker, Silas, and Myer walk in.

"Whoa," Charlotte gasps and grabs ahold of my shoulder to steady herself. "Who's that?"

I hang on until she is stable and reply, "That's Braxton, Sophie's fiancé, and his friends—Walker, Silas, and Myer."

"Damn, no wonder she stayed in Colorado," she muses as her eyes go wide.

"Yep. That Braxton Young is a looker. Sophie came along and snagged him right out from under the noses of all the single gals in Poplar Falls," I reply.

We walk over to the table where the guys are crowding around.

As we make it to our seats, Sophie is introducing Brax and Charlotte, and Myer pulls my stool out. He has his eyes at the bar where Russ and his friend still sit.

"You need another drink?" he asks.

"Yes, please. Teaching the city girl how to dance is going to require more alcohol." I laugh.

"I'll be right back," he says before walking off toward the bar.

"Now, which one is that one?" Charlotte asks as she leans in and watches Myer's retreating form.

"That's Myer," I inform her as I follow her eyes.

"Is he single?"

"Um, yeah, I guess so," I answer.

She turns her eyes back to me. "You guess so?"

"I mean, yes, he's single, but he's not the one-night-stand kind," I explain.

"I'm here for almost two weeks. It doesn't have to be just one night," she says with a grin.

A sudden case of protectiveness prickles in my chest.

"He's not the two- or three-night-stand kind either," I say a little more forcefully.

She raises an eyebrow at me. "Okay, hands off, he's yours. I get it. Just point me in the direction of one who is available."

"He's not mine." I sputter, "He's just … he's Myer."

"*He's Myer*. What exactly does that mean?"

"It means, I don't think of him that way," I say as I look back over my shoulder at him.

He's leaning over the bar, whispering something into the bartender's ear. The female bartender.

When did she start working here?

"Right," she says on a laugh.

"What?" I ask as I bring my attention back to her.

"First of all, that beautiful, tall, blue-eyed man is not 'just' anything. What he is, is sexy as hell, and you're a tiny bit possessive of all that hotness."

"I am not," I protest.

I'm not. Am I?

"Girl, you turned red when I asked if he was single," she says as she points to my face. "I thought fire was going to come from your nostrils, and the bartender should have burst into flames from the look you just gave her."

"I did not turn red. Myer and I are just friends," I argue.

"Okay … then you won't mind if I take that cowboy for a test spin tonight," she says as she takes a drink of her beer.

Just as I'm about to answer, an arm comes around me and places a mason jar and bottle in front of me.

"Here you go, Dal. I brought you a water, too, so you stay hydrated," Myer says into my ear.

A shiver runs through me.

What the hell was that?

"Hi. I'm Myer," he says as he reaches his hand in Charlotte's direction.

"Charlotte," she says as she smiles up at him in a flirtatious way.

"Sophie's friend from New York, right?" he asks as she takes his hand.

"That's me," she answers with the smile still plastered on her face. Her eyes don't leave his face.

I look up at him. He is beautiful. His eyes are a deep blue-gray, like the color of storm clouds. He has long, dark eyelashes that brush his cheeks when he looks down at you. His jawline is defined, and it's covered with a dark stubble that always shows up when he doesn't shave for a day or two. His black hair is unruly, and he doesn't try to tame it; he lets it do whatever the hell it wants to do. Most of the time, it's covered by a ball cap or an old, worn-out cowboy hat.

I watch as he chats with Charlotte, and I realize that I've never paid attention to how attractive he is. My gaze travels down to his strong arms. His tee is pulled tight across his broad chest and is tucked into his jeans, which ride low on his hips.

She's right. He is sexy as hell. *Why have I never noticed that before?* No wonder the bartender was practically crawling across the bar to talk to him. *Huh.*

"Dallas?"

His deep voice penetrates my thoughts, and I blink up at him.

"What?"

He chuckles.

"Braxton asked if you girls want to play a game of pool," he says as he curiously looks at me.

"Oh." I look down at myself and back up to him. "Not sure it's such a good idea in this dress."

His eyes slowly move down my body. He brings his hand to my side and slides it down to my hip.

"Yeah, maybe not," he says and brings his eyes back to mine, "but it'd sure be fun to watch you try."

I smack his arm, and he chuckles.

"It looks good on. That's all I'm saying."

"Thank you," I say as I meet his stare.

Heat.

Is that heat dancing between Myer and me? Surely not. I've just had too many cocktails, and Charlotte has gotten into my head.

Eleven

MYER

"THAT'S THREE TO TWO, LADIES," WALKER TAUNTS AS HE pockets the last ball.

"You just got lucky." Dallas pouts.

She changed her mind, and she and Elle decided to play us after all. I've spent the last hour making sure no one can see her panties when she bends over to take a shot. It's been sweet torture.

"Baby, that's pure skill," he says with a wink in Elle's direction. "I have lots of skills."

"Yeah, you're a skilled cheater," Elle pipes in.

He gives her a playful grin. "Me? I don't cheat," he says as he places his hand over his heart.

"Please. You did whatever you could to distract me every time I went to take a shot," she accuses.

"Woman, it's not my fault you're so easily distracted."

She rolls her eyes. "You're a devil," she says with a shake of her head.

"That I am, baby girl. That I am," he agrees.

Braxton is standing to the left beside Sophie, who is seated at one of the pub tables, and he is watching their exchange.

"Walker, quit being an ass to my little sister. We all know you cheat," he interjects.

"Fine. I'll prove my innocence. Best out of seven, and I'll be on my best behavior," he says as he crosses his heart with his finger.

"No way. It's getting late, and I'm beat," Elle says.

"Chicken," Walker mumbles at her, and she sticks her tongue out at him.

"Come on. I'll take my girls home," Braxton offers. He cuts his eyes to me. "I got Sophie, Elle, and Charlotte. You got Dallas and Sonia?" he asks.

"Yep," I answer.

"What about me? Who's taking my drunk ass home?" Walker asks as he looks between us.

"Chloe's coming to pick you and Silas up," Braxton informs him. Chloe is Silas's ever patient wife.

"I'm not tired. I can stay a while," Charlotte says as she walks over to Walker.

He puts his arm around her neck. "Well then, I will buy you another drink while we wait on Chloe to arrive," he says as he turns her and leads her back into the bar area.

Sophie watches them and shakes her head.

"We can stay if you want," Braxton offers.

"No, she's a big girl, and I know you're exhausted. I'll just have Aunt Doreen leave the door unlocked for her." She walks over and hugs Dallas. "I'll come by in the morning and pick you up. We are going on a surprise road trip," she says.

"Payne can bring me. He has to bring Beau home anyway," Dallas says.

"See if he can keep him a couple extra hours. If not, I'm sure Aunt Doreen and Aunt Rita wouldn't mind watching him. We have a party mission." She grins.

"You got it. I'll ask him. See you tomorrow—and hopefully not two of you, like I'm seeing now," Dallas says as she sways on her feet.

They say their good-byes, and I corral her and Sonia into my truck.

We drop Sonia off first, and then I head to Dallas's. About halfway there, she starts yawning. She kicks her boots off and curls her legs up in the seat of the truck.

I do my best to keep my eyes on the damn road. That dress has been driving me crazy all night. It fits her perfect and hugs her curves in all the right places.

"Myer, I think I might be drunk," she says as she closes her eyes and lays her head back against the seat.

"You think so, huh?" I say playfully.

She peeks one eye open and looks at me. "You're handsome," she says with a slight slur.

"Thank you." I chuckle.

"I'm serious. You are. You had Charlotte all hot and bothered tonight," she insists.

"Is that right? Must be why she stayed with Walker." I smirk.

"No, no, she stayed with Walker because I told her to back off you," she says, and then her eyes fly open and meet mine. "I mean, I told her you weren't that kind of guy," she tries to explain.

"You mean, the kind of guy who would want to go home with a beautiful woman?" I ask just to tease her.

"You think she's beautiful?" she asks and then shakes her head. "Of course you do; she is beautiful."

"She is," I agree. "But you're right. The only beautiful woman I want to take home is the one in my truck," I say as I smile over at her.

She bites her lip. "You think I'm beautiful?" she asks as if she doesn't believe me.

"Dallas Stovall, I think you are the most beautiful girl I've ever met," I answer honestly.

She blinks at me as if the words aren't registering.

"Really?" she breathes.

I grin and cut my eyes from the road to her. "You know you're gorgeous."

Her forehead crinkles, and she shakes her head.

"I'm a mess," she whispers into the cab.

I reach over and take her hand into mine. She lays her head back down, and before we make it to her house, she is fast asleep.

I put the truck in park, and I walk to her side and open the door. I give her a gentle jostle to wake her. She barely rouses.

"Hey, we're home," I tell her.

She mumbles something incoherent and hands her keys over to me.

I unlock her front door and turn the lamp beside the door on. Then, I go back for her.

I pick her and her boots up. She wraps her arms around my neck. I carefully walk her to the house and to the couch. She curls up on her side and immediately passes back out. I walk into Beau's room and grab a pillow from his bed. I bring it and place it under her head.

I throw the blanket off the back of the couch over her and kiss the top of her head. I whisper, "Good night," and quietly let myself out, taking her keys and locking the dead bolt behind me.

Twelve

DALLAS

I WAKE TO BANGING ON THE DOOR. I SIT UP AND LOOK AROUND. I'M ON the couch, still in my dress from last night. I don't remember coming home. *Damn Walker and his shots.*

I get up and open the door to Sophie and Charlotte. Soph is all bright-eyed and bushy-tailed, but Charlotte is wearing a pair of dark sunglasses and looks about as good as I feel.

"Good morning," Sophie sings as she pushes past me with a bag in hand.

"What's so good about it?" I ask as I follow them to the kitchen.

"Someone's grumpy," Sophie notes as she starts pulling the contents from the bag.

Charlotte raises her hand. "That would be me. I'm grumpy," she groans as she sits down on one of the stools.

I laugh as I take her in. "You too, huh? Need a little hair of the dog?" I question.

"Whatcha got?" she asks as she removes the glasses and grabs one of the muffins Sophie has arranged on a plate.

"I can whip up some Bloody Marys," I offer.

"Sold, bartender," she agrees as she takes a bite.

I start a pot of coffee and then head to the liquor cabinet to grab the vodka and Bloody Mary supplies and proceed to make our hangover cures.

"Did you have fun last night?" I ask Charlotte as I top her glass with a celery stalk and slide it in front of her.

"If the pounding in my head is any indication, I would say, yes, yes I did," she admits as she takes a huge gulp from the glass.

"I have a bit of a headache myself. This is what happens when Walker wants to win. He keeps buying shots until we see two cue balls on the table instead of one. Getting me plastered is the only way he can beat me, and he knows it," I complain.

"He didn't force you to drink them," Sophie butts in.

"You hush. The only reason you aren't in the same boat we are is because Braxton threatened to hurt him if he brought one more drink to you," I whine.

"He knew we had a lot to do today, and he didn't want me to be suffering."

"How thoughtful of him," I say snarkily as I shake two ibuprofen into my hand and offer the bottle to Charlotte. "What's on the agenda anyway?" I ask.

"Once we finish here and you pull yourself together, we're going to Aurora to shop for engagement party dresses. Then, we're going to go sample cake flavors at your mom's bakery this afternoon," she says excitedly.

My mother is a master of cake decorating. She can make anything you want. I would put her up against any of those fancy bakers on the TV; plus, hers actually taste amazing as well.

"Braxton doesn't want to help pick the cake?" I ask.

Sophie gives me the *are you kidding me* look.

"Right. Never mind," I say as I finish my drink.

"Just let me call Payne and check on Beau and ask if he can bring him to the bakery later. Then, I'll go wash my face and put on real clothes, and we can go."

I grab my phone from my purse.

There's a text from Myer. He has my keys. I send him a message back that the girls are here to pick me up. He offers to swing by and bring them to me, but I have spare house keys upstairs, so he's just going to go by the bar with Payne, pick up my truck, and drop it off at the house later.

After I pull myself together, the three of us pile into Braxton's truck and head to Aurora. I called Payne and he said Beau wanted to stay and help him on the farm this morning, which was perfect, so he's going to bring him to me at Momma's bakery later.

"All right, spill," I command Charlotte as I stare her down in the backseat.

"Spill what?" she asks innocently.

"Did you go home with Walker last night?" I ask.

"I did not," she answers.

"Really? I thought he was in there for sure," I say, crestfallen.

"He's fun. We stayed at the bar a little longer. Drank a little more. Then, Silas's wife picked us up and took him home and then dropped me off at Rustic Peak," she informs.

"I bet he was disappointed," I muse.

"I don't think so. He didn't seem all that interested," she says with a shrug.

"What? Walker not interested in taking a girl home for the night? That's not possible," I say in disbelief.

"He didn't make his move, so I just assumed he wasn't."

"That's odd," Sophie agrees.

"What about you? Anything juicy to share?" Charlotte wags her eyebrows at me in the rearview mirror.

"No. I didn't even remember how I got home last night," I admit.

"Myer took you," Sophie says.

"Yes, I know. He had to fill me in this morning."

"What's his story anyway?" Charlotte asks.

"Myer?"

She nods and expectantly looks at me.

"His family's ranch, Stoney Ridge, backs up to our orchard. He and my brother, Payne, have been friends since they could walk. They spent the better part of my childhood torturing me in some capacity or another," I start the tale.

"Dallas and I both crushed on him hard when we were little. We'd follow him and Payne around like puppies. Drove them crazy. Then, when we were about eight years old, we were in the barn at Dallas's house, playing a cutthroat game of Spin the Bottle with a bunch of kids from school, and Myer's spin landed on Dallas. She kissed him for a whole minute. Broke my heart," Sophie says, reminiscing as she places her hand over her wounded heart.

"Yeah, I remember. It wasn't a whole minute. I was eight, and he was ten. It was an awkward peck on the lips that lasted two seconds, tops. Then, you wouldn't speak to me for an entire week. Like I'd used some sort of telepathic power to cause the bottle to land on me," I say as I roll my eyes at the memory.

She sticks her tongue out at me.

"Anyway," I continue, "in middle school, he started playing football and was damn good at it. Coaches, girls, and practically the whole damn town started fawning all over him. He kind of got himself a big head and then a hot girlfriend. So cliché—the quarterback and the head cheerleader. Meanwhile, I was going through my awkward phase."

I lift my hand and start ticking the list off on my fingers. "I was short and painfully thin, I had braces, you could play connect the dots on my face, I wore Coke-bottle glasses—poor Beau gets his shitty eyesight naturally—and my best friend left me all alone to face puberty."

I end my rundown by giving Sophie the stink eye.

"Needless to say, my crush was unrequited, and I eventually got over it, but I was still a fan. Myer was scouted by every college in the Midwest. He won a scholarship to the University of Colorado Boulder; the cheerleader followed him, and so did Payne. I was left here to finish my senior year, and that's when Travis rolled into town. He was new, kind of edgy, and a handsome devil. *Devil* being the operative word. He hadn't been here for my awkward phase either. I fell head over heels. Married him the second I graduated and moved to Denver."

Charlotte is listening with rapt fascination. "And …" she asks.

"And?"

"How did you both end up back here, in Poplar Falls?"

"Myer took a hard hit in a bowl game against UCLA his second year. It was illegal contact. UCLA was losing and they wanted to rough him up a bit, and boy did they. Blew his ankle out. It was bad. He had to have surgery, and it required metal rods and pins. He came home to recover and rehab, and when he went back, his agility on the field was never the same. He knew his chances of being drafted were slim, so he returned home to work the ranch. Sans the cheerleader. That disloyal hussy stayed and hitched her wagon to the backup quarterback, from what I heard."

"Damn, that sucks," she says.

"Yeah, he doesn't talk about it much, but I know it had to hurt terribly to lose your dream when you were that close to it coming true."

"He doesn't seem that broken up about it though. If you hadn't told me, I'd never have guessed that he hadn't wanted to be a rancher his whole life. He's great with the horses and cattle," Sophie adds.

"He is. It's in his blood, like the rest of us, I guess," I agree.

"What about you and Beau? What happened there?" Charlotte continues her questioning.

"That's another tragic tale. My husband ended up a scoundrel who was dabbling in selling illegal drugs that then led to laundering drug money through our auto repair shop, unbeknownst to me. And one day out of the blue, federal agents showed up at my door and proceeded to inform me of all his dirty deeds. They indicted him on too many charges to count and seized everything we owned, but luckily, they didn't take me down with him—which they could have because my name was on everything. But they had a guy in deep cover, working for Travis, and they knew he was keeping me completely in the dark. He was convicted and sentenced to fifteen years in prison and a half-a-million-dollar fine," I say.

"Whew, that's steep," Charlotte says as her eyes go round.

"Apparently, he had gotten caught up over his head with a pretty big ring that the Feds had been investigating for a while. Travis wasn't necessarily dangerous, just stupid. So was I. I didn't see it. I knew he was pulling in money from somewhere, but I just thought he was somehow screwing insurance companies out of crazy amounts of cash when he worked on accident claims. Anyway, he went to prison. I filed for divorce, and then I came home to Momma and Daddy, in debt up to my eyeballs. Then, Beau was born three months later," I finish my sordid story.

"Do you hear from him at all?" she asks.

"Who? Travis?"

She nods.

"No. He used to write letters and send them to Momma and Daddy's house, but I didn't open any of them. Amanda down at the post office knows to mark anything coming from the Fremont Correctional Facility as *Undeliverable* and *Return to Sender* now.

"I don't want him to have any part in our lives. I've been trying to get his rights to Beau taken away for years. He's never even laid eyes on him. You'd think he'd be more than willing to give up any responsibility, but no, his stubborn ass wants to fight it just to piss me off."

"Wow, that's … just wow. The most exciting thing that has ever happened to me was when I stumbled into Jason Momoa in Central Park. He was shooting scenes for a movie, and I was going for my morning run," Charlotte states.

"Um, what about meeting me and, I don't know, starting a successful, global jewelry empire?" Sophie says, affronted.

"Soph, it was Jason Momoa—aka Khal Drogo or Aquaman," she says slowly. Then, she looks at me and mouths, *So needy*.

I giggle.

Sophie stares at her and then relents. "Yeah, okay, I'll give you that one."

"So, now, both you and Myer are back in Poplar Falls, and you guys are, what?" Charlotte asks.

I look up at her, confused. "What do you mean?"

"You said last night that you guys were just friends, but you're, like, friends with benefits or something, right?"

"No, we're just friends, no benefits. Unless you count driving my drunk ass home all the time a benefit. Which it kinda is for me," I answer.

"Wait, I'm confused. He bought your drinks and stayed by your side all night, and he took you home," she points out.

"Yeah, so?"

"You aren't sleeping together?"

"No."

"Hmm," she muses.

"What?"

"Nothing. You're just awfully possessive of him. I assumed you two had hooked up," she says with a shrug.

"No, I'm not," I protest.

"Oookay," she says.

She and Sophie give each other a look in the rearview mirror.

Whatever. I start playing with the radio in the truck to find us some music to change the subject.

"Hey, Dallas, do you recognize that car behind us?" Sophie asks as she looks in her side mirror.

I turn around and check out the dark blue coupe that's about five car lengths behind us. "I don't think so. Why?"

"It's been behind us since we turned off your road. It keeps speeding up and then falling back, but I'm pretty sure it's the same one," she says with a little alarm in her voice.

"That's strange."

"Right? What are the odds?" she says nervously.

Aurora is about sixty miles from Poplar Falls, and we've been on thc road for almost an hour.

"Slow down. If we get a little closer, maybe I can see it better and figure out who it is," I say as I turn completely around in the seat.

Charlotte scoots to the far right, so I have a clear line of sight.

Sophie lets off the gas, and the distance between us and the other car narrows. I can't quite see the driver's face, just that it looks to be a male with a ball cap on.

"I can't tell. Pull over to the shoulder, and maybe they'll go around," I suggest.

She slows down even more and turns her left blinker on. Just then the car makes a sharp turn on a side road that shoots off into the woods.

We come to a stop.

"They bolted off," I say.

"Do you think they were following us?" she asks.

"It was probably just a coincidence. Are you sure they got behind us near my place?"

She nods her head. "I think so. I mean, it looked like the same car. I guess it could have been another one. I wasn't paying really close attention until about twenty minutes ago."

"Yeah, I bet it wasn't the same car. My guess is, it was probably a local who lives down in those woods," I say.

We get back on the road and make our way into town.

We stop and park in front of a quaint little boutique.

"Janelle told me about this place," Sophie says as she parks the truck.

"Janelle? You took shopping advice from Janelle?" I ask her in disbelief.

"Don't worry; I went online and checked it out. It's really nice. The owners have a shop in Denver and opened this one last year. I'm sure we'll be able to find something we like."

We walk inside, and the place is stunning. Chandeliers hang above the counter, and velvet furniture is sprinkled throughout. Two young salesclerks greet us as we enter and offer us champagne while we shop.

"Fancy," I quip as I take the glass and start to peruse the racks.

"What about this one?" Sophie asks as she holds up a gorgeous pink slip dress.

"Maybe for you. Pink and red hair, not so much." I grimace.

"I like these. We can all wear shades of yellow. What do you guys think?" Charlotte asks as she stands in front of a rack of bright spring dresses.

"Oh, I love that one," Sophie squeals and grabs a pale yellow number.

I shrug. "Okay, matchy-matchy it is. Let's try them on," I say as I select a low-cut one in a bold hue.

One of the salesclerks leads us to the back where there is a large, open room with a settee and standing mirrors. She pulls the curtain closed and leaves us to try on our finds.

I undress quickly and pull mine over my head. It's a perfect fit, but I'm unsure about all the skin showing.

"Um, there's no way I can wear a bra with this thing. It dips practically to my belly button," I grumble.

Sophie steps back and assesses me. "True, but, Dallas, it looks amazing on you. You have to get that. You can use fashion tape to hold the girls in."

I look to Charlotte to see what she thinks.

"What in the hell do you have on?" I ask.

She is standing there, wrapped up like a mummy from her breasts to her thighs. She looks down at herself. "What? My Spanx?" she asks.

"Is that what you call that straitjacket you're wearing?"

"It's awesome. It holds in all your jiggly bits," she explains. She reaches down into her pile of dresses, pulls out a package, and hands it to me. "Here, try a pair. It will give you the perfect hourglass figure," she suggests.

"I don't think so. I like my jiggly bits to live wild and free," I say as I try to hand it back to her.

"I'm telling you, Spanx are life. Just try it on and then put the dress back on. You'll thank me."

I decide to give in. I pull the dress over my head and set it aside. I open the package, maneuver my way into the openings, and start to pull it up my legs. It takes all of my strength to yank it over my hips. Once it's pulled up to my navel, I start yelling for Charlotte.

"Help me! I'm stuck," I call.

I keep tugging, trying to get it up, and my arms are getting tired.

"Oh no," Charlotte says. "You have it twisted. Hold still, and I'll get it straightened."

She starts jerking and rotating the offensive garment and calls Sophie to help.

"Owww," I cry as I lurch forward when I feel a pinch in my nether regions. "My hoo-ha is trapped in there. Be careful."

"Hold still," Charlotte demands.

I look in the mirror over her shoulder, and the three of us look ridiculous.

"There you go," she says as she finally gets it pulled up under my breasts.

We're all sweaty and out of breath now.

"What do you think?" Charlotte asks.

"What do I think? I think you're batshit crazy. It's like we just wrestled an alligator for fifteen minutes."

"Yeah, but see how good you look." She beams.

"I can't breathe in this damn thing, and forget about eating, drinking or dancing. My stomach is in a vise grip," I complain.

"You mountain girls are soft," she says with a frown.

"Jeez, how do I get out of this thing?" I ask as I start tugging it down.

"I'll help," Charlotte says as she rolls her eyes.

I lift my hand to stop her. "No. Go ask that salesgirl for scissors," I command as I continue to paw at the offensive garment.

"The things we do for fashion. Wait till you see the shoes I picked out," Sophie says before bursting out laughing.

City girls are nuts.

Thirteen

DALLAS

After our morning of shopping in Aurora, the three of us come back with gorgeous new dresses for the party. We head over to Momma's bakery next. She isn't open on Sunday, but she came in after church to bake several options for us to try, so we have the place to ourselves.

Sophie's aunts and stepmom join us for the fun.

"Mmm, I think this one is my favorite. Dottie, you have outdone yourself," Doreen gushes as she looks up at my mother and takes another bite of the carrot cake with lemon cream cheese frosting.

"You've said that about the last three we tasted," Ria tells her.

"They're going to have several tiers," Doreen says with a shrug.

"Great. So, we've decided on nine flavors," Sophie says as she looks down at the chart in front of her. "That's too many. We can't have a nine-tier cake. We only have fifty people coming. That's three tiers, tops."

"Okay. Let's narrow it down," Doreen offers. "The carrot cake stays for sure. You loved the vanilla with the raspberry puree filling. Braxton is a chocolate fan, so let's keep the German chocolate with the bourbon peanut butter ganache filling for him."

She takes the paper from Sophie and starts scratching out other options.

"But that cinnamon marble with the maple-bacon buttercream was amazing," she says as she erases the X mark over it. "Oh, and the strawberry with the lemon curd filling is to die for. Maybe we could do cupcakes in addition to the cake. You know, a dozen in each flavor. That way, we can get them all, and what isn't eaten can be boxed up for guests to take home. What do you think?" She expectantly looks up at Sophie.

"Works for me. Mrs. Henderson, can we get the chocolate and peanut butter one for the engagement party next week as well?" she asks Momma.

"Sure thing. You still want the pecan tarts too, correct?" Momma asks.

"Is that the miniature pecan pies?" Sophie clarifies.

"It is."

"Yes. Braxton loves those," she confirms.

"If I lived here, I would be so fat," Charlotte adds as she pops another cake bite into her mouth. "Between Doreen and Ria's cooking and this bakery, my thighs wouldn't stand a chance."

"You outdid yourself, Momma. I can't believe you did twenty flavors for us to taste," I praise as I start gathering plates to help clean up.

"I bet she's just practicing for the day she gets to bake your wedding cake," Doreen adds with a wink.

I give an amused laugh. "Yeah, right. I don't think I'll be having another one of those," I declare.

The mood of the room instantly changes, and all their eyes come to me.

"Oh, Dallas, don't let your heart harden to the possibility of something more," Momma says from behind the counter.

"It's too late, Momma. My heart's already turned to stone."

"Good thing God has a history of turning stone into something better," Doreen muses.

"Not sure I'm that high on God's list of priorities. He has better things to worry about. You know, war, hunger, disease, that sort of thing," I try to deflect.

"Oh, he cares very much about you, and he has a plan for your life. A good plan," Momma says as she starts opening boxes for the remaining goods.

"Well then, maybe it's just not in his plan for me to be a married woman, Momma. If it were, why would he have let my marriage to Travis fail so epically?" I try again.

She stops and looks up at me. "Oh, baby, because God doesn't interfere with your choices. He gave you free will after all. Besides, I don't recall you asking for his opinion—or anyone else's for that matter—when you ran off and married that boy."

She gives me a pointed look and then adds softly, "There comes a time when every parent has to let go and let their child make their own way. That doesn't mean they stop caring. It doesn't mean that they can't see the storm coming. You just have to be patient and wait and watch and be there to help guide them and protect them through it. It's the same with God. You have to stop blaming him for your own messes and start asking for his help to fix them and to make better ones going forward. You'll see one day when Beau starts stumbling around, trying to become his own man."

"It's true. Braxton used to say the same thing after that Morgan ran off. He was never going to get married. Never put his heart out there again. He was done with women. Then, God brought Sophia right to his front doorstep," Madeline adds with a smile.

Just as I open my mouth to respond, the bell above the door chimes, and in runs a little blond blur. He stops in front of me and pulls a handful of colorful weeds from behind his back. White clover and dandelions.

"Are those for me?" I ask as I brush the hair from Beau's sweaty forehead.

"Yes, I picked them for you," he says as he hands them to me.

I bring them to my nose. "Thank you, baby. They are so pretty."

He beams his snaggletooth grin at me, and I bend down to kiss his cheek.

"Come on, Beau. Nana will help you get some water for them,"

Momma offers as she takes his hand and one of the paper cups from the counter and leads him to the kitchen.

Payne comes in next, carrying Beau's overnight bag and Fritz's aquarium.

"You sure you don't want to keep that thing at your house?" I ask as he sets it on one of the tables near the door.

"What, and rob Beau of all the joy of caring for his slimy little friend? No way," he says as he tries to stifle a laugh.

"Well, who do we have here?" Charlotte asks from her spot next to Doreen.

"That pain in the ass is my brother, aptly named Payne," I introduce. "Payne, this is Sophie's friend Charlotte."

"Nice to meet you," he greets.

"The pleasure is all mine," Charlotte purrs.

Payne gives her a half-grin before he brings his eyes back to mine. "Momma got any cake left, or did you hens eat it all?"

"There's plenty left. Just grab what you want," I say as I hand him one of the boxes.

"Awesome. I'm heading out to Braxton's spot to help the guys finish adding the deck. Hopefully, we'll have it done tonight. I'll take extra for them."

"In that case, raid the display and take whatever you like. I'll bake fresh goodies in the morning," Momma says as she comes back with my flowers in the tiny cup of water.

"Thanks, Momma," he says as he kisses her cheek.

"You be good, little man, and make sure you feed Fritz when you get home," he tells Beau and reaches his hand out for a fist bump. "Ladies," he says as he tips his head and walks into the kitchen.

"Maybe I should move to Colorado too," Charlotte says as she watches him go.

"Did you not hear the 'pain in the ass' part?" I ask her.

She just shrugs. "Aren't they all?"

A collective, "Yes," comes from the room at large.

Fourteen

MYER

"I got it," I yell up to Braxton as I balance the heavy beam on my shoulder.

I hoist it up over the anchor and hold it in place as he uses the nail gun to secure it.

"You can let it go," he says, and I release it. "We're almost done. A couple more," he says as Walker brings another.

We've been at it since noon.

As soon as the cattle were taken care of this morning, I headed straight here. The deck is pretty amazing. I should add one on the back of my cabin overlooking the mountains and apple trees.

Once we're done, I climb back up the back side of the house and join them inside. Payne showed up a few minutes ago with coffee and a ton of baked goods from his momma.

"I stopped and got cold cuts, so we could make sandwiches," he says as he unloads a cooler.

"Thank you, man. I'm starving," Walker says as he forgoes the coffee and grabs a beer from his own cooler.

We all make a plate and head out to the new deck to eat. It still needs a railing and to be stained and coated, but it looks good.

"Sophie is going to love this," I say as I sit down in one of the portable stadium chairs.

"I sure hope so," Braxton says as he looks out over the gap.

"Speaking of, what were the girls up to?" he asks Payne as he, too, takes a seat.

"They were there, tasting cakes, but it looked like they were done and just gabbing to me."

Braxton lets out a long, frustrated breath. "Sophie's stressed out about all this wedding stuff. I'm just ready for it all to be over and for us to get moved in here. I swear, I never knew girls needed to throw so many parties to celebrate one marriage," he huffs.

"How many are we talking?" Walker asks.

"Engagement party—whatever the hell that's for—then the rehearsal, and dinner party." He stops mid-sentence and looks up. "Why the hell do we need a rehearsal? We stand up with the reverend and repeat what he tells us to say. We don't need to practice that shit. We don't even have to memorize our lines; he feeds them to us."

We all look at each other and shrug. Makes no sense to us either.

"Then, there's the actual wedding and reception. Which is fine. Throw in our branding and yours"—he nods to me—"and trying to get this house finished by June, I barely get to see Sophie, and when I do, I'm dog-shit tired," he grumbles.

"The things we do to keep our women happy," Walker says as he turns up his bottle.

Silas throws a chip at him. "Like you'd know," he says.

"I'll have you know, I do what I must to keep several happy." He wags his eyebrows at us. He turns to me and asks, "What about you?"

"What about me?" I ask as I open a sugar packet and add it to my cup.

"You left with Dallas last night. Anything happen there? Did you finally make your move, man?" he asks.

"Nah, she ain't ready," I answer as I take a swig from my cup.

Walker shakes his head. "Dude, you are in the friend zone. You've been friend-zoned for a long time. It's hard to come back from that. You're going to have to do something drastic to get her attention," he informs me of something I already know.

"And just what would you suggest?" I ask.

"This ought to be good," Braxton says on a laugh.

"I don't think I want to hear this," Payne grumbles under his breath.

"I'm just saying, Dallas needs a man to take charge and show her who's boss, or she'll run all over them," Walker explains.

"Is that right?" I ask.

"Yep, she's a pistol, and it will take a real man to tame her."

"What makes you think I want to tame her?" I ask.

"Don't you?"

"Hell no. She had a man who was high-handed with her. He tried to lock her away in an ivory tower and control her. I don't want to put her fire out. I want to sit back and enjoy the burn. She doesn't need to change a thing. She just needs someone to love her and love Beau with all he has, just the way they are."

"You that man?" Payne asks, all the amusement gone from his voice.

"If she lets me be, I'll be that man every single day for the rest of both their lives—or the rest of mine at the very least."

He nods and then grasps my shoulder.

"Well, damn," Walker adds.

"You'd better make that move soon, man. Or you're risking some other guy sliding in there and making it," Braxton says before he stands.

"I know."

And I do. Every man who crosses her path wants to try.

"Come on. Let's get back to it. Doreen and Ria are feeding us dinner again tonight, and I'm pretty sure I smelled pot roast simmering this morning."

"My favorite," Walker exclaims as he takes one last drink from his bottle and stands.

Fifteen

DALLAS

"WAKE UP, SLEEPYHEAD," I SAY GENTLY AS I SMATTER Beau's face with kisses.

This is our morning routine. I open his blinds to let the sunshine in, and then I kiss him awake.

I get him dressed and ready for school. Then, I feed him a quick breakfast, and we pile into the truck.

"Nana is going to pick you up today and bring you to Miss Madeline after school for your first riding lesson," I tell him.

"Yay!" he squeals from the backseat.

"You have to be good and obey her and listen closely to everything she says, okay?"

"I will, Mommy. I promise."

"After your lesson, we're gonna have dinner at her house. Aunt Doreen is making you chicken fingers and mac 'n' cheese."

His two favorite things.

His face lights up.

He is so easy to please.

"We have Doc scheduled for the branding weekend, right?" I ask Sophie as I update the office calendar.

"Yes, and he's bringing the new guy, Dr. Haralson. We need to call and make sure the new branding cradle is delivered on time too," she says from her side of the desk.

We work in a cramped room off the kitchen in her family's farmhouse, but as soon as she and Braxton move into their new home, we're relocating the office to the loft they live in now. I can't wait. We'll have our own kitchenette and bathroom and a lot more space.

"Okay, I can do that." I add it to my calendar. "Who all is coming to help?" I ask.

"Myer and his dad are helping Walker and Braxton rope. Silas and Payne are going to do the cutting, and Pop, Emmett, and Daddy will be using the branding iron," she says. "Aunt Doreen and Ria are in charge of the picnic. All the ladies from the church are coming and bringing a potluck dish."

Branding season is a big deal in Poplar Falls. All the ranches coordinate the schedule so that everyone is free to help serve their neighbor. We take pride in our cattle and in our community, and this is our opportunity to show it. The ladies make a ton of food, and the kids play while we all watch the herds being roped and branded. It's a celebration like no other.

"By the way, Mom gets in tonight," she informs me.

I look up, and she's chewing on the end of the pencil in her hand.

"I thought she wasn't coming in until Saturday?"

"She decided she needed more time to prep for the party. Which means she will have more time to get under Braxton's skin and drive me crazy," she huffs. "She wants to have a luncheon with the bridesmaids on Friday."

"A luncheon? For what?" I whine.

"Wedding talk, I guess," she says.

Ugh. The last thing I want to do is spend the afternoon listening to Vivian railroad her into things she and Braxton don't want, but I see the tension written all over Sophie, so I relent. This should be an exciting time for her, and I want her to enjoy every minute even if it means I have to suck it up and play nice with her overbearing mother.

"That sounds like fun," I say as I finish up the calendar.

"Really?" she asks as she looks up at me.

"Really. We get to hang out, eat, drink, and talk all things wedding. What's not to like?" I say, infusing my voice with as much honest excitement as I can.

She smiles huge. "Yeah, and she'll have all our dresses, so we can try them on. I can't wait for you girls to see my gown."

There's the radiant glow I wanted to see.

"I thought your gown was staying in New York?"

"I begged. I truly don't have time in my schedule to fly back and forth, so I'll have to be extra strict and not gain or lose a single ounce before the wedding. But it's here!" She beams.

Ugh, watching your weight that closely. That sounds dreadful.

"Well, I can't wait to see it. I bet you really will look like a princess."

We work in silence until we hear the back door open and tiny feet scurry in rapid fire.

Beau appears in the doorway a second later with Hawkeye, Sophie's pup, skidding to a stop at his feet.

"Hi, fellas," I say as I take in Beau's dirty face and jeans.

Madeline appears next, carrying his backpack.

"How was the lesson?" I ask as I stand to take it from her.

"Awesome!" Beau says as he jumps up and down.

Madeline smiles down at him. "He did really well. He's a good listener, and he follows directions. We matched him with a gentle mare who has a lot of experience with children," she informs me.

"Her name is Natasha," Beau tells me.

"Natasha. That's a great name."

"I know. She's brown, like Thumper."

Hawkeye starts yapping and running around Beau's feet, riled up by Beau's excitement.

"Go grab a cookie off the table, and then you and Hawk go out in the backyard and play until Miss Sophie and I are finished in here. I'll call you when it's time to come wash up for supper," I say.

He bolts for the kitchen.

"*One* cookie. And you stay in the backyard where I can see you out this window," I call after him.

"Yes, ma'am," he replies, and we hear the back door slam.

I look back to Madeline. She usually doesn't take kids one-on-one. She hosts riding camps in the summer and runs a renowned nonprofit equestrian therapy center for children with disabilities.

"Thank you. He was so excited last night that he barely slept a wink. Riding is all he has talked about for weeks now."

"You're welcome. He was a delight and no trouble at all. I think he's a natural too. He'll be riding on his own in no time."

I mentally add a horse to my growing list of expenses I need to save for because I know that is going to be added to his wish list for Santa one Christmas in the near future.

Sixteen

DALLAS

"What is it?" Sophie asks.

"It's a vision board the wedding planner and I put together. It turns out, the elegant farmhouse theme is quite the rage this year. Even in New York City. Who knew?" Vivian says in disbelief.

We arrived at Momma's bakery for the bridal party luncheon about half an hour ago. Vivian had a restaurant in Cedar Ridge cater in food for the eight of us. Apparently, Faye's Diner does not serve sufficient luncheon foods. So, we are sitting here with teacups and tiny finger sandwiches of which it will take an entire tray just to fill us up.

The bridesmaids consist of me, Charlotte, and Elle, but Doreen, Ria, and Momma were also invited. Madeline should be here, too, but she and Sophie agreed that it might be awkward for her and Vivian, so she decided to sit this one out.

The board has photos of chalkboard signs; tables set with burlap runners and wildflower centerpieces; mason jars with ribbons, holding candles; chalk-paint signs for the food tables; wine-cork place-card holders and the like.

"Elegant farmhouse, you say?" I ask as I take it all in.

"Yes. It's an upscale-rustic motif. Classy country, like my Sophia," Vivian explains as she smiles lovingly at her daughter.

Charlotte elbows me in the ribs. "See, I told you bougie cowgirl was a thing," she says with a wink.

"Apparently so," I reply.

"I actually like all of that, Mom," Sophie says in astonishment. She and Viv have disagreed at almost every turn on the wedding details.

Vivian's eyes tear up, and she nods. "I thought about it. It's your big day, and I want both you and Braxton to be happy with everything. So, I called the wedding planner, Niles, and told him to scrap all we had planned and to start from scratch. I told him my daughter is elegant and beautiful, but her fiancé is rugged and handsome, so he put the two together and came up with this," she gushes.

Charlotte leans in from the side and whispers to me, "Wow, I can't believe Mrs. Marshall gave in that easily."

"Me neither. She must be going soft. Either that or she's worried Braxton won't let her see her grandchildren if she makes him eat sushi at his reception," I say on a giggle.

Next, we discuss the plans for the engagement party, which is next weekend at the ranch. It will be tented, and there will be a DJ and a makeshift wooden dance floor. The same restaurant that brought over these pitiful sandwiches is catering, but Viv assures Sophie that they have an excellent and substantial buffet coming.

"Good, because if you try to feed our boys tea sandwiches, there will probably be a riot," Doreen informs her.

"Butch is providing iced-down kegs, and the restaurant will have both a red and white wine selection," Sophie adds.

"Red and white wine," I say as I wrinkle my nose.

"Yes. If you want anything else, you'll have to brown-bag."

"You should try the wine, Dallas. I picked a couple of excellent vintages. It might surprise you," Vivian suggests.

I'm not betting on it.

Once we finish our lunch and motif discussions, we move on to the dresses.

Charlotte, Elle, and I try ours on first. They are a lovely, sleeveless A-line chiffon in sienna with an antique lace overlay. Perfect to pair with cowgirl boots.

"Oh my," Doreen gushes. "You girls look stunning."

"The color is perfect. I don't think any of you will even need alterations," Ria adds.

"I gave the designer their exact measurements, and he is a master." Vivian beams. "Okay, girls, go sit. Don't spill anything on those dresses. Doreen, Ria, you want to help me get Sophie into hers?" Vivian asks as she shoos us to the tables.

After about twenty minutes, the aunts return, and I can tell they have both been crying. Then, Sophie comes in with Vivian tailing her, holding the train of her gown off the floor.

The gown is a fitted vintage lace bodice with half-sleeves and a full champagne silk skirt and train. I have never seen anything so beautiful in my life. With Sophie's gorgeous blonde hair pulled up and her tanned skin aglow, she looks like she belongs on a runway.

"What do you think?" she asks nervously.

"It's exquisite," I breathe.

She looks down and smooths the front before looking back up.

"You think?" she asks again, her eyes growing wet.

"What I think is that, when Braxton Young sees you in that dress, he is going to march down the aisle, pick you up, and throw you over his shoulder, caveman-style, before running off with you," I exclaim.

"Oh, no, no, no, he can't do that," Vivian states firmly.

We all giggle.

"The men will be wearing dark jeans, crisp white shirts with French cuffs, and sienna-colored silk ties, as will Beau—although his is a bow tie. I have the ties and shirts with me," Vivian explains.

"And I had a matching outfit made for Hawkeye," Sophie adds.

Beau is going to be the ring bearer. He's excited to be dressing up like Braxton, Payne, Myer, and Walker. Hawkeye is going to walk with him down the aisle.

"Sophia, are you seriously going to have that dog be part of the ceremony?" Vivian asks in disbelief.

"Yes, Mom. We've discussed this. He had a big role in Braxton and me getting together, and we want him to be a part of our big day."

Vivian rolls her eyes but doesn't protest any further.

After we finish with the fashion show, Vivian gathers all our dresses and carefully bags them back up to take to her hotel for safe-keeping because we obviously can't be trusted with them.

I pick Beau up from school, and we head home for supper. I help him with his homework, and then we get ready for bed.

He climbs in, and I settle in beside him.

"How was your day, baby?" I ask him the same question I ask every night before I start his bedtime story.

"Great!" he answers.

"Tell me all about it," I prompt.

"Mrs. Perry taught us how to spell our names in crayon. I got mine right the first time 'cause Nana already showed me how. I got a gold star on my locker for being quiet at naptime. Josie shared her chocolate pudding with me at lunch, and I get to take Fritz to school on Monday for show-and-tell," he rattles off his list of good. "Oh, and I made a new friend on the playground. His name is Stanley."

"Stan Lee or Stanley?" I ask him to clarify.

"Stanley."

I don't remember any kids in his class by that name.

"Is he new?" I ask.

"He was just visiting."

"Visiting? He visited your class?"

"Yes. He has a kid who goes to school too."

"Oh, he's an adult?"

"Yep."

"Whose father is he?"

He just shrugs as he yawns big. I make a mental note to ask his teacher next week and grab a book off his shelf.

I only get a chapter into Fly Guy's latest adventure before he is fast asleep.

I tuck him in tight, kiss his forehead, and tiptoe out.

I grab my phone and dial Myer's number.

"Hello?" His sleepy voice comes over the phone.

I look over to the clock above the television and see it's nine o'clock.

"Crap, I'm sorry. I didn't realize it was so late," I apologize.

Ranchers keep early-to-bed and early-to-rise hours.

"It's okay. I wasn't asleep yet. What's up?"

"Beau had his first riding lesson this week. It's all he's talked about for days," I tell him.

"That's great," he says.

The line goes silent. I don't really have anything else to say.

"That's actually all I had to tell you. He's just so proud, and he's asked me a million times if I told you. He wants you to come watch him one day. I know it's hard with the timing. He goes on Tuesdays and Thursdays, right after school," I babble.

He stops me. "Dallas?"

"Yeah?"

"I'll be there. Tell him I'll come by next week and watch him ride."

"Thanks," I say softly.

"You're welcome."

I hang on the line a few more minutes and then offer him a good night.

"I'll see you tomorrow night. Apparently, we're all going camping," he informs me.

"We are?"

"Yep. Braxton called Payne this evening, and Payne called me."

"Sounds like fun. I hope Momma can keep Beau."

"If not, bring him. He can sleep in the tent with me and Payne."

I smile at that. They are never bothered to have my little man tag along.

"Okay. Night," I say again.

"Good night, Dal."

Seventeen

MYER

"MYER, YOU IN HERE, SON?" POP CALLS FROM THE entrance to the barn.

"Back here, Pop," I answer as I continue to load bags of grain onto the trailer.

Most of our cows are grazing cows, and they get the majority of their food off the land, but we do supplement with a hay and grain mixture on Saturdays for added nutrients.

"Whatcha got left for today?" he asks as he approaches.

"Just gotta get this feed into the troughs and ride the fence before I call it a day," I answer.

"Bells is coming in for spring break. Any way you can swing by and pick her up this afternoon?"

Bellamy is my little sister. She's in her last year at the University of Chicago. Swing by and pick her up means a four-hour round-trip trek to Denver and back.

I look up at him with a grimace. "What time does she get in?"

"Plane lands around three p.m. I'd go, but your momma took my truck into town for her ladies' auxiliary meeting down at the church, and I'm not sure she'll be back in time."

His excuse is flimsy at best. We have other trucks, but I know he is not a fan of long road trips anymore. His eyesight isn't what it used to be. Winston Wilson is a proud man though, and he'll never admit it.

"You ride the fence, and I'll go get her after I load the troughs," I suggest.

"Deal," he agrees.

"You gonna be home for supper tonight?" he asks.

That means Momma plans to cook a big dinner for Bellamy, and they'd like me to be there.

My cabin is on our ranch about half a mile from my parents' house. I usually fend for myself, but occasionally, I still join them for meals.

"I'm supposed to meet the guys down at the river. We're going camping tonight. I suppose I could eat a quick bite with you all before I head that way."

"Bev would like that. She's planning on making all of your and Bells's favorites. Eat around six p.m.," he throws the blame on Momma before slapping me on the back and heading to the stables to saddle a horse and ride the perimeter.

Stoney Ridge is a thirty-eight-hundred-acre cattle ranch my family has owned for generations. We are about half the size of Rustic Peak. Pop and I run the show, and we employ a half-dozen ranch hands and hire seasonal workers during calving season. We work twelve-hour days, seven days a week, three hundred and sixty-five days a year. Sometimes, those days are grueling, and sometimes, they are laid-back, but they are never boring. The work is hard but satisfying. I like working with my hands, and I love the animals. Respect them. Take care of them, love them, and feed them until it's time for them to feed us. Our beef cattle are of the highest quality, and we make a good profit when we go to auction every year.

It might not have been my dream to work the ranch when I was younger, but I wouldn't have it any other way now. This is what I was born to do, and I'm damn good at it.

After I finish with the feed, I take a quick shower, and then I head to Denver. Traffic is fairly light since it is Saturday, and the drive up is easy. I pull into the pickup lane and spot Bells with her hair piled on top of her head and earbuds in her ears, pulling her suitcase behind her.

I throw the truck in park and hop out.

"Hey, big brother," she squeals as she spots me and comes running. "I didn't know you were coming to get me. I thought Momma and Pop were."

She wraps her arms around my middle, and I squeeze her tight and kiss the top of her head.

"Momma was busy at the church, and Pop is waiting to help her with supper. Are you hungry?"

"Starving!"

"Good. She has a feast planned."

I load her suitcase and open the door for her.

"How are classes?" I ask once we are back on the road.

"Good, I guess. I'm on the homestretch now. Only a couple months left, and I'm done," she says with relief.

"Ready to come home, huh?"

"I don't think I can survive another Chicago winter. I mean, Colorado can be bad, but Chicago is insane. This past year, there was a winter advisory, and we were told not to leave our homes. With the wind chill, the temperature was negative twenty-five. That's almost double freezing," she says with her eyes wide.

"Sounds awful," I agree.

"It was. Classes were canceled for over a week. Chicago is great in the warm months. It's a really fun city, but we were trapped inside for days."

"So, what's the plan when you finish school? You going to come back to Poplar Falls?"

She shrugs. "I haven't decided. I can use my degree in environmental science to work with the farmers and ranchers near home, or I could apply for a position at the Denver Zoo."

"That'd be fun," I encourage.

"Yeah, and if I go that route, I could work a few days a week from home and commute to the zoo the other days. That way, I have the option of living in Poplar Falls or maybe somewhere in between. I've missed home though. I miss the ranch, you guys, Elle, and Sonia."

The kid has been homesick since the day she left. I'm proud of her for sticking it out and finishing.

"Speaking of which, we are all camping down by the river tonight. Braxton and Sophie and her friend from New York, Elle and Sonia, Dallas and Payne, Silas and Chloe and Walker. You want to come with us?"

Her eyes light up. I knew she would.

"Yes. That sounds like fun. I'm dying to meet Sophie. Elle has told me all about her."

"Good. After supper, we have to slip out before Momma realizes what's happening and tries to guilt you into staying home with her."

"I'm here for over a week. She can have me later."

"Two weeks? That means you'll be here for the engagement party and Stoney Ridge's branding party."

"I know. It's gonna be a great spring break," she says with a grin.

Eighteen

DALLAS

"You sure you don't mind him staying the night?" I ask Daddy as I drop Beau off with him.

"Of course not. When Dottie gets home from the ladies' meeting, we're going to eat supper and then make homemade ice cream," he says as he cuts his eyes to Beau.

"Ice cream? Yay!" Beau screams in delight.

"What do you say you and I go pick some fresh strawberries for our ice cream before Nana gets home?"

"Okay, let me go get my gloves and bucket." He lets go of my hand and races into my parents' house.

"That boy sure loves farming," I muse as I hand Daddy his overnight bag.

"It's in his blood," Daddy agrees.

Beau comes running back out with a bucket about as big as he is with gardening gloves on his hands.

"Come give me a kiss," I command.

He drops the bucket on the porch and comes to me, and I bend down on one knee.

"You be a good boy for Nana and Pop-Pop tonight, okay?"

He nods his head. "Yes, ma'am."

"Don't give them any trouble when they say it's bedtime. Make sure you brush your teeth and say your prayers too."

"I promise, Mommy," he says as he wraps his little arms around my neck and kisses my cheek over and over.

"I love you the mostest," I tell him, and he grins.

"No, I love you the mostest," he replies.

"Y'all have fun," I say as I stand and kiss Daddy's cheek.

They wave to me as I drive off. Hand in hand, they head out into the field.

Two peas in a pod.

I pull up in front of Sophie's place, and it looks like the gang is all here. I park my truck out of the way and grab my overnight bag and sleeping bag from the bed. I toss them in the gravel and reach for the tent.

"You need some help?" I hear Myer's voice behind me as I tug.

"Yes, please. This sucker is heavier than it looks," I grunt.

He reaches over top of me, easily plucks it from the tailgate, and tosses it over his shoulder.

I look up at him with a scowl. "Nobody likes a show-off," I huff.

He laughs as he carries the tent over to his truck and tosses it in. I follow with my bags and add them to the pile already settled in.

"Myer, you got room for another cooler in your truck? Mine is full, and Walker's is loaded down with firewood and the grill," Braxton calls from the porch.

"Yeah, bring it on," he answers.

"Do I need to take my truck too?" I ask as Brax sets the cooler on Myer's tailgate.

"Nah, we should be good. You, Charlotte, Bellamy, and Myer are in this truck. Sophie, Elle, Sonia, Hawkeye and I are in my truck. Walker's got Payne, Silas, and Chloe in his truck. That's everyone, isn't it?" he asks as he counts heads.

"That's all of us," Myer answers him.

"I didn't know Bellamy was home," I say to Myer as he shuts the tailgate.

"Yep, I picked her up at the airport this afternoon. It's her spring break. She's somewhere in the house with Elle and Sonia."

Those three have been thick as thieves for as long as I can remember. It's odd, seeing Elle and Sonia without Bells tagging along.

Once Silas and Chloe finally make it and we're all packed, the caravan heads out.

Our favorite place to camp is in a clearing at the bottom of the gap by the river's edge. We've all been coming here since we were in high school. It has a large, open space for all our tents, a huge stoned-in area for a campfire, horseshoe pits, a rope swing secured to one of the large Ponderosa pine trees that balances over the water, and an outhouse that Braxton and Walker dug out and built for us in the woods about a hundred feet from the clearing.

As soon as we pull up, the boys start unloading the trucks and putting up tents while us girls get the charcoal going on the grill and start a fire. Next, we set up all our lawn chairs around it.

The days are warm now, but the nights still get pretty cold. The fire, as well as the dozen jars of moonshine Walker brought with him, should keep us comfortable.

"This is quite the setup," Charlotte observes as she looks around.

"Yeah, we don't play around when it comes to camping," I agree.

"This is my first time. You guys are popping my camping cherry," she informs us.

"What? Are you serious? Never?" Elle asks in disbelief.

"Never," she confirms.

"How is that possible?" Sonia asks. "Don't you have Girl Scouts or summer camps in New York?"

"Nope. They probably have Girl Scouts, but I wasn't one."

"Church camps?" Bellamy chimes in.

"We have theater in the park and Tavern on the Green." She shrugs.

They all look at each other in confusion.

"It's the closest we get to outdoor activities. That and ice-skating in the winter."

"That's sad." Elle grimaces.

"Quite," Charlotte agrees. "That's why I'm here though. To have a true Colorado adventure."

"You start with this," Sophie says as she passes out red Solo cups filled with shots of apple moonshine, homemade by Walker's grand-daddy, using apples from my family's orchard. It's the best in the county.

She raises her cup to toast. "To the full Colorado Mountains experience."

We all raise ours and repeat after her. Then, we down the shots.

Once the tents are up, Braxton and Myer man the grill while we cook beans over the open fire. Doreen and Ria loaded us up with potato salad and banana pudding in the cooler.

We all get our bellies full, and then we start passing the moon-shine jars around.

Walker grabs his guitar and starts to absentmindedly strum it, and before long, he's effortlessly playing it like it's an extension of himself. I sit back in my chair and close my eyes as I listen to the melody. He starts to softly sing the words, and I let them flow through me. He is really talented. He doesn't perform for us often, but when he does, it's always a treat. I love country music. I love the honesty and the emotion in the lyrics. Walker sings them like the pain is a living, breathing thing for him. It's beautiful.

We enjoy each other's company. It's simple. It's free. It's the best. The only thing missing is a little six-year-old rascal. He loves camping and fishing.

"Hey." Myer sits down next to me and says, "You look lost in your thoughts."

I open one eye and look over at him. "I was thinking about Beau.

He would like this. He gets a kick out of Walker playing that guitar. He begged him to teach him how to play it last time," I say as I close my eyes again.

"We should have brought him," he agrees.

I really wish we had.

"Next time," I sigh.

"What are the sleeping arrangements?" Charlotte asks.

"Me, Braxton, and Hawk in one tent. Bellamy, Sonia, and Elle in one tent, Payne and Myer in a tent, Silas and Chloe in their tent, you and Dallas in a tent, and that puts Walker in the small single tent," Sophie answers.

"That's me, always sleeping alone," Walker moans.

"Please, you get more action than the cleanup bull on the ranch," Braxton says on a laugh.

Walker grins at him. "I do what I can for the poor lonely women of Poplar Falls."

"That's you, Walk; you're a giver," Myer says as he tips his bottle in Walker's direction.

"Damn straight."

Nineteen

DALLAS

"I'M OUT," I SAY ON A YAWN AS I STAND.

Braxton and Sophie retired about half an hour ago. I hung in there as long as I could. I look down at Myer. His eyes are heavy too.

"You've been up since dawn; you should get some sleep too," I suggest.

"Just waiting for you to say when," he says as he stands.

"She ain't the boss of you," Walker says as he grins at the two of us.

"No, but I didn't want to be the dude who punked out first," Myer says and chucks his bottle cap in Walker's direction.

Elle, Sonia, and Bells are all still chatting away, and Payne and Charlotte look to be cozying up.

"I'll leave the tent unzipped for you, Charlotte. Just so you know, I'm a snuggler," I warn as I head to our tent.

"That's good because I'm a cuddler too," she calls after me.

I turn to Myer. "Good night. I hope these guys aren't too rowdy and keep you up."

"Nah, I'm beat. Once I hit the mattress, I'll be out. You sleep tight," he says before disappearing into his and Payne's tent.

I grab a flashlight and trek down to the outhouse before I settle in.

The tent is large with room to walk around. The queen-size blow-up mattress is made up with our sleeping bags and covered in the pillows I never leave home without. A girl has to have her own pillows to sleep well.

I snuggle into the sleeping bag, throw the extra quilts over me, and fall fast asleep.

I feel the mattress shift, and I roll further to my side to allow Charlotte more room.

A few seconds later, I feel a light tap on my shoulder.

"Dallas, are you awake?" she whispers.

I don't respond. I just pull the blankets up over my head.

"Dallas," she says a little louder this time.

Ugh.

I roll over and blink my eyes open. "What?"

"Um, can you switch tents with your brother?" she asks quietly.

"Switch tents? Why?"

"Well, we have been out there talking for a while, and, um … we would kind of like to continue getting to know each other better," she explains.

"So? Just keep talking outside until you're ready to go to sleep," I suggest as I turn back on my side. My groggy mind having trouble catching up.

"We want to continue getting to know each other"—she pauses—"privately."

"Okay." Then, it finally registers, and I say, "Ohhhhhh."

"I'm sorry to ask, but it's that, or we drive back to his place," she apologizes.

I close my eyes for a second and consider making my stupid brother drive all the way back home to fool around.

"Please," she says sweetly.

Who am I to stop anyone from having a good time?

"Oh, all right," I huff as I throw the covers off.

"Are you mad?" she asks, and a hiccup escapes. She covers her mouth and giggles.

She's a lightweight, like Sophie.

"No, it's fine," I say as I gather up my sleeping bag and pillows.

"Thank you. I owe you one," she says excitedly.

I exit the tent, and I see my brother adding more wood to the fire. Everyone else has retired to their tents and are all zipped in for the night.

He looks over his shoulder at me and comes to grab my pillows.

"You owe me, Payne Henderson. It's like high school all over again," I say as I shove the pillows into his chest and stomp off into the direction of his tent with him close on my heels.

"Yeah, but instead of you switching bedrooms with me, it's a tent, and I won't wake up to Momma standing over your bed with me snuggled up to Peggy Clemmer," he agrees.

I laugh. "I'll never forget you running around in a circle in your underwear with Momma holding on to your arm with one hand and swinging a rolling pin with the other. Poor Peggy was horrified, and she was never allowed back to the farm either."

"It was just as well. She kissed like she was trying to eat my face," he says with a shudder.

"Well, just keep in mind that Charlotte is Sophie's New York bestie. So, you'd better be careful because she's not going anywhere."

"Don't worry, sis. We're both grown-ups, and I made sure we were on the same page," he assures me.

"All right. Have fun, I guess," I say as I kiss his cheek and duck into his tent.

He hands my pillows off to me and heads back.

I zip the tent closed to keep any critters from climbing in with us, and I crawl up the mattress beside a sleeping Myer.

I try to settle in as lightly as I can, but he stirs anyway.

He squints up at me. "Dallas?" he asks, confused.

"I'm sorry. Go back to sleep," I whisper.

"What are you doing?"

"My brother and Charlotte booted me from my tent, so it looks like you're stuck with me," I explain.

He smiles. It's a sexy, sleepy smile.

"I knew that was going to happen," he states.

"Yeah, once she sat down between his legs while roasting marshmallows, I kind of figured it too," I admit.

I start shivering. I'm wearing a large sleep shirt, but my legs are bare, and the night has gotten chilly.

He notices and opens his blanket, gesturing for me to get in.

I slide in beside him and snuggle into his warmth. He's wearing flannel pajama pants and nothing else. He wraps his arms around me and pulls me in close to tuck my head under his chin. The shivers stop, and in no time at all, I'm cozy and falling fast asleep.

Twenty

DALLAS

I'M LOST IN THE MOST AMAZING DREAM. I'M ON THE DECK OF A GORGEOUS home. Beau is playing in the yard just beyond the railing, and I'm watching from my lounge spot. Two strong arms are holding me, and I have an overwhelming sense of serenity.

Giggling. I hear giggling. Girls.

I look out into the yard, and Elle and Sonia are swinging Beau between them. *Where did they come from?*

The arms around me tighten and shift, and I feel warm breath on the back of my neck. A shiver runs down my spine, and I burrow in closer.

That's when my eyes pop open.

I'm in the boys' tent. The giggles I hear are the girls starting to stir outside, and those arms in my dream are securely pinning me to a sleeping Myer. He rolls onto his back. My face is pressed against his bare chest, which rises and falls with his deep breaths. He has a smattering of dark hair on his chest. Curiosity gets the better of me, and I take my hand and run it through it. It's soft. I sigh, close my eyes again, and cuddle in closer. I haven't slept beside a man in six years. It feels nice. Comfy, warm … content.

I start to doze back off to sleep when I hear the tent unzip, and Payne pokes his head in. He stops and does a double take as his eyes find Myer and me wrapped around each other.

"Morning," he says with a question in his voice.

Myer stirs and opens one eye. He tilts his face down to me and smiles a sleepy smile.

"Hey," he says as his hand roams down my back.

Payne clears his throat.

I untangle from Myer, sit up, and stretch.

"Good morning," I mumble.

"How was your night?" Payne asks.

"Uneventful, compared to yours," Myer answers for us.

Payne grins a wicked grin and reaches in to grab his duffel bag. "It was eventful. You guys get up. We're cooking breakfast, and as soon as it warms up a bit, we're throwing the inner tubes in the water," he tells us before ducking out.

I feel shy all of a sudden once he zips the tent back up. Looking down at Myer with his sleep-mussed hair feels too intimate.

"Did you sleep okay?" he asks.

I nod as I focus my eyes across the tent and not on his chest. "How about you?" I manage to ask.

"Like a baby."

"That water is too cold," I exclaim as I dip my big toe in the river.

"Don't be a baby; it's not that bad," Walker taunts from his perch on an inner tube.

"Sorry, I haven't ingested as much antifreeze as you this morning," I gripe.

"Then, get to drinking, woman. Don't make me chase you down and toss you in," he threatens.

I narrow my eyes at him. He grins, but I know his ass would do it, so I take a deep breath and cover my nose and mouth and jump in.

Ice-cold water pricks my body like a hundred tiny knives, and I scream as I surface.

"You liar. Not that bad, my ass," I yell as I splash water up into his face.

"Calm down. You'll get used to it in a minute," he says as he throws his hands up to defend himself against my assault.

Braxton ties off a tube for the cooler, and we all spend the next couple of hours floating in the water and drinking beer. It's tranquil—other than the chattering of Elle and her friends.

Did I talk that much when I was their age? Don't they know every second doesn't have to be filled with conversation? I think that's just a sign of maturity—to be able to spend time with your best friend in complete silence and still feel the connection.

My body finally acclimates to the water temperature, and I decide to dive in for a quick swim. Walker suggests a friendly game of chicken, and we are all just drunk enough to oblige.

"Hop on," Myer says as he goes down to his knees in the water.

I jump up and wrap my legs around his head. When I clamp my thighs to the sides of his neck to hold on, he stands. Sophie is on Braxton's shoulders, and Charlotte is on Payne's. Walker looks around and then grabs Elle's hand and tugs her off her tube.

"Come on, Elle. Partner with me," he pleads.

"No, you'll let me fall," she protests.

"I'd never let you fall, woman," he exclaims and kneels down.

She hops up on his shoulders.

"Hey, you be careful with my sister," Braxton calls out as he frowns at them.

"You and your girl had better watch out; we're coming for you," Walker calls back, and the battle begins.

I lean down and talk into Myer's ear, "Let's kick some ass."

"Yes, ma'am," he replies, and we charge into the midst of them.

It doesn't take long for us to dismount Charlotte. The city slicker in her is too worried about her nails getting ripped off to put up much of a fight. She goes sailing into the water with a splash two minutes in. Elle is a little harder to tackle. Mainly because Walker is too stubborn to let her go. He holds her legs on to him by sheer force of will until Sophie and I gang up on her and finally tear her from his grip. She goes into the water, squealing, and surfaces, laughing.

Left to face off is me and Myer and Sophie and Braxton. It is a pretty even match between Myer and Braxton. Both are a little over six feet tall, built strong. Their shoulders, chests, and arms have been sculpted to perfection by the hard work on the ranch, but we have the advantage because I'm definitely more of a scrapper than Sophie.

"Don't let me down, Dal," Myer calls up to me.

"I got this," I state assuredly.

We charge them, and Sophie and I lock into a hold. We wrestle until my arms and thighs are burning. Finally, I am able to snake my right arm out of her grasp, and I wrap it around her shoulder and throw my entire body into a twist. She lets out a yelp and dismounts. Braxton tries to hold her on, but all he can manage is to keep one of her legs pinned to the side of his neck.

I throw my arms up in victory. "Yes! We are the champions," I bellow into the air.

Everyone starts clapping, and Myer drops a shoulder and plunges me into the water. I come up sputtering and jump at him. He effortlessly catches me. I wrap my legs around his middle and try my damnedest to pull him down. He doesn't budge. He's like a freaking tree trunk.

"I can't believe you did that. You're supposed to be on my team," I complain.

He laughs as I splash water into his face.

Everyone starts to exit the water, but he just stands there, clutching my bottom and holding me to him. Then, he brings his forehead to mine, and my breath catches.

"You cold?" he asks against my lips.

I nod.

"Come on. Let's get you up to the fire," he says, his voice husky.

He doesn't let me down. He keeps his hold and walks me right out of the river and up the bank to the firepit. When he sets me down on my chair, I look around, and every set of eyes is watching us.

"What?" I ask loudly.

They all quickly look away.

Twenty-One

MYER

AFTER A LATE DINNER OF BURGERS AND HOT DOGS ON THE grill, we all pack up and head toward Rustic Peak.

Payne and Charlotte ride back with Walker, and the three of them plan to head out to Butch's Tavern tonight. I'm beat from the day in the water, and that early morning alarm I know is coming is sending me home.

"Hey, Myer. Do you mind picking me up tomorrow afternoon? I want to stay the night with Elle. Doreen and Ria are having a *Gilmore Girls* marathon," Bellamy says as her eyes light up, "but I promised Momma I'd go to Janelle's with her after lunch."

"What time? I have Doc coming out to look at one of the heifers tomorrow," I ask as I unload Dallas's tent from my truck.

"Around eleven?"

"I don't think he'll be done by then, Bells. Momma will just have to pick you up," I answer.

Her face falls. "She's giving a piano lesson from ten thirty to eleven thirty. That won't leave her enough time to come all the way out here before our appointments. It's fine. I'll just go on home. I can stay another time," she says, disappointment clear in her voice.

"Why don't I just leave you my truck?" Dallas offers.

Bells looks to her. "Really?"

"Sure. Myer can drop me off on the way home. My parents are keeping Beau another night, and Momma will take him to school in the morning on her way to the bakery. I have the lunch shift at Faye's, so you can swing by and get me, and I'll drop you off before work." She fishes her keys out of her bag and hands them to Bellamy.

"Thank you, Dallas," she squeals and hugs her neck.

"You're welcome. Just make sure you leave by eleven fifteen, and we should have plenty of time."

Bells hurries back to the house, and I start picking Dallas's things back up and loading them in my truck.

"I guess I just volunteered you to chauffeur me home without asking. I'm sorry," she apologizes.

I slam the tailgate shut and turn to her. "You never have to ask, Dal. I've always got you. Besides, you're on the way home," I say as I slip her bag from her shoulder.

Her eyes find mine. She's wearing an odd expression.

"You do, don't you?" she asks softly.

"Do what?"

"Always have me," she answers.

I lean in, brush the hair from her face, and tuck it behind her ear. "Yes, ma'am. Always."

She's silent the entire drive. I'm not sure what's going on in that beautiful head of hers, so I leave her to it.

When we get to her house, I put the truck in park and start to get out to walk her safely to her door, like I always do. Before I can exit, she places her hand on my thigh to stop me.

I look over just as she hesitantly pulls herself over to my side.

"I need to try something," she says as she moves both of her hands to my chest, takes a deep breath, grasps my shirt, and tugs me to her. Then, her mouth is on mine.

It's an unsure kiss at first, but after a few stunned minutes, my brain starts to fire again, and I wrap my arms around her, bring her in closer, and take control.

She opens for me on a moan, and I deepen the kiss, our tongues gently wrestling. She tastes like cinnamon. My left hand slides into her hair and grabs a fistful while the other glides down and caresses her lower back.

She feels like heaven.

A groan escapes my lips as she starts to pull away and gasp for air.

I adjust myself, and just as I'm about to apologize for losing control, she grabs me by my ears and pulls me back to her mouth as she crawls into my lap.

This time, her kiss is wild. Like a dam breaking and finally letting go of the weight held behind it for too long, she throws her whole body into the kiss.

My body reacts, and I know she can feel me growing hard beneath her.

I grasp her hips.

I try to keep ahold of her, but she starts moving frantically against me. Her flesh begging for something more. Then, she suddenly bears up, and her head smacks hard against the roof of the truck.

"Ow," she howls as she rubs the top of her head and sits back against my thighs, trembling. Her back presses into the steering wheel, and the horn begins to blare. "Shit!" she cries and leans back into me.

"You all right?" I ask, trying my best to hold back laughter.

"Yes. No," she says breathlessly. "I hope I didn't wake up Momma and Daddy or Beau."

She looks nervously over my shoulder toward the farmhouse.

"Hey, let's go inside," I suggest as I draw her attention back to me.

I reach around her for the door handle.

She doesn't move, just watches me. Chewing on her bottom lip.

"Dal?"

"If we go inside, it's gonna change everything," she whispers.

What she doesn't realize is, everything already has changed.

"Yeah," I agree. "You ready for that?"

"I don't know," she answers honestly.

I sit up and take her mouth again. She opens and melts into the kiss.

When I pull back, I look her in the eyes and whisper across her lips, "Yes, you do."

Twenty-Two

DALLAS

When we make it inside the house, I drop my bag on the floor beside the door and stand there, uncertain what to do next. I don't know why I'm so nervous. It's not like I haven't made out with boys in trucks before or even invited one in, but this is different.

This is Myer.

I'm not sure what possessed me to kiss him like that, but it's all I've thought about since I woke up in his arms this morning.

I hear him walk in behind me and shut the door. Then, he waits. I know he wants to make sure this is what I want.

Is it?

Still facing forward, I reach behind me and offer him my hand. He takes it and walks into my back. I can feel my heart beating rapidly against my chest, and I take a deep breath, trying to calm it.

His arm snakes around my middle and pulls me into him. He lays his chin on my shoulder. "Relax, Dal. If all I get to do is kiss you tonight, it'll still be the best damn night," he says softly, assuring me.

I close my eyes and turn to face him. His heat feels so good. I lay my forehead on his chest and let him hold me for a minute. Then, I make my decision. I bear up on my tiptoes as I wrap my arms around his neck, and I kiss him.

After a couple of beats, he starts to back us up toward the couch. I want to touch him. To feel his skin against mine again.

I grab the hem of his tee and start yanking. Our mouths disengage just long enough for him to step back and pull it over his head. It drops to the ground at our feet. I watch as it falls, and then I bring my eyes back to him. I really, really like his chest. I step in and lightly run my fingertips over his torso. I memorize every muscle as it contracts under my touch. With a growl, he picks me up and deposits me on the couch.

He kneels beside me and slides his hand down the inside of my thigh to my calf. Then, he holds it up and tugs my boot loose. He repeats the move with the other leg, and I watch as my body starts to hum with anticipation.

He sets the boots aside and then joins me. The heat of his body covers me, and he brings his lips back to mine. I love the weight of him.

He tears his mouth away and kisses a line across my jaw to just beneath my ear where he whispers, "You taste so damn good."

Then, he slowly glides his mouth down the column of my throat as he laces a finger in the strap of my tank. He tugs it down, giving him access to my chest.

I writhe underneath him as he wraps his hand around one mound and starts to knead lightly.

"God, you're beautiful, Dallas," he says before he wraps his mouth around my nipple and sucks gently.

My hips buck from the couch in response, and I cry out at the sensation.

My core turns to molten liquid as he continues to lavish attention on my breasts.

I glide my hands down his back into the waist of his jeans.

His heated gaze finds my eyes, and he watches my reaction as his hand slides my tank up, exposing my stomach. He crawls down my body and twirls his tongue around my belly button as he pops the button to my jeans. He looks up, his eyes asking for permission.

I raise my hips to allow him to slide my pants down my legs.

He presses a kiss into the curls at the top of my thighs, and then he spreads my legs apart and sits back to look at me.

"Gorgeous," he says reverently as he kneels back down and swipes his tongue across me in one unhurried lick. The scruff on his face lightly scoring the inside of my thigh.

My breath catches, and I grab the sides of the couch to keep from coming up to my feet.

He does it again, and I let out a tortured moan.

I need him to touch me. I start circling my hips, trying to reach his face, and he grins. He tucks his large hands under my hips and raises me. Then, he moves his body under mine and pulls me fully on top of him.

For a second, I'm confused and a little bereft. He was right where I wanted him. Then, he tugs my hips forward till I'm sitting upright against his face. I clasp the back of the couch to steady myself as he securely holds me up in his grasp. Then, he leans in and brings his mouth back to me again.

That's when I lose all self-control.

He wraps his lips around my clit and firmly sucks it as he finds my opening with his finger.

Finally.

I slowly start to ride his face, but I can't hold back as he presses another finger inside. I begin wildly bucking against him as I feel the pressure rapidly building within me. My fingers find his hair and grab a fistful of it as I move faster against his tongue.

He softly bites down on me as I explode around his fingers, and his name escapes from my lips.

He grasps hold of my hips as I tremble from top to toe, panting to catch my breath.

After my shudders subside, he releases me, and I crawl back down his body until my chest is flush with his. He watches me as I bring my mouth to lick the beads of salty sweat that have gathered at the hollow of his throat.

I proceed downward. Exploring him with my tongue with every intention of making him feel as good as he just did me when, all of a sudden, there is a pounding at my door.

My head shoots up as I hear my mother's voice calling to me from the other side.

I leap from the couch, pull my shirt down and frantically look around searching for my jeans.

"Just a minute, Momma," I call. I look to Myer and whisper, "I'm so sorry."

He shakes his head. He reaches up and places his hand on the side of my face, and then he quickly kisses me.

Once we are both semi–put together, I open the door.

Momma is standing there with Beau in her arms, wrapped in a quilt. "I'm sorry to interrupt your night, but he woke up with a stomachache about an hour ago, and he's been asking for you," she says apologetically.

"No, that's okay," I say as I reach out and take him from her arms.

All thoughts of embarrassment evaporate as I take him in. He is white as a ghost, and his little body is shivering.

"Mommy," he cries weakly.

"I'm right here, baby."

I lay my lips against his forehead.

"He's burning up," I say. I turn to Myer, who got up to stand behind me. "Can you get me a bottle of water from the fridge?" I ask.

"Sure," he says as he lays his hand on Beau's head. "Hey, little man."

"Are you having a sleepover?" Beau asks as I turn to walk him inside.

Just as I start to answer, he makes a pitiful retching noise, turns his head, and vomits all over himself and me. Then, he starts to cry harder.

"Shh. It's okay, Beau. Mommy's got you."

I head toward the bathroom.

"I'm getting him into a cool bath," I yell over my shoulder.

Twenty-Three

MYER

Mrs. Henderson walks quickly to the kitchen and opens the door beside the back door. She retrieves a mop and a pail. I come to her side.

"I'll take care of it," I say as I take them from her hands.

"Oh, Myer, you don't have to," she says wearily.

"I want to. You look exhausted. You need to go back to bed," I tell her.

She smiles up at me. "I guess I am a bit tired. It's been a long time since my children were little and needed me in the middle of the night."

"Go on home. He'll be okay, and I'll stay with them until he is settled," I assure her.

She lays her cool hand against my cheek and looks up at me through watery eyes. "You're a good man, Myer Wilson."

"I just care about your daughter and grandson," I admit to her.

"I know you do," she says. Then, she kisses my cheek.

I walk her to the door, careful to avoid the mess.

"Please tell Dallas I'll be back by to check on him in the morning. I'm not sure he'll be up for school tomorrow though."

"I'm guessing not," I agree.

She reaches into the pocket of her night coat and hands me a pair of small, round glasses. Then, she heads down the steps, and I stand in the doorway and watch as she crosses the drive to the farmhouse.

"Good night, Myer," she calls from her porch.

I wave as she disappears into the house.

I shut the door and get busy, cleaning up the vomit.

Dallas comes back into the living room about twenty minutes later, carrying Beau, who's wrapped in a big, fluffy towel.

"His fever broke," she says as she looks to the place where he got sick. "Did you do that?" she asks as she takes in the clean floor.

"Yeah, I didn't want you to have to deal with that too. Beau needs you," I tell her.

She looks up at me with tears in her eyes. She's exhausted too.

I walk to them and take Beau's weight from her arms. She still has puke in her hair, and her clothes are soaked.

"I'll get clean pajamas on him while you get a shower," I offer.

Her lips tremble, as she nods at me.

"Thank you," she says as she brushes the back of her hand against Beau's forehead. "Baby, Myer is going to help you get clothes on while Mommy gets cleaned up, okay?"

"Okay," he mumbles.

She heads back into the bathroom, and I take him to his room. I stand him on his bed, tucked in the towel.

"Which drawer has pajamas?" I ask, and he points to the top one.

I fish out a Batman footed onesie. After I get him dressed, he wraps his arms around my neck, and I carry him back to the couch.

I sit and turn the television on the Disney Channel, and he lies down, propped against me.

Dallas emerges, wrapped in a fluffy bathrobe with her damp hair piled on top of her head.

She stops short and takes us in.

Beau lifts his head. "Mommy, can we have a sleepover in here?" he asks hoarsely.

"You and I can, but I think Myer has to get home. He has to be up really early to feed the cattle," she gently breaks to him.

He brings his eyes to me, and his bottom lip quivers as he nods his head.

"Okay," he says as he leans up off of me.

I look up at Dallas. She still looks worried.

"I can stay for a sleepover. I'll just slip out in the morning."

Beau looks to his mother for her reaction. "Please, Mommy. Can he stay?"

She brings her eyes to him and smiles weakly. Indecision written all over her.

"I want to stay in case he gets sick again," I tell her.

"Are you sure?" she asks.

"I am," I say as I tuck Beau back into my side.

"All right, I'm going to go put on pajamas, and I'll be right back." She gives in.

Before she returns, Beau is fast asleep. His arm is wrapped around my middle, and his little head is resting on my chest. She has pillows in her arms, and she hands me one before she grabs the quilt off the back of the couch and settles in on the other side of Beau.

She checks his temperature with the back of her hand one more time.

"I gave him Tylenol. I think the worst is over," she whispers.

"Yeah, he seems to be sleeping peacefully now," I agree.

I hoist him up a little higher and open my arm wider, so she can cuddle into us.

She lays her head against my side and covers the three of us with the quilt.

Before long, her even breaths join his. I click the television off, and then I lay my head back against the top of the sofa and close my eyes.

I could fall asleep like this every single night.

My internal clock wakes me a few minutes before four in the morning. Beau's entire body is wrapped around my middle, and his head is up under my armpit. Dallas's head is lying on his legs on the opposite side. Both are softly snoring. I sit still and enjoy the sight of them cuddled up before I try to disengage and slip out.

I wish I had my phone to snap a photo before disturbing them.

I carefully lift Beau and attempt to hurry to the side, but the arm of the couch is blocking my exit.

Dallas feels me shifting, and her eyes blink open. Her confused expression is adorable as I see her mind working to figure out where she is.

"Myer?" she asks groggily.

"Shh." I gesture down at Beau, who is still sleeping like a rock. He's a deep sleeper, just like his momma.

She blows a wayward curl from her face and looks down at her son. She reaches over to brush her hand through his hair, and then she sits up, bows her back, and stretches her arms above her head as she yawns.

"What time is it?" she asks.

"Almost four," I answer as I slide completely clear of Beau and tuck him back into the couch on his tummy.

She stands with me. "Want me to make you some coffee or something?" she asks as she looks around the room, trying to wake up fully.

"No," I say as I take her shoulders and lead her back down to the couch. "I want you to go back to sleep."

She lays her head back against Beau's behind and wraps herself around a pillow. "You sure?" she says as her heavy eyes start to close.

I don't answer her. I just lean down and press a kiss to her mouth.

She smiles in her sleep.

My heart melts.

Twenty-Four

DALLAS

"How is he?" Momma asks as she comes through the front door, carrying her purse, a thermos, and a basket of fresh muffins. She marches past me and unloads everything onto the kitchen island and turns for my answer.

"He's still sleeping, but he's feeling better. No fever this morning."

I woke around nine when Beau stirred and needed to go to the potty. I forced him to take another dose of Children's Tylenol and drink a glass of Pedialyte before he fell back asleep, and I carried him to his bed.

"I'm keeping him out of school today to be on the safe side though. That fever took it out of both of us," I tell her as I pluck one of the muffins from the basket and start to butter it.

"Yes, I think that's best. Don't you have to work today?" she asks.

"Yeah, I already texted Faye to tell her I couldn't come in. She was okay with it. They had a slow morning, and Kim didn't make that many tips, so she was happy to pull a double."

Kim is Faye's other waitress and the two of them are always willing to cover for me when something unexpected arises and I do the same for them when I can. I'm incredibly lucky that both my bosses are lenient with me when it comes to Beau's needs. Not all single mothers are as lucky.

"I notice your truck isn't in the drive."

"No, Bellamy wanted to stay at Rustic Peak with Elle last night but needed to be home early to meet her momma, so I left her my truck, and Myer gave me a ride home," I explain that last part unnecessarily, as she knows Myer was here.

"That was awfully nice of you," she says while looking down and stirring the coffee I just placed in front of her, "and Myer."

There it is. I know she's dying to quiz me on what exactly she walked in on last night. I'm sure our disheveled appearances left no question as to what we were up to.

"It was—if that old truck actually starts for her this morning and doesn't leave her stranded out there," I deflect.

She catches it and looks up at me. Her keen eyes taking me in.

"Myer sure was helpful last night. He wouldn't let me clean up, and he promised me he'd stay until you had Beau settled," she says, the question definitely in her voice.

"He did. He cleaned everything up and even rinsed the mop and pail outside. He got Beau dressed while I showered the vomit off of me, and then we let Beau talk us into a sleepover in the living room," I tell her, but she already knows.

She lives forty feet from my door and gets up with the chickens. I'm sure she watched him pull off this morning while she was baking these muffins.

"He was always a good boy, and he's grown into a good man. I prayed he would rub off on your brother," she sighs.

Payne is a good man too. He works hard, running the farm, and he helps me with Beau, but he does have a wild streak in him. So do I. I'm surprised she survived either of our adolescence.

"Yep," is all the response I offer as I turn to the sink and start rinsing the muffin from my fingertips.

"And he grew up to be a handsome devil too." She keeps digging.

"He did," I clip, giving her nothing because, honestly, I don't know what last night was.

We were all hot and bothered and pawing at each other like hormonal teenagers one minute, and the next, we were tending to my son like responsible adults. We didn't exactly get the chance to finish what we'd started, much less discuss what it meant.

Oh God. We are going to have to have a conversation. I hate those.

"You know, Dallas, you don't have to have everything figured out all the time. You can relax and let things happen naturally. Life has a way of working itself out exactly as it should," she consoles, uncannily reading my thoughts.

"I know, Momma. I just have to be careful now. What I do doesn't just affect me anymore," I tell her. I prop a hip against the island and face her. "I don't want to bring someone into Beau's life and let him get used to them if I don't have it all figured out."

"Oh, honey, Beau already loves Myer. We all do."

"I know." I look up to her and whisper my biggest fear, "What if I do something to screw it up, and he goes away?"

She walks over to me and wraps her arms around me. I stand there and let my momma's comfort seep into my bones.

"You can't go into it, expecting to screw it up, or that's exactly what you'll do. You'll sabotage yourself. It's okay to be scared. You've been through a lot, but, baby, Myer is not Travis, and it's not fair to make him pay for the mistakes Travis made. Myer knows who you are. He knows all your flaws, all your insecurities, and all the emotional baggage you carry. He knows you. If he's here, it's because, knowing all of that, he wants to be here."

I let my momma hold me a few more minutes, and then I pull it together and back away.

"It might not have meant anything anyway. So, I don't know why I'm freaking out."

"Oh, if that boy finally showed his cards, then it meant something," she says matter-of-factly.

"Finally? What does that mean?"

She smiles a secret smile that mommas tend to do when they know something their children don't. A smile that comes from a wise place that we can't reach.

She grabs her purse and starts to head for the door.

"Momma?"

"Tell Beau his nana made those muffins special just for him. I love you both and I'll come back to check on him after work," she says over her shoulder, ignoring my question.

I sigh.

I have a feeling my life just got interesting or messy … or somewhere in between.

Beau seems himself after waking and devouring three muffins and a glass of milk. He hates to miss school but loves when I play hooky from work because he gets to spend the day with me.

We color, and he builds castles out of Legos for a while. Then, he plays in my walk-in closet, which he calls his Batcave, while I throw our clothes from last night in the laundry.

Bells picks us up around eleven thirty, and we pile in the truck to take her home.

Beau chatters the entire way.

"Mommy, is Myer gonna be there?" he asks.

"I think so," I answer.

"Can I help him feed Thumper?" he asks.

"Baby, Myer is working. He might be busy," I say to prepare him.

"I can help him work," he offers sweetly.

Bellamy turns in her seat to face him and smiles. "You want to be a rancher, Beau?" she asks.

"Yes! I'm gonna be a cowboy and ride a horse just like Myer when I get big," he excitedly starts telling her his future plan.

"I thought you wanted to be a superhero like Batman?" I ask.

"I do!"

"Well then, you can't be a cowboy," I explain.

"Yes, I can. Batman is Bruce Wayne and wears a suit when he isn't fighting bad guys. I'll just wear my jeans and cowboy boots," he informs me without missing a beat.

"He told you," Bells says as she turns back around.

I guess he did.

I look at him in the rearview mirror. He has his Batman cape on and his Harry Potter glasses with his cowboy boots. That's my little man—pure magic.

"You can be anything you want to be, Beau Stovall," I agree.

He grins at me, and I blow him a kiss in the mirror.

Twenty-Five

MYER

I'M ON HORSEBACK, CORRALLING ONE OF OUR HEIFERS FOR DOC AND his new protégé from Oregon, Brandt, to take a look at. She has me worried, as she hasn't been grazing normally and appears to be losing interest in eating. Usually, loss of appetite is the first sign of illness in cattle.

I get her through the holding yard and into the forcing yard before I dismount. I tie off Bolt—he's a handsome Appaloosa stallion and my favorite horse on the ranch—and head into the yard. I get her roped fairly quickly because she doesn't have the energy to resist. I lead her into the cow crush and guide her to the head bail.

"There you go, girl, nice and easy." I soothe the animal.

Once her head is safely secured, I slide the gate closed and join Doc and Brandt.

"You're right. She is a smidge thin. How's her gait?" Doc asks as they both snap on gloves.

"She's been a little unsteady, but I'm not sure how long. She calved week before last," I tell him what I know.

He takes his time walking around the crush and examining the animal. I hear the sound of tires against gravel and look up to see Dallas's truck coming down the drive toward the barn.

"I'll be right back," I call to them.

Doc's grunt lets me know he heard me, and I walk toward the house.

"Hey, big brother," Bells greets as she hops from the passenger side.

I give her a quick hug, and she wrinkles her nose.

"Ew, you're sweaty, and you stink," she observes as she backs away.

"Sorry, Truett, Foster, and I have been driving the herd in closer all morning to get ready for sorting," I apologize as Dallas rounds the truck with Beau.

Truett and Foster are our two full-time ranch hands. We employ a couple part-time hands as well and take on extra day laborers during the calving season.

Beau sprints to me when he sees me and wraps his arms around my legs.

"Hey, little man. How are you feeling?" I ask as I rustle his hair.

"Good. Can I help you ranch?" he asks as he disengages and looks up at me, pushing his glasses up on his nose.

"All I'm doing right now is waiting for Doc to finish looking at one of the cows that's not feeling real good," I tell him.

"Does she have a tummy ache too?" he asks.

"Yep, I think she does, but hopefully, Doc will have medicine to make her feel all better, like you," I answer.

He catches sight of Bolt tied to the fence. "Mommy, can I pet the horse?" He looks back at Dallas.

"Only if Myer has time to take you over there," she tells him and then looks at me. "We don't want to get in the way."

"You're not," I assure her.

She's holding herself funny, stiff, like she doesn't know how to act at the moment.

I expected as much.

"Come on," I say to both of them.

Beau runs ahead and straight for the horse.

"Wait for us, Beau Stovall. Do not get close to that horse," she calls to him, and he stops his strides and impatiently looks back at us.

We catch up, and I pick him up and walk him over.

"This is Bolt," I introduce him.

"Hi, Bolt," he greets the animal, and Bolt nickers and stomps his back leg.

"Easy," I say to the animal as I take the reins in my hand.

"Can I pet him?" Beau asks.

"Sure. Remember to go real slow. Make sure he sees your hand and then pet above his nose. Be gentle," I instruct.

He releases my neck and holds his little hand up and waves it around. "Hey, good boy. I'm Beau, and I'm gonna pet you," he says as he gradually eases his hand to the horse's muzzle and lightly strokes him.

Bolt whinnies.

"That's good, Bolt," I encourage the horse to be nice.

"I like him, and he loves me," Beau declares proudly. "Did you see, Mommy?" he asks.

"I saw."

I hear Doc bellow to me.

"Here, I'll take him." Dallas opens her arms for Beau.

"I want to go see the sick cow," he says as he wraps his arms back around my neck.

"I told you, Myer has to work," she starts.

"It's okay. Walk with me." I incline my head in the crush's direction.

She gives in on a sigh. Indulging both of us.

We round the corner to where Doc is crouched over his bag.

"Hi, Doc," Dallas says, and the old man looks up and smiles wide.

"Well, hello, Dallas," he returns.

Beau starts waving.

"And you too, Beau," he says as he removes a glove and reaches out to shake his hand.

"What's the conclusion?" I ask as he pulls a needle from his bag.

"Retained placenta. Looks like she's having a hard time shedding it," he informs.

"She got an infection?"

"Nah, doesn't look to be infected, but I surmise she is in some pain, and that's why she's not grazing. Brandt went to the truck to grab the cooler. I'm gonna give her a shot for the pain. It'll ease her for tonight at least, and maybe she'll eat some. I suspect she'll shed on her own in the next day or so," he says as he rubs the needle down with alcohol.

"Anything I can do to help her?" I ask.

"I'd just keep her in the holding yard for now. Feed her hay mixed with a little grain. Bring it high and make it easy for her. And keep an eye on her. You'll know when she sheds and starts feeling better."

Brandt walks up from behind us, carrying a small cooler.

"Look who it is. How are you, Dallas?" he greets her.

How do they know each other?

"Well, if it isn't my second favorite vet in the county," she flirts as he passes the medication off to Doc. "How are y'all settling in?" she asks.

"Good. Everyone's been very welcoming."

"You two meet already?" Doc asks as he loads the needle.

"Yes, sir. She makes the best blueberry pie I have ever eaten for breakfast," he says with a grin.

What the hell?

"Yes, he and his lovely momma came into Faye's. I'm afraid the credit for the pie goes to my momma though. She owns the bakery two blocks down from the diner. You'll have to take Miss Elaine and go in and try her other pies."

"I'm sure Mom would enjoy that." He smiles down at Beau in her arms. "Who do we have here?"

"This is my son, Beau. Beau, say hello to Dr. Brandt," she prompts.

"Hey, Dr. Brandt." He obliges.

"You find a place yet?" she continues her banter with the good doctor.

"Actually, I'm thinking about converting the storage space above the medical office into an apartment. It's two floors, and it has a lot of space and a separate entrance. It'd be convenient to be right upstairs when after-hours emergencies call; plus, Mom loves downtown."

"You should talk to Myer about that. He practically built his cabin with his own two hands, and the boys are all pitching in to get my best friend's house built. He can probably give you some pointers," she volunteers for me. When I don't say anything, she elbows me in the side. "Right?"

"Yeah, sure, anytime," I say tightly, and she gives me a quizzical look.

After Doc finishes administering the shot, he loads his bag back up. "That oughta do it," he says.

We walk him and Brandt up to his truck.

"All right, I'll see you at the shindig this weekend," he says as he shakes my hand, "and we'll be here the next Saturday for the branding. If she doesn't improve, just call, and I'll swing back by to see her again before then."

"Thanks, Doc."

He turns and tips his hat. "Dallas."

"Bye, Doc. See you this weekend," she replies.

"It was good to meet you, Myer." Brandt offers his hand, and I take it.

"You too."

He moves to Dallas. "A pleasure seeing you again and meeting this young man," he says to Beau.

Doc starts the truck, and he hops into the passenger side. Then, they drive off, leaving us alone.

"Well"—she blows out—"I guess we'll also head out and leave you to it."

"No," Beau protests. "I wanna stay and ranch with Myer."

She gives him a stern look. "Beau Stovall, did you just tell me no?"

His eyes widen slightly. "I'm sorry, Mommy."

"You tell Myer good-bye and thank him for letting you pet the horse," she commands.

"Thank you, Myer," he says as he wraps his arms back around my neck and squeezes.

"You're welcome, buddy," I say as I hug him again.

He pulls back in my arms. "Bells is right; you do stink." He starts cackling.

Dallas laughs with him.

"Thanks for calling me out in front of your momma," I say as I stand him on his feet.

Momma and Bellamy come out the door, and he trots off to tell them good-bye, leaving me and Dallas alone for a brief moment.

"So," she says as she chews nervously on her bottom lip.

"So," I repeat, letting her take the lead.

"Last night was … interesting," she says as she looks off to the side, not meeting my eyes.

I reach, gently clasp her chin, and turn her back to face me. "Last night was amazing. It's all I've thought about the whole damn day," I assure her, and I don't miss how her breath catches.

"Yeah," she agrees.

Beau comes running back to us, his cape blowing behind him.

She looks down at him. There's a long, loaded pause.

"I guess we're gonna go to Rustic Peak for lunch," she finally says and looks back up at me.

"Yay!" He jumps and does a fist pump in the air.

"Okay. Be careful."

"Okay," she says and awkwardly spins toward the truck.

"Dal?"

She turns back, and I reach out, snake my hand around her neck, and draw her face to mine.

I briefly kiss her. Not a peck, but not a deep kiss.

Then, I step back. "I'll call you later."

"All righty," she says as Beau, who stands between the two of us, looks up at us and giggles.

I turn and stride back down to Bolt.

Twenty-Six

DALLAS

"OH MY GOD, YOU WOULD NOT BELIEVE MY DAY," I SAY AS I take a seat at the kitchen table beside Sophie.

"What happened?"

Do I tell her?

"I just got back from dropping Bellamy off at Stoney Ridge," I start.

"Yeah, I knew she was picking you up," she prompts me to continue.

"Well …" I stop mid-sentence.

Doreen walks in with Beau on her heels.

Sophie looks up from the papers she has in front of her. She reads my face and looks over at her aunt. "Aunt Doe, do you think you could let Hawk out for me?" she asks sweetly.

"Sure," Doreen agrees without hesitation.

"I bet Beau would like to help. Wouldn't you, Beau?" she adds.

"Yes, ma'am." He turns to me and asks permission, "Can I?"

"*May I*," I correct him. "And, yes, you may, but you listen to Miss Doreen," I instruct him.

"I promise," he says, and Doreen takes his hand.

"Grab a treat for Hawk," she says as they pass a basket on the counter.

Beau reaches up and pulls out three dog biscuits.

"Braxton is gonna have a fit if that pup weighs too much at the vet again." She shakes her head.

Charlotte walks in, yawning.

"Where have you been?" I ask.

"Napping," she answers as she shuffles in and starts to pour herself a cup of coffee.

"Out late, huh?" I ask.

"Yep, we couldn't get Walker out of the bar and Payne wouldn't leave without him," she says as she sits down.

"That's why we don't go out with Walker on school nights. He's always fine the next day, but the rest of us are the walking dead," Sophie tells her.

"Where was that voice of reason yesterday?" Charlotte groans.

"Some things you just have to live through to learn." Sophie pats her back. "Anyway, back to you," she says as she swings her gaze back in my direction.

"Me?"

"Yes, you. What's up? You're acting all squirrelly," she accuses, her eyes closely assessing me.

I bite my lip.

"Spill," she commands.

I take a deep breath and just come out with it. "I might have made out with Myer last night," I mumble.

"What?" she pants.

I put my head in my hands. "I know," I wail.

She gets up, pours me a cup of coffee, and sits in front of me. "We're gonna need details," she says as she eyes me expectantly.

"We, uh … shared a tent Saturday night. Because *somebody* forced me from mine," I say as I side-eye Charlotte. "And … I don't know. It was nice, being held all night. And he looks really good without a shirt on," I admit.

"He sure does," Charlotte pipes in.

Sophie shushes her friend and takes a sip of coffee.

I continue, "After we woke up on Sunday, it just felt like something had changed between us, and I was hyperaware of him all day at the river. When he dropped me off at home, I just … I kind of threw myself at him. I wanted to kiss him, so I could see that there was nothing there. I thought it would be awkward and gross, like kissing my brother, and then we'd laugh it off," I ramble.

Charlotte interrupts again, "There is nothing awkward or gross about kissing your brother." She grins.

"Ew, gross," I throw in her direction. "Anyway, it was …" I search for the right words. "It was like my body caught fire, and I needed to claw my way up him to quench it," I spew.

Sophie's mouth falls open, and she just stares at me. "What?"

"I don't know," I yell. "I've never had it happen before. One minute, I'm climbing over the cab into his lap, and the next, we're on my couch, doing things that couch has never seen before."

Charlotte leans in and asks, "Like what?"

"Stuff," I say hesitantly.

"I'm going to need more than *stuff*," Sophie demands. "Were either of you naked?"

"Half-naked," I admit.

"Which one of you?"

"Both."

"Top half or bottom half?" Charlotte cuts in.

"Him top, me bottom."

Sophie leans back and starts trying to piece it together. "I don't think I understand how that would work," she says.

"I was naked from the waist down," I say pointedly, leading her.

"Okay."

"And he didn't have his shirt on."

"I'm following you." She nods.

"Oh, for goodness' sake, Soph. He went down on her," Charlotte blurts. Then, she lowers her voice and asks, "Is he good with his tongue?"

"Yeah," I admit.

"How good?"

"To be honest, I haven't had an orgasm that wasn't self-induced in years, and I'm shocked he didn't suffocate … or drown."

"Wow," she says with admiration. "That good, huh? Wait, did you say *years*?"

I just nod because it's the truth.

"How is that possible?" Charlotte asks, stunned.

"Travis and I were teenagers when we got married. We were all hormones back then. All he had to do was say *boo* to me, and I was a quivering, wet mess. It takes a little more than that now. I need at least a wink and a shot of tequila to get my motor started, and then I need a whole lot of tinkering to keep it running. No one I've dated in the last six years has been able to get me there. Not that I've given them much opportunity to try."

"But Myer got your motor started with a kiss and then drove you all the way home?" Charlotte asks.

"Yep."

"Is that it? He just curled your toes and left?" Sophie asks, clearly disappointed.

"I was going to return the favor, but we were interrupted when Momma brought Beau home with a fever in the middle of it." I bang my head against the table.

"Oh no. What did you do?" she asks.

"I took care of Beau," I say as I lift my head and shrug.

"And Myer?"

"He helped. He cleaned up puke. Then, Beau asked if he could stay the night, and the three of us cuddled up on the couch and slept."

Sophie just blinks at me.

"Say something," I demand.

She grins. "It's about time."

"What's that supposed to mean?"

"It means, you two are perfect for each other."

"Perfect for each other? Sophie, I'm a divorced mother with a ton of debt who lives in her parents' backyard. I'm nobody's perfect. Least of all Myer's," I say out loud what I have been thinking all day.

"Dallas Stovall, did you just talk down about yourself? Fishing for compliments is so unbecoming," she says as she crosses her arms over her chest and shakes her blonde locks at me.

"I'm not looking for anything other than a casual relationship. I don't have time. I'm a hot mess. You know it. I know it," I point out.

"And Myer knows it," she adds.

She sounds like Momma.

"Do you like him?" she asks.

"Of course I do."

"Do you wish you hadn't been interrupted last night?" she asks.

"I wouldn't have wanted Momma not to bring Beau to me. He needed me," I answer quickly.

"Not what I asked. I want to know if you wanted things to go further."

I bite at my fingernail and think about her question.

Do I wish things had gone further?

"I did last night, but today, I think I'm relieved they didn't," I admit.

"That's normal. I mean, the first time I made out with Braxton, I was a confused mess the next day, but trust me, you'll know for sure before too long."

"How's that?"

"Because, now that you've crossed that line, neither of you will be able to stay away."

Twenty-Seven

DALLAS

I agreed to work for Faye this morning, being as I missed yesterday's tips. I drop Beau off at school and head toward town.

Myer called last night after supper. He had just finished his day and wanted to check in and make sure Beau was still feeling okay.

They chatted for a few minutes before I took the phone. I asked how the rest of his day had gone, and he told me a few cows had gotten out of a fence and wandered onto the apple orchard, so he and Payne spent the last couple of hours wrangling them back onto his land.

I could hear how exhausted he was through the line, so I told him I had to get Beau to bed and let him go.

Before we hung up, he asked if he could see me tonight. I reminded him that Beau had his riding lesson this afternoon with Madeline and told him that I would be working there tonight to make up for missing this morning so that I could pick up the shift at Faye's. He asked about the rest of the week, but I promised Sophie I'd help with last-minute party details on Wednesday and with setup on Thursday evening but that I'd see him at the party.

Friday seems so far away.

I tie my apron as I walk into Faye's. Kim is filling the cream and sugar boxes on the tables, and Andy is prepping the kitchen.

"Morning, Dallas," Kim chirps as I fall in behind her with jelly and pancake syrup.

"Morning. Thanks for yesterday, I truly appreciate you covering for me," I offer.

"No problem. Lunch was a little busier, so it made up for the lousy morning."

"Unlocking the doors in five, ladies," Andy bellows from the pickup window.

We hurry and finish our prep work, and I start the coffeepots as Kim lets the waiting customers in.

"By the way, some guy came in here and asked about you yesterday," she says as she waggles her eyebrow at me.

I frown. "Guy? What guy?"

She shrugs. "Didn't catch his name. He said you two used to be a thing or something," she continues.

"Really? What did he look like?"

"A couple inches taller than me, dark eyes, dark hair. He was a looker," she says with a whistle.

"Russ Eastman?" I ask.

She thinks for a minute. "Why does that name sound familiar?"

"We went out a couple of times the end of last year. Remember?"

"That's right. I don't think he ever came in here though, did he?"

"Maybe not," I say. "He is about six-two with a close-cropped beard."

"It was probably him then. This guy definitely had facial hair. Kind of wild, unkempt," she says before walking off to take an order.

Unkempt? Russ? He must have had a hell of a Sunday night too.

After my shift, I head to Rustic Peak. Vivian is meeting us there for the last-minute party prep, Doreen and Ria are cooking for us girls, and we are going to go over everything at supper. Sophie called me this morning, all nervous because Madeline will be there, and she doesn't know how her mother and stepmother are going to get along. They've never been in the same room together, and Vivian has not hidden her jealousy of Madeline and Sophie's budding relationship very well.

I guess Viv and I are alike in that regard. You always know where you stand with us, good or bad. It's our face. I can't control mine any more than she can hers.

When I arrive, Sophie, Charlotte, and Elle are on the front porch.

"Oh, good, you're here. Come join us," Sophie says as she pats the seat on the swing beside her.

I walk up and take a seat. "What's up? Anyone throw a punch yet?" I ask.

Sophie rolls her eyes. "No. Mom hasn't even made it here," she answers.

"Good. I was afraid I'd missed the good stuff. By the way, my money is on Madeline. I know Viv's got a mean streak and all, but Madeline works with horses. Have you seen her biceps? I bet she throws a mean punch," I add.

"I'll take those odds. I've seen Vivian lose her shit on more than one occasion in New York. She might be refined and elegant on the outside, but that woman still has some straight-up Colorado mountain woman in her; plus, like you said, she's mean, and I don't think Madeline has a mean bone in her body," Charlotte says.

"Oh my God, would you two stop? I'm nervous enough," Sophie whines.

I elbow her in the ribs. "It'll be fine."

"I hope so anyway. I have something for you three. Technically, it's your bridesmaid gifts, but I wanted to give them to you before the party." She plucks three jewelry boxes from the bag beside her. "I designed them and had our shop make them."

She hands each of us a box. "Go ahead; open them," she says excitedly.

We open at the same time, and nestled inside is a gorgeous necklace with a pearl pendant surrounded by a halo of tiny diamonds.

"The chains are white gold, and each one has either a white, black, or pink pearl. The pearl represents you. You each have a different color, and that's the one that reminds me of you," she explains.

"It's stunning," Elle says in awe.

"Mine has the pink pearl in the middle," Charlotte observes. "What does it mean?"

"Pink pearls represent energy, success, and good fortune. I chose it for you because I'm so fortunate you found me in New York and made me your best friend. We built a company together. Success is who we are. Elle, your center is the white pearl; it represents innocence, beauty, and sincerity. All the things that you are."

Elle wipes a tear from her cheek as she says, "Thank you."

"Let me guess. Mine's the black pearl because it represents wickedness and badassery," I tease.

"No," she answers as she rolls her eyes.

"It's more smoky gray than black, so it could represent my heart of stone," I say as I hold it up to my neck.

"The black pearl is my favorite one of all," she says. "It represents mystery, independence, and strength. It's beautiful but edgy. All of the things you are and all of the things I admire about you."

"Well, damn. Now, you're gonna make me cry like a little girl, just like Elle," I say as I close my hand around the necklace and bring it to my heart.

"The diamonds are because I love you all. You're all diamonds, and the extra bling makes them look amazing." She beams.

I wrap her in a hug. "Thank you, Soph. It really is special. I'll treasure it always."

As I let her go, I hear a peal of laughter and look to see Madeline and Beau walking up the drive.

"Mommy!"

He takes off in a run and bounds up the porch steps. "I rode all by myself today," he squeals.

"You did?"

"We put him in a saddle and taught him how to hold the pommel. I walked beside him and held the reins the entire time while the horse did a four-beat round. And Beau did really well," she explains.

"It was so cool, and next time, I get to hold the reins and steer her," he states excitedly.

"That's wonderful. I'm very proud of you," I say as I squeeze his chin with my fingers and bring his mouth to mine for a kiss.

My little cowboy.

Twenty-Eight

DALLAS

"Beau, come on. Nana and Pop-Pop are waiting on us," I call as I put the back on my earring and slide into my heels.

He comes running out of his room.

"Where are your shoes? I thought you went to get them?" I ask as I look at his sock-covered feet.

"Sorry, Mommy, I forgot. I had to feed Fritz," he says as he throws his arms in the air, exasperated, and trots back toward his room.

His white dress shirt is tucked into his little khaki dress shorts. His socks are a pale blue with the tie and suspenders to match. Watching his booty strut to his room is the cutest thing I have ever seen, so I can't even be agitated. I just want to eat him up.

He returns with his cowboy boots in hand.

"You're supposed to wear the dress shoes Nana bought you," I remind him.

"But I like these better. The party is at the ranch. They won't care if I wear my boots," he protests.

I put my hands on my hips and huff. "Oh, all right, but when Nana asks you to wear them to church, you can't complain. Deal?"

"Deal!" he agrees.

He grins and pulls on his boots, and we meet Momma and Daddy in the driveway and ride with them to the engagement party.

We don't have that many fancy occasions around here, so the whole town has been abuzz all day. Janelle's salon was packed all afternoon with ladies getting gussied up. Everyone is looking forward to seeing one another and eating, drinking, dancing, and celebrating Sophie and Braxton. It's like the prince of Poplar Falls is getting hitched.

"You look so handsome, Beau," Momma says as she looks back at us.

"Like Bruce Wayne?" he asks.

"Just like him," she agrees.

When we pull up to the ranch's gate, a young guy in a suit greets us and guides us where to park.

"Oh my, fancy," Momma declares.

We all hop out and walk to the two tents at the side of the barn.

They are massive, and all day yesterday, there was a crew of two dozen men out here, setting them up and laying the wooden dance floor.

The decorations are exquisite. Vivian made sure every single detail was perfect. It's all pink roses and crystal. Sophie let her have her way with this party, being as she gave in on the actual wedding. The roof is strung with twinkling lights and draped in white hydrangeas and lavender wisteria. The candlelit tables are covered with white tablecloths.

She might be a bit overbearing, but the woman sure knows how to throw a party together.

It's stunning.

Sophie and Braxton are seated at the table at the head of the tent, and waiters are serving them. She looks up as we walk in, and she grins huge and waves. She's wearing a soft yellow summer dress, and her hair is braided around the top like a crown. She has a sunflower behind her ear, and she's glowing.

My dress is a bold, golden yellow with a plunging neckline. It's fitted up top, but it flares at the hips. It swings when I walk or dance around. I wore my hair down and loose, and my nude stilettos match Sophie's and Charlotte's. I have been practicing walking in them all week. I pray I don't break my ankle.

Momma is ahead of us, searching the tables for our name cards.

"Here we are," she bellows when she finds our seats.

I take Beau's hand and lead him to our chairs. As soon as we settle in, the wait staff has our drinks filled, and the first course is served.

"I don't think I've ever been served a meal in shifts before," Daddy complains as a bowl of lobster bisque that he never touched is removed from in front of him and a salad is set in its place.

"It's courses, dear," Momma tells him as she picks up the salad fork and hands it to him.

He takes it from her hand and starts picking out the dried cranberry and candied pecans. I giggle at his effort to fish the fancy out of his plate.

"At this rate, we won't finish eating until midnight," he grumbles.

"Mommy, do I have to eat this?" Beau asks as he stares at his plate in disgust.

"No, baby. Here, just have another roll."

I reach in the basket to get a roll, split it open, and butter it for him. He happily takes it from my hand and bites into it.

Myer, Bellamy, and his parents arrive, and their table is across the tent. His eyes scan the tables until they find us. He smiles a sexy smile. Then, he pulls the chair out for Bells to sit, and once she and his parents are settled, he makes his way over to us.

He looks good.

He's wearing black dress pants that fit him oh-so well. He has on a crisp white tailored shirt and black tie. His dark hair is a little wild on top of his head. I never noticed how it wants to curl on the edges if he lets it get a day or two past time for a cut. I like it. It looks like he just woke up and ran his hands through it. He looks amazing in jeans and tees, but damn, this works too.

"Myer, look," Beau calls when he spots him. "I have on a tie too!"

"I see that. You look sharp," he says as he reaches our seats.

"I know," Beau agrees.

Obviously, I have not done well at teaching him modesty.

"You look beautiful," he says as he leans in and kisses my cheek.

"Thank you."

"Mr. and Mrs. Henderson," he greets my parents.

"Hello, Myer. Have you seen that wayward son of mine?" Momma asks.

"I believe he pulled in behind us. He should be here any minute."

"That boy will be late for his own funeral," Momma complains.

The DJ starts to play "It Had to Be You," the Harry Connick Jr. version, and calls Sophie and Braxton to the dance floor.

"Oh, I bet he's gonna love this," Myer says.

He folds his arms across his chest, and we all watch them make their way to the floor.

Braxton takes her hand, quickly twirls her, and pulls her into him, and then they start slow-dancing to the music.

"Damn, he looks like a natural out there. He's been holding out on us," I say in astonishment.

"Right?"

I look up to see Charlotte standing beside me. I guess I know what was keeping Payne.

My brother is behind her with his eyes on the happy couple too.

"Ha, he just never wanted you girls drunkenly pulling him on the dance floor at Fast Breaks and pawing all over him," Payne says.

"That was probably smart," I admit because I would have done just that.

"I'd better go join the family and eat before the beer starts flowing," Myer says as he slaps Payne on the shoulder. Then, he looks back down at me. "Save me a dance," he says with a wink before walking over to his seat.

I let out a breath.

I have no idea how to act or feel around him.

I reach for my glass and take a gulp. I guess I'll just drink this fancy wine and let whatever happens happen.

Twenty-Nine

DALLAS

AFTER DESSERT IS SERVED, THE WAITER BRINGS AROUND GLASSES OF champagne.

We're all mingling now, mixing, sitting, and chatting at all the tables.

I sit down beside Vivian and introduce myself to Sophie's stepdad, Stanhope, who footed the bill for this shindig, before he excuses himself to take a phone call.

"I'll be right back, sweetheart," he says as he kisses her cheek and walks out of the tent.

"That man is always working," Vivian says with a shrug. It doesn't seem to bother her in the least. "What do you think of the champagne?" she asks.

I look down at the glass in my hand. "It's really good. Not as sweet as I'm used to, but I think I like that, and the bubbles are tickling my nose," I say.

She smiles. "The bubbles are the key to a good champagne," she educates me.

I look down into my glass. "Hmm, good to know," I say before taking another sip.

To everyone's surprise, Braxton walks up to the DJ and takes a microphone.

This should be good.

"Is he that drunk?" I ask Walker, who is sitting beside Elle across from us.

"Maybe. We have had him drinking all day." He shrugs.

"Oh, Jesus." I start to stand, but Vivian puts her hand on my knee.

"Let him talk, dear," she says as she watches Sophie.

Sophie has a look of unbridled love and expectation on her face.

"Um, hey, everyone," he starts as he nervously looks around the crowd. "I'm not one to give toasts or speeches. I even refused to write my own vows because I didn't want to have to share that in front of a bunch of strangers, but I have just enough shine in me tonight."

He grins, and we all laugh. Damn, he is beautiful, especially when he lets his guard down.

He waits for us to settle and continues, "I'm not good with words, so instead, I'm going to quote one of my favorite movie characters, the ever-eloquent Rocky Balboa."

More laughter.

"When Rocky decides he wants to marry the love of his life—the lovely Adrian—her brother, Paulie, asks him why he wants to marry his sister. Rocky answers his question with—fills gaps. Paulie doesn't get it, so Rock explains. He says that she has gaps and he has gaps and together, they fill gaps.'

He takes a drink from the glass in his hand and continues, "I understand those words because that was me. I was walking around as a man full of gaps for a long time. I've had good people come into my life who have loved me and tried to fill them, but it wasn't until a beautiful, sexy, pain-in-the-ass princess in ridiculous shoes came waltzing into my life that I felt whole again."

He raises his glass in Sophie's direction. "You fill my gaps, baby, and I'm going to spend the rest of my life trying to fill all of yours. I love you."

As we all raise our glasses in toast with him, Sophie stands, runs, and leaps into his arms.

I look beside me, and tears are streaming down Vivian's face, just like they are on mine.

"Well," she says as she wipes at her cheeks, "that was unexpected."

"Yep, that boy can surprise us sometimes. Sophie is very lucky," I agree.

"He is very much like Jefferson. He loved me like that," she muses.

I turn to face her, and she has a bittersweet look on her face as she looks in Jefferson and Madeline's direction.

"My Sophia, well, she's not like me at all. She'll be able to appreciate that and hold on to it. Give it back to him and not destroy it the way I did."

"You're not the only one to royally mess it up the first time. I think some of us just aren't meant for marriage," I confess.

"Oh, Dallas, that's not what I'm saying at all, sweetheart," she says as she grasps my hand in hers. "I loved Jeff, and I tried to put myself in a box to be what he wanted me to be in order to hold on to that love. I just never really fit in there. I was suffocating. Then, Sophia came along, and instead of making things better, the box just felt smaller. While we were filling Jefferson's gaps, mine got bigger and bigger."

I know how that feels.

"That's me. I'm one big, cavernous gap. I don't think happily ever after is in the cards for some of us," I say as I down my glass.

"No, ma'am. You listen to me, Dallas. You are a free spirit, just like I was, and that man you married tried to put you in a box you weren't meant to be in. You have to find the one who lets you be you."

She nods toward Braxton and Sophie, who are now holding each other and slow-dancing. "That's what they have. He lets her be herself, and she lets him be himself. They aren't pretending to please each other. I found that in Stanhope. He's a wonderful man. He dotes on me. Makes sure I have everything I could want or need. I can be me with him, ridiculous as I am, and he accepts me. He has his businesses and his career, which demand a lot of his time and attention, and he thrives when challenged; I accept that. It takes all the pressure off of me to be the perfect wife. I am but a splash in the pool that is his happiness."

I wrinkle my nose. That doesn't sound all that great to me.

"I know. It's not the relationship for everyone, but it's the one that suits us. That's what you have to find. The relationship that lets you be unabashedly you. I think it might be closer than you realize," she says with a grin just as I feel a tap on my shoulder.

I look up to see Myer standing there with his hand outstretched.

"Dance with me, Dal?"

I turn back to Viv, and she gives me a wink. Then, I take his hand, and he leads me to the dance floor.

"I didn't know you danced," I say as he twirls me.

"I do tonight. Besides, you looked like you needed rescuing."

"She's not so bad. She loves Sophie," I reply. Seems I have softened to Momma V.

"And she throws one hell of a party," he points out.

"She sure does."

He pulls me in tighter.

"Are you having a good time?" I ask.

"I am now," he answers.

He nods his head toward Braxton. "Making sure the groom makes it home okay and doesn't get too inebriated. We have to be out at his cabin bright and early to get tar paper on the roof before the roofing guys show up to lay shingles."

"You're a good friend, Myer Wilson. I don't know how you fellas do it. You work so hard," I say, admiration clear in my voice.

"Says one of the hardest-working humans I know," he replies.

"I might work two jobs, but they aren't as physical, and they aren't from sunup to sundown."

"Maybe not, but yours are more mentally demanding than wrangling cattle all day; plus, you are raising a little man, and that is a twenty-four/seven job," he says as he pulls me in close. Then, he whispers into my ear, "And you are a rock star at that."

I melt at his praise.

Just as the song ends, Beau comes rushing up to us, Hawkeye on his heels. He is covered in chocolate icing. It's on his fingers, his chin, the front of his shirt, and Hawkeye is jumping up, trying to lick it from his face.

"Mommy, can I have another cupcake? Hawkeye stole mine," he asks sweetly.

"Then, why do you have chocolate all around your mouth?" I ask.

"I licked the icing off first, and then he snatched the cake out of my hand."

I look at the overgrown puppy, who is hopping at our feet.

"Hawkeye," I call to him.

He stops and sits, panting up at me.

"Did you steal Beau's cupcake?"

He yaps up at me.

"See," Beau says as he throws his hands up in exasperation.

I give in. "Okay, one more. One."

He grins and takes off toward the dessert table. Momma walks over, watching him as he goes.

"Your daddy is getting tired. I think we are going to head home. Beau can come with us. I'll throw him in a bath and get the sticky off of him," she offers.

"I can come," I start.

She waves me off. "No, no. You stay and enjoy the party. We're gonna curl up and watch one of his Disney DVDs. He can stay with us tonight."

She tilts her head and looks past me. "Myer, you'll give her a ride home, won't you, dear?" she asks.

"Yes, ma'am," he answers.

"Thank you." She looks back at me. "Have fun, sweetheart."

Then, she disappears.

Real subtle, Momma.

I never realized my mother had such a sneaky streak.

Thirty

DALLAS

We spend the next two hours drinking, dancing, laughing, and enjoying the night.

Sophie, Charlotte, and I are all on the dance floor, wrapped in each other's arms, and they're both crying.

They are happy tears, I think. Drunk tears for sure. We shot right past the drunk-girl *I love you so much* stage about an hour ago. Now, we are in the staggering, holding-each-other-up-so-we-don't-fall stage.

"You guys are sloppy drunks. Neither of you can hold your liquor," I complain as I'm stuck in the middle of their emotional sandwich.

"You've drunk as much as we have," Charlotte accuses.

"Yep, but you city girls are lightweights."

"You love us," Sophie slurs.

"Yeah, I do," I admit.

They have me locked in between them as they are swaying.

"The song ended, like, five minutes ago, y'all," I inform them.

"So?" Sophie hiccups as she snuggles in deeper.

I look off to the side of the dance floor and Braxton, Walker, Payne, and Myer have gathered, watching us.

Help, I mouth to them.

Four wide grins flash at me.

Great.

They find this amusing.

Finally, Braxton breaks away from the pack and heads our way. He wraps his arm around Sophie's shoulders and tugs. "Come on, Princess. Time to get you home," he says as he turns her into him.

"I'm tipsy," she whispers at him.

He smiles down at her. "I'd have never guessed. Let's go tell the rest of the guests good night," he suggests.

"Okay. Bye, girls. I love you," she says as he leads her away.

I walk over to Myer. I look up at him and pout.

"Are you ready to go?" he asks.

I nod as I step into him and lay my forehead against his chest.

"My feet hurt," I whine. "I don't know how they wear these dang shoes all day. My toes hate me."

"Take them off," he suggests.

I grab his arms to balance myself and kick them off to the side one at a time.

"Ahh, relief," I moan as I move up and down on my toes and stretch my aching arches.

I bend and pick the offending footwear up.

We say our good-byes to everyone and head out to his truck.

"Ouch," I cry as I try to gingerly walk on the gravel.

Myer reaches around my waist, scoops me up into his arms, and starts carrying me.

"My hero," I sigh and lean in to kiss his cheek.

He tilts his head, so my kiss lands on his lips instead. I melt into him, and the kiss turns from a quick thank-you to something passionate. I wrap my hand around the side of his neck and hold him to my mouth.

I wondered if the second time would feel as fiery as the first. I worried that I wouldn't respond to his touch again. That last weekend was a fluke, but all I want in the moment is his mouth on mine.

A clear whistle floats through the air from behind us.

I break from the kiss and look over Myer's shoulder to see Walker and Silas carrying boxes.

As they pass, Walker casually remarks, "It's about damn time." Then, he looks back and grins at us.

"Why do people keep saying that?" I ask out loud.

Myer just laughs and carries me to the truck.

This time, on the way home, I don't even try to fight my anticipation. I practically sit in his lap the whole time, and my mouth is on his neck and nipping at his ear while my hands roam.

He bursts from the door before the truck comes to a complete stop in my driveway and plucks me from the driver's side.

I get the door unlocked, and then we are all hands. I pull his shirt-tail loose from his pants as he guides us to the couch.

He sits down and tugs me into his lap. I lean back on his thighs and continue my efforts to unbutton the shirt. Once it's open, my mouth finds his chest, and I run my hands over his sides and around his back. He is solid and warm, and he tastes so good. He lets me explore his skin, and I can feel him growing hard beneath me. I start to move my hips against him, and he lays his head back against the couch and groans.

I love that sound. It's a deep, guttural reflex that lets me know he wants this as badly as I do.

One second, my tongue is climbing the column of his throat as I writhe in his lap. The next second, he laces his hands under my ass and hoists me up as he stands to his feet.

"What are you doing?" I ask breathlessly.

"Taking you to bed," he growls as he heads toward the stairs.

He takes them two at a time, and once we are in the loft, he deposits me on the bed and quickly strips his shoes and slacks and tosses them on the floor. He crawls up the bed and kisses me again.

I wrap my legs around his hips, the hem of my dress riding up to my waist. He is hard and ready against the silk of my panties.

He takes a finger and tugs aside the plunging neckline of my dress so his mouth can reach my breast. As he takes my nipple between his teeth and gently bites down, I cry out his name.

I plant my feet, raise my hips, and circle them. *Oh, yes, sweet contact.* I don't think I've ever been this turned on before. My body is coiled tight and screaming for release.

I feel the vibration of his chuckle against my sensitive skin.

"My impatient girl," he says as he sits up on his knees.

My legs fall open for him.

He sits there, looking down at me almost reverently.

He hooks his fingers into the sides of my panties and gently slides them down my thighs.

I'm totally exposed to him and so damn ready.

His finger glides through my wetness before he comes back on top of me.

I rake my fingernails down his back as he finds my entrance and slowly moves inside me.

Finally.

We keep a slow-building pace. His eyes never leave mine until his control snaps, and he can no longer hold back. I lock my knees to his sides as his powerful hips move urgently. I raise to meet his thrusts, chasing the burning sensation that's crawling up my spine, till an explosion of pleasure sweeps me up. I score my nails down his back, and he covers my mouth with his and takes my muffled cries until I'm panting and sated.

I'm in trouble.

I think I might love him, and it's both terrifying and exhilarating.

Like jumping off a cliff and free-falling.

Thirty-One

MYER

I WAKE TO A TANGLE OF STRAWBERRY CURLS TICKLING MY NOSE. Dallas has her arm slung over my chest and her face under my chin, and she's snoring lightly.

Sunshine is bleeding in from the windows downstairs.

I have no idea what time it is. This is the first time the sun has beaten me up in years. Nature calls, but I like the feel of her wrapped around me so much that I don't want to disturb her sleep.

The sound of a text message alert starts chirping from the closet and causes her to stir. It takes her a few tries before she's able to blink her eyes open.

"Is that my phone or yours?" she mumbles as she snuggles in closer.

"Yours."

She grudgingly untangles herself from me and the sheets, and I watch as her beautiful, naked form stumbles sleepily into the closet to retrieve her purse.

"It's from Momma. They're on their way to church with Beau," she says as she lies back down and closes her eyes.

I brush her hair from her shoulder and start kissing a trail down her spine.

"Mmm," she hums.

"You need to get up, sleepyhead," I say as I reach the dip in her lower back.

"It's your fault I'm so exhausted," she murmurs on a sigh.

I slide my hand up the inside of her thigh. "Then, I'll have to find a creative way to wake you up. Come take a shower with me," I beckon as I find the spot that makes her moan my name.

She squirms beneath my touch until I have her fully awake. Then, I lead her to the shower.

After getting each other thoroughly clean, I help make toast as she cooks eggs and bacon and brews a pot of coffee.

She is awake enough to be freaking out again. I can see it as her eyes follow me around her kitchen, but I'm done handling her with kid gloves. She's going to have to get used to the fact that I'm here and I'm not going anywhere.

I grab ketchup from the fridge, make a plate, and sit at the island across from her where I start eating.

"You put ketchup on your eggs?" she asks as she watches me do just that.

"Yep," I answer.

"Why?"

"Because I like it. Been doing it since I was a kid." I shrug.

She starts to say something else just as the door swings open, and Beau comes stomping in. I see the immediate panic cross her face before she tucks it in. She wasn't expecting them to get home so soon, and I'm pretty sure she was hoping I'd be gone before they did.

"You're home early," she says as he climbs up in the stool beside me.

"Pop-Pop got a bellyache at church and made us come home. He told Nana he needed to sit on his own throne. Did you know he had a throne, Mommy?" he asks.

She chuckles as she pours him a mug of chocolate milk and places it in front of him. "I did not," she replies.

"I asked Nana if I could see it, and she said nobody wants to follow him in there."

Dallas loads him a plate with scrambled eggs and butters a slice of toast while he chatters away.

He looks over at me as he pulls his mug of chocolate milk to him and blows on the top of it, just as I'm doing with my coffee.

Then, he snags the bottle of ketchup and squeezes a dollop on his eggs. He takes a bite, makes a face, and then continues to dig in.

Dallas watches him closely as he mimics my actions.

After a few minutes, he starts filling us in about his Sunday school class's upcoming field trip to a dairy farm. What Jesus has to do with milking cows is lost to us, but we listen intently as he continues.

He stops mid-sentence and looks at me in question.

"Did you and Mommy have a sleepover without me?" he asks as he blinks up at me.

Dallas's pleading eyes fly to me.

"Nah, I just came over to have breakfast with you guys," I lie.

He looks at me funny and then asks, "Why come your hair is wet?" He takes another bite.

"It's *why is your hair wet*, baby. Not *why come*. And his hair is wet because he took a shower right before he came over, and it hasn't had time to dry yet," Dallas answers as she pours herself a cup of coffee.

He points down at my bare feet.

"Why come—I mean, why don't you have any shoes on?"

He's an observant little devil.

"I mopped the floor last night, and I didn't want him tracking in dirt," Dallas says without skipping a beat, "so I made him take his boots off like I try to get you to do before you come in the house."

She carefully watches him as the next question hits the air.

"Why aren't you wearing any socks?"

I lean in and answer low, "Sometimes, I like to go without socks. My feet get sweaty."

I do my best to hold in my laughter as Dallas's eyes meet mine.

He nods. Then, he leans in and whispers, "Mine too, but Mommy won't let me wear my boots without socks. She says it makes my feet stinky."

"Is that right?" I ask.

"Yep, so you'd better put some on, or she won't let you have sleepovers here anymore."

Then, he takes the last bite of his breakfast and hops down.

"May I be excused, Mommy?"

"You may," she says, and he scurries off toward his room.

Dallas's eyes follow him, and then she says, "I think he might know."

It's then that I burst into laughter.

Thirty-Two

DALLAS

Sophie hugs Charlotte as we drop her off at Denver International Airport.

"I can't believe you're leaving already. Two weeks flew by," Sophie says as I unload the bag from the back of the truck.

"I know." Charlotte pouts. "But it's time to get back to the real world where vanilla soy lattes with extra foam and spin class exist. Besides, I'll be back in a couple of months for the wedding."

I place her bag at her feet, and she turns and opens her arms wide.

"Dallas, I'm so happy I got to finally meet you. Take care of our girl," she says as I step into her embrace. Then, she pulls back and adds, "And that hunky cowboy of yours."

She winks at us before she slides her designer sunglasses onto her face, grabs the handle of her suitcase, and sashays into the airport. Her full New York attitude snapped firmly back in place as we watch her disappear into the crowd.

We get back into the truck to head home.

"You know, I think I'm going to miss her," I say.

"She's good people. A little nutty, but that's part of her charm. And I love her and Mom to death, but honestly, having them both in town has been exhausting. I'm ready for them to leave," Sophie admits. "Maybe now, we can get back to normal."

Normal.

"I'm not even sure what that is anymore," I tell her as we pull off.

She peeks a sideways glance at me while trying to watch the road ahead.

"Yeah, about that, how did the rest of your weekend go?" she asks stealthily.

"Exactly how you think it went," I say pointedly.

"Yay," she clips. "How was it?"

I sigh. "Amazing."

"Your place or his?" she asks.

"Mine."

"Did he stay the night?"

"Yep."

"How many orgasms are we talking?" she asks, and clearly, my nosy nature has rubbed off on her.

I look over and narrow my eyes at her. "Three, if you count the one in the shower the next morning. And might I add, you are enjoying this little interrogation an awful lot."

She grins. "I sure am. So, where did you guys leave things?"

"It's weird. We got up Sunday, and we showered. Then, he started helping me make breakfast, and before I knew what was happening, we were taking Beau to the park in town, having a picnic, and he was teaching Beau how to hold and throw a football properly," I spew.

"That sounds like fun to me," she says carefully.

"It was fun," I agree.

"Then, why do you sound so put out?" she asks, confused.

"Because I was freaking out, and he acted like it was the most natural thing in the world to wake up and spend the day together. No discussion. No, *what are we doing*? Nothing."

I throw my arms up in exasperation.

"And the worst part is, Beau did the same damn thing. When he came in from Momma's and saw Myer sitting there, having breakfast, he didn't bat an eye. Little turkey even called us out when we lied about having a sleepover. No, *why are you here? What's going on?* Just a shrug, and *let's go play*."

She bites her bottom lip as she fights a laugh.

"What's so funny?" I snap.

"I remember when I was the one freaking out after spending the night with Braxton and you having to talk me down. It's nice, being on this side of the equation," she says.

"Grr, not helping."

"Okay, look, Beau's not acting weird because it's Myer, and there is nothing strange about Myer being at your house. He knows him, he loves him, and he trusts him, so he's completely comfortable with waking up to Myer in the kitchen. And Myer is not acting weird because he's a man. Men apparently don't have the freak-out gene that we do. They decide they want something, and they take hold of it. Bam. No fuss. No long-drawn-out discussion needed. Braxton sent me a thumbs-up when I texted him about my dad seeing me leave his apartment one morning. It's frustrating, I get it, but if you're waiting for him to feel the same panic you do, you're gonna be disappointed."

"Yeah, well, he sends me a stupid thumbs-up emoji, and I will break his thumb off his hand and shove it somewhere extremely uncomfortable," I huff.

"That's what I'm saying," she agrees.

We make it back to Poplar Falls just in time to get an hour of work in before I have to pick Beau up from school.

When I pull into the passenger pickup line, Mrs. Perry meets me at the truck with Beau.

"Hey, Mommy," Beau greets cheerfully.

"Hey, baby. How was your day?"

"I made Josh laugh at lunch, and milk came out of his nose," he says excitedly.

"Ew, nasty," I say as I strap him in.

"It was great. So gross."

I shake my head. The things boys like.

Once I have him in the truck, I shut the door and turn to his teacher. "What's up? You never walk him all the way out."

She usually stands at the head of the pickup line and watches for the children to make it to their parents.

"We had some unusual activity today. A gentleman sat on the bus bench across the street most of the afternoon. I could see him out the window. He wasn't doing anything wrong per se. It was just odd to show up hours before your bus is scheduled and just sit there. He was finally picked up about half an hour ago. I'm sure he was just passing through, but I felt it better to walk each child out today."

"Thank you. I'm sure you're right, but I appreciate you caring so much about the kids' safety," I say as I hug her.

"They're my babies too. Every one of them," she says as she leans down into the window and waves at Beau. "I'll see you in the morning, Beau."

"Bye-bye, Mrs. Perry." He waves back.

Thirty-Three

MYER

I'M IN THE BARN, TRANSFERRING BALES OF HAY FROM THE TRAILER TO the floor. We ordered extra this week to use for seating for the branding this weekend. Branding is a tradition here in Poplar Falls. Every May, friends and family gather on a ranch and watch the branding of the calves before the summer grazing season begins. Horsemen and wranglers from other ranches volunteer to help.

It's been nonstop prep for the last few days. Pop, Truett, Foster, and I have been getting the ranch ready and the corrals set up while Momma, Bells, and the other ladies in town have been picnic-planning.

Braxton, Walker, Emmett, and Jefferson will be a part of our branding this year, and Pop, Truett, and I will be at Rustic Peak to help the following week.

Our branding day here on Stoney Ridge usually pulls in about fifty to seventy-five spectators. After which, we serve a feast. There's something special about gathering with your neighbors, giving thanks to God for his provision, having the reverend bless our land, working hard, and then spending the evening eating and drinking in fellowship. We are a community based in support for one another. It's a beautiful thing.

In addition to getting everything ready for Saturday, we have to prepare our fences and watering systems to move the herds into the summer grazing pastures after the branding.

Ranchers get very little sleep in the spring.

I hear footsteps and look up to find Dallas walking into the barn.

The sight of her takes my breath away damn near every time she walks in a room.

I drop the bale in my hands, wipe the sweat from my brow, and walk over to greet her.

"Hey," she says, looking around. "Working hard, I see."

"Yeah, just getting everything ready for the weekend."

"I tried to call. I hope it's okay I dropped by," she says nervously.

Is she kidding?

"Of course it is. You can drop by anytime," I tell her.

"I know you're busy and probably really tired, so I thought maybe Beau and I could come here for supper tonight. I mean, if you want, I could make supper at your cabin, so you don't have to cook. I can have it ready when you get done working." She's babbling now.

"I'd love that," I cut her off.

She smiles. "Okay. I'll make spaghetti. I'll just bring everything I need with me."

"Let me get you the keys," I say as I remove my gloves, and we walk in the direction of my truck.

"Are you guys ready for Saturday?" she asks.

"As ready as we can be, I guess. Foster pulled a muscle in his back, so he can't do the roping. That leaves just me and Brax on horseback, but Emmett called and said he'd help Truett with cutting, so Walker can ride. Pop and Jefferson are going to be doing the branding," I share.

"At least the weather is going to be nice this year. Remember last year, we all sat in the pouring rain, watching you guys slip and slide around, roping calves in mud all day," she says, laughing at the memory.

"It's funny now, but it wasn't at the time," I recall.

I open my truck and fish my keys from the console, and then I start removing my spare cabin key from the ring.

"What time do you think you'll be finishing up?" she asks.

"I should be wrapping up around five."

"Okay. I'm going into town to help Momma in the bakery for a couple hours. She's trying to get all the cakes and pies done for this weekend. Then, I have to swing by Rustic Peak and pick Beau up from his riding lesson. We'll run by our house and grab all the stuff we need to cook and meet you at your place."

Momma and Bells emerge from the house, and Momma spots us and calls out to Dallas.

I place the key in her hand, and she trots off to say hello to them while I grab my phone. I have three missed calls.

One is from Dallas, and two are from Doreen.

I dial her number back.

"Myer?" Her frantic voice comes over the line.

"Yeah. What's wrong?" I ask.

"Is Dallas there? She told Sophia she was going to Stoney Ridge when she left here."

"Yeah, she's up at the house, talking with Momma and Bells. Do you need her?"

"There's been an accident. We're getting in the truck now and heading to the hospital."

I listen intently as she explains.

Dallas waves to the girls and comes jogging back over to me. The smile drops from her face as she takes me in.

"We're on our way. Yes, I'll drive her," I say as I disconnect. "Go grab your purse and lock up your truck," I tell her as I start toward the house.

"Momma, tell Daddy the back barn door is open, and the trailer bed has half a stack of bales on it. I have to run Dallas into town, and I don't know when I'll be back," I yell up to the porch.

"Everything okay?" she calls back, concern in her voice.

"Yeah, I just need him or Truett to pull the trailer all the way in and close up. I'll finish unloading it in the morning. I'll call you later and fill you in."

"Okay, son," she says as I turn and see Dallas fumbling in her truck.

She emerges with her phone in her hand. She raises it in the air. "I've got a bunch of missed calls from Rustic, but nobody is picking up now," she says.

I rush to her. "Come on. Let's get in my truck," I say as I shut her door.

She stands in place, distress written all over her. "What's wrong?"

Thirty-Four

DALLAS

"I NEED YOU TO STAY CALM," HE SAYS AS HE PLACES HIS HANDS ON my shoulders.

"Calm? Why? What happened?"

"There was an accident over at Rustic Peak," he says as he looks me in the eye.

"What kind of accident?"

My mind starts whirling in a hundred directions. *Was there a fire? Did someone turn over a bush hog? Fall from the barn?* It could be anything.

"A tractor backfired out in the field. Apparently, it was sudden and loud. They were too close to the stables …"

Oh God, no. Beau is at his riding lesson this afternoon.

Myer can feel the sudden shift in my body, and he moves in closer.

"Please," I whisper as I close my eyes tightly.

"It's okay. Everyone is okay," he says as his lips touch my forehead.

I feel my body relax at his reassurance.

"Beau was on one of the horses. It bucked him. He was wearing his helmet, and Madeline was able to get him clear of the animal before his rear came down. She took his back legs to her hip," he says.

I open my eyes and look up at him. "Is she okay?"

"She might have a fracture in her hip, but she's going to be fine."

"Beau?"

"They think he broke his arm," he says gently.

"Where is he?" I say in a panic.

I have to get to him. I have to get to my baby right now. I move around him and open my purse and start frantically searching for my truck keys. The purse slips from my hand, and its contents scatter across the ground.

"Dammit!" I scream as I fall to my knees and start gathering my mess. "Where is he?"

He kneels down in front of me. "Doreen took him straight to the emergency room down at County General. Come on. I'll take you," he says as he tugs me up from the gravel.

He reaches down and grabs my wallet and keys.

Bells comes running down the steps of the porch. "I'll get the rest. You guys go on," she says as she gets to us.

I hand her my purse. "Thank you," I say as I take off running to Myer's truck.

"Mommy!"

I hear his cry as I burst through the door. Three sets of eyes fly to me. Doreen, who is sitting beside Beau's bed, stands and gives me space as a nurse sets up a tray by the opposite side. I take a deep breath and calm my shaking nerves before I walk to him.

I look at his left arm, which is an alarming shade of purple and has an unnatural bow from his elbow to his wrist. My stomach rolls, and I have to look away.

"Hey, baby," I say softly as I run my hand through his hair. It's what I always do to soothe him. It is wet and matted to his head. He sweats when he is scared, same as me.

"Mooooommy," he continues to cry.

"Shh, it's all right. Everything is going to be okay. The doctors here are super smart, and they know exactly what to do to make you all better," I whisper to him as I lean in and kiss his forehead.

"It hurts," he says with trembling lips.

I have to bite the inside of my cheek to keep mine from trembling too.

"I know, baby, but it won't for long. You just have to be strong for a little bit longer. Can you do that for Mommy?"

He purses his lips together and brings his watery eyes up to mine as he nods.

My brave boy.

The nurse clears her throat, and I look to her.

"We're going to give him a shot that will ease the pain and make him very loopy before the doctor sets the bone."

I nod my acceptance, and she begins to load the syringe as the door opens behind me. I turn to see Myer walk in.

"Hey, little man. I hear you took a tumble today. How are you doing?" he asks as he comes up beside me.

"I hurt my arm," he says and starts to lift it to show Myer.

"No, no. We want to keep it still, remember?" the nurse reminds him.

"I see it, buddy." Myer draws his attention back to us.

"Miss Madeline was mad at my horse. I don't want her to get into trouble," he says as tears spill down his cheeks.

"I'm sure Miss Madeline was just scared, not mad," Myer reassures him.

"Okay, here we go," the nurse says as she raises the needle, and Beau's eyes go as round as saucers. "This is going to pinch just a little."

His eyes fly to me, and I can see the pleading in them. He wants me to help him.

I sit down in the chair Doreen has vacated, and I place both my hands on his good arm. "Look at me, baby."

He does, and I see the fear shining back at me.

"This is like every other time you have gone to the doctor to get your shots. Remember how it's never as bad as you think it's going to be? It only lasts a second, and then you're all done."

He nods and squeezes his eyes closed.

The nurse gives him the quick shot, and he starts to cry again.

"You're all done, little man. Look at that," Myer says over my head.

Beau's eyes pop open, and he looks over at the nurse, who is removing her gloves.

"I did it," he says as he turns back to us and smiles.

"You sure did. Just like a big boy," I praise.

The nurse cleans up her tray, and before she leaves, she tells us that the medicine will take about fifteen minutes to set in and that the doctor will be in soon.

Doreen places her steady hand on my shoulder. And I look up at her. Her eyes are closed, and her head is bowed. She's praying over my son. When she is done, she looks at me and smiles.

"It's his first accident, isn't it? Oh, it never gets easier. I swear, between Sophie breaking her arm when she was little and Elle knocking out her front two teeth and busting her nose open when she wrecked her bike in kindergarten, I have endured a scare or two," she says as she looks me in the eye. "He is going to be fine. Kids scrape knees, chip teeth, and break bones, but they are resilient."

I know she's right.

After about ten minutes, the giggling starts.

"Mommy, I got a fishy in my tummy," Beau slurs.

"You have a what in your tummy?" I ask.

"A fishy, and it's swimming round and round."

He starts laughing, but it's a half-laugh, half-gurgle. Then, he opens his eyes wide and tries to put his finger in my nose.

"What are you doing?" I ask as I take his wrist in my hand and pull my head back.

"My nose itches," he says slowly.

"That's my nose, not yours, silly," I say as I playfully tug his fingers.

More sedated giggles.

"He's high as a kite," I say as I turn to Myer, who is smiling at my son.

"Yep. You should record it and show him later. Use it as blackmail when he starts dating," he suggests.

I gasp in horror. "That's just wrong."

The doctor comes in a few minutes later, and I stand to greet him. Beau is super relaxed but still awake.

"Ms. Stovall," he acknowledges as he shakes my hand. "Your son has a fracture in his left arm, and I need to set it. Then, we'll put a cast on, which he'll need to wear for six to eight weeks. The nurse will give you care instructions," he says as he writes on a chart. Then, he looks up at me.

My expression must show I'm panicking because he continues, and his voice takes on a compassionate lilt rather than the matter-of-fact one he was using.

"There is no need to worry. Children's bones are soft and heal very easily. The break is clean, and I don't expect he'll have any trouble recovering quickly and completely."

I let out a breath.

"That being said, this next part isn't pleasant, and you guys might want to step outside for a few minutes," he finishes, and then he walks to the other side of Beau's bed and starts talking to him.

The hell I'm leaving the room.

I stay seated beside his bed and grasp his hand.

The doctor looks over at me.

"I'm not leaving this room. If you want me to leave, you're going to have to force me out, and you'd better have an army waiting to do it," I tell him.

He looks from me to Doreen and Myer.

"She's not kidding," Myer informs him.

"Okay, Ms. Stovall. You hold his hand, and I'll set the bone on a count of three."

It's the worst thing I have ever had to endure. Holding my baby as he cries out in pain and hearing the snap of his arm.

I'd rather break every bone in my body and have them snapped back one by one than to ever have to watch Beau go through that again.

This Mommy business is not for the faint of heart.

Thirty-Five

MYER

We pull up to my cabin. The sedatives wore completely off about halfway home, and Beau is chattering away in the backseat about his Hulk arm. He was a little freaked out about the cast until the doctor explained that he could give him a green one like The Incredible Hulk and he could have all his friends sign it.

I throw the truck in park, hop out, and round the hood to help them out. Dallas looks exhausted. Beau is full of energy.

Once they exit, I say the one thing I know she doesn't want to hear.

"Dal, why don't you go inside and relax a bit before you guys head home? Beau and I are going to take a ride on Thumper before the sun sets."

"We are?" he asks nervously.

She immediately turns around on her heels.

I meet her eyes as I answer him, "Yeah, buddy. You've been wanting to ride him, right?"

"He's not getting on the back of another horse," she starts, and I walk to her.

"Dal," I begin slowly.

"No!"

"Listen to me for a minute," I say as I take her hand.

She starts to pull away, but I hold on tightly.

"He just broke his arm, Myer, and it could have been worse," she grunts under her breath as tears well in her eyes.

Her chin starts to quiver, and I can feel the fear rolling off her in waves.

"I know," I say carefully. "And if he doesn't get back on a horse right now, he will be scared of them for a long time, maybe forever," I explain gently.

She starts to shake her head as she looks down behind me.

"Mommy?" he calls to her in question with a tremble in his voice.

"Do you trust me?" I ask.

She snaps her eyes back to me. "Yes, but …"

"Then, you need to go inside and let me take him for a ride. I won't let anything happen to him. I promise you."

She stands there, indecision making her breathing uneven.

She looks back down at him. "It's okay, baby. Myer is going to take you for a ride. You have fun. Mommy will be here when you guys get back, and we'll make supper."

He looks up at me, and I see the apprehension on his face, but he doesn't cry, and he doesn't ask not to go.

He looks back at Dallas and says, "Okay, Mommy. Can we eat here?"

"Yeah, we can eat here."

He reaches up and places his good hand in mine, and we turn and walk toward the stables.

"Come on, little man. Let's chase some wind."

I look over my shoulder and see Dallas standing on the porch, watching us until we are out of sight.

We ride for about an hour and a half. He was scared at first, but once I was seated behind him and we trotted out past the house and into the clearing before the woods, I could feel the tension leave his body. I let him hold the reins with me with his good hand. Before long, I had Thumper in a full gallop, and Beau was giggling and asking to go faster. In the end, I have to force him off the horse, so we can go inside and eat.

I missed lunch today, and I'm starving. The aroma of garlic and tomato sauce wafts through the air as we climb the steps to the porch, and my stomach lets out a tortured growl.

I open the door and see Dallas behind the island with one of Momma's aprons on. She is cutting up veggies and tossing them into a bowl while dancing to the country song coming from the radio in the corner.

Her eyes dart up, and I see the flash of relief that passes on her face before she smiles wide.

"How was it?" she asks.

"It was awesome!" Beau exclaims as he flies past me into the kitchen. "We rode superfast, and Myer let me help lead Thumper," he says as he tries to pull himself up onto a barstool with just one arm.

I help boost him up and scoot him to the counter as he continues, "Myer's going to get me my own saddle. I'll be able to ride with him and Uncle Payne. Madeline says I need goggles, too, so my glasses don't fall off anymore."

"I'll call and order you a pair tomorrow," she says.

I walk around the island and kiss the side of her head. "Smells good. How'd you pull this off?" I ask as I take in the pasta feast.

"I called your momma, asked if she had what we needed at her house, and she did. She even sent your dad to the garden to pull fresh vegetables for the salad. We owe her a meal," she says as she walks over and turns off the stove.

Then, she takes a towel and pulls out a freshly toasted loaf of garlic bread from the oven.

"Are you hungry?" she asks as she sets it down and leans a hip against the counter.

"Starving," I answer.

"Thank you for today. I don't think I could have driven myself to the hospital. I know you had work to do."

I stop her there. "Dallas, the work can wait, and even if you hadn't been here when that call came in, I would've stopped what I was doing and gone straight to the hospital."

She lets out a breath and places her head against my chest.

I bring my hands to her shoulders and gently massage them as she finally releases some of the tension.

"Do you love each other?"

The question comes out of nowhere, and it hits us both like a physical blow.

Her head pops up, and she looks at Beau with stunned eyes. "Uh, um, no … I mean, yes, of course we do—what?" she stammers.

"Like a boyfriend and girlfriend love each other?" he asks.

Dallas turns several shades of red as she searches for the right words.

"You know what, buddy?" I interject and round the island to sit down beside him.

His eyes come to me. "What?"

"I like your momma very much," I tell him honestly.

"And you like kissing her," he states, "like how Braxton likes kissing Miss Sophie and Pop-Pop likes kissing Nana?"

"Yeah, buddy, kinda like that. How do you feel about that?"

He looks up at me and thinks for a moment. Then, he shrugs. "Mommy should have somebody to kiss her. She's pretty, and she's nice. She smells good, and she cooks really good. Better than Nana, but don't tell Nana."

Dallas lets out a muted sob.

"I won't. That'll be our little secret," I agree.

"Mommy smiles a lot when you're around. I think she wants you to be her boyfriend," he whispers and then looks at Dallas. "Don't you?"

"I …" Her voice cracks, and I try not to laugh at her distressed expression.

"Promise you won't make her cry," he says.

"How do you mean?"

He shrugs. "Josh's mommy's boyfriend makes her cry all the time. It makes him sad. I don't like it when Mommy cries."

I bend and look him in the eye. "I promise," I tell him.

"Okay," he says.

Dallas stares at him for a minute, and then she looks to me and shrugs.

I ruffle his hair and stand to go wash up.

He just made that awkward conversation easy for us.

God, I love that kid.

Thirty-Six

DALLAS

W*hat just happened? Did Beau just declare us a couple, and Myer agreed?*

I turn to the stove, grab the pot of noodles, and drain them. Trying to keep myself from freaking out.

When he returns from the bathroom, Myer helps me load plates, and we sit at his dining table to eat.

It's a beautiful table. He made it himself from reclaimed wood of a barn he and his dad had torn down to rebuild. Its finish is fantastic, and it has two matching picnic-style benches for seats.

It suits this space perfectly.

The log cabin is spacious. The kitchen and living room are open with a long concrete island separating the two. There is a large stone fireplace with the stonework climbing all the way up to the two-story ceiling against the far wall. Towering floor-to-ceiling windows open the back of the cabin up to a breathtaking mountain view, and to the right and over the hill, you can just catch a glimpse of our orchard. The master bedroom and bath are off the back of the first level, and upstairs are two bedrooms and a single bathroom.

I can remember when he was building it. He started the summer after he returned from college. I think the work distracted him from the fact that his football dreams had been crushed.

It's big, but the rich, dark woods and sand-colored stones give it a cozy, warm feel.

I've always loved it.

Beau chatters away while we eat. I have to help him with his glass of water, and he ends up wearing as much of his spaghetti as he eats. The doctor said there would be an adjustment period for him with the cast, but since the break was not in his dominant arm, he should get the hang of it after a few days. He'll have it for six weeks, which means, barring any further accidents, it will come off just in time for Sophie's wedding.

Once we're done eating, Myer helps me clear the table and wash the dishes. I catch him mid-yawn, and I know we've overstayed our welcome.

"We'll get out of here soon so you can get to sleep," I say as I towel the last plate.

"We're leaving?" Beau asks.

I turn to see him standing by the table, covered in noodles that must have gathered in his lap. He even managed to get them in his hair.

"Look at you; you're a mess. We have to get you home and in a bathtub right away, or we'll never get the orange off of you," I tease.

He looks down at himself and giggles. "I'm sorry, Mommy."

"It's okay. The doctor said your aim would get better."

"Why are we leaving? Can't we have a sleepover here?" he asks as I make it to him with a rag and try to scrape as much loose from him as possible.

I wipe his mouth first and then his hands. "Myer needs to go to bed. He has to get up very early in the morning for work," I explain.

His face falls.

"You need to get to bed too. You've had quite a big day. Your first broken bone. It's worn you and your momma out."

"Stay," I hear Myer's request from behind me.

I look over my shoulder.

"We'll give him a bath in my tub. The doctor said you needed to tie off his arm with a plastic bag and keep the cast dry. You'll need help the first time. I'll start a fire, and we'll all sleep out here on the sectional. The ends open to recliners. He might be more comfortable sleeping upright tonight."

"Thank you, but you've done enough today. I don't know how well he'll sleep, and I don't want us keeping you up half the night. We've imposed enough already," I tell him.

"Please, Mommy. I'll sleep real good, I promise," Beau begs.

"Yeah, please, Mommy. I will be good too. Cross my heart," Myer joins in.

"Y'all are going to gang up on me, huh? So, that's what's happening?" I ask, looking between the two.

"Yes, boys against the girl," Beau squeals.

I poke him in the side. "Hey, Mommy's vote counts double," I declare.

He purses his lips. "No fair. You make up rules," he complains.

"Seriously, Dal, stay. I'll be fine in the morning," Myer encourages.

"Please," Beau says as he wraps his good arm around my neck.

I sigh dramatically and give in. "Oh, okay. If Myer will let both of us borrow a shirt to sleep in, we can stay tonight."

To be honest, I'm too drained to tackle the bath alone.

"I've got you two covered," Myer agrees.

"Yay!"

My six-year-old celebrates like we just told him he was going to Disneyland.

"All right, I got the bag. Let's go get you hosed off, little man," Myer insists as he waves a plastic grocery bag in the air.

Beau takes off, running in the direction of the bathroom.

"I'll get him started, and you grab a couple of T-shirts from the dresser across from my bed," he says and follows after Beau.

I sit back on my heels in the middle of, I guess, my boyfriend's floor, watching him chase after my son, and I think to myself, *What a crazy couple of weeks it's been. Life changes on a dime and when you least expect it.*

I take an extra minute to just sit and collect myself. Then, I grab shirts from Myer's drawer and join my boys in the chaos that is bathing a six-year-old with a broken arm that's covered in spaghetti. It's not easy.

Once we have Beau clean and towel-dried, I pull Myer's tee over his head, and he looks like he's wearing a tent. Which he thinks is cool.

Myer loads the wraparound couch with blankets and pillows and builds a fire.

I open one of the reclining ends, Beau hops up, and I tuck him in, snug as a bug.

"You comfy?" I ask him, and he nods enthusiastically. "Who's my favorite boy in the whole wide world?"

"Me!"

"That's right."

He grins.

"I don't have a book with me," I tell him.

"That's okay. I'm ready to sleep now," he whispers.

"Good night," I say as I kiss his forehead.

I look up, and Myer is standing there, watching us. He's changed into a pair of lounge pants.

"Good night, Myer," Beau calls.

"Good night, buddy."

One more yawn, and his little eyes start closing.

I tiptoe away.

"I'm going to change. I'll be right back," I whisper to Myer.

I make my way to the bathroom and decide to step into the shower quickly. I grab the soap to lather, and it smells like Myer. Woodsy and clean. I love the way he smells.

I'm out in minutes and return to the living room. It's dark with only the glow from the fire lighting the room, and both Myer and Beau are fast asleep.

I take a pillow and curl up beside Myer. His arm comes around me in his sleep, and he turns into me.

In no time, I drift off too.

Thirty-Seven

DALLAS

"CAN YOU CLIMB DOWN?" I ASK AS I OPEN THE TRUCK DOOR for Beau.

The doctor suggested I keep him out of school today just to give him time to adjust to the cast.

Everything takes a little longer, but he's maneuvering around reasonably well.

I have to fight the instinct to do everything for him.

Once he's out of the truck, I hand him the bouquet of flowers we picked up in town. He wanted to bring something to Miss Madeline to make her feel better.

I follow him up the stairs, and when he gets to the screen door, I can see the frustration well up. He usually bursts through doors at warp speed, but holding the flowers in his good hand, he can't manage the door.

I reach around him and open the door, and he trots in.

We find Doreen, Ria, Sophie, and Madeline in the kitchen.

"Hi, Beau. How are you feeling?" Madeline asks as soon as she catches sight of him.

"I'm good. I brought you flowers." He proudly presents the bouquet he picked out himself.

She takes them from him and brings them to her nose, making a big show of inhaling their scent. "These are beautiful, and they smell so good. Thank you," she praises as she hugs his neck.

"See my Hulk arm?" He holds up his cast for all to see. "Isn't it cool?" he asks, and they all answer in the affirmative. "Mommy, can I go show Emmett?"

"Yes, but be careful and watch your step," I warn, and I walk and open the back door for him.

"Dallas, I'm—" Madeline starts.

I put up a hand. "Don't apologize. It was an accident, and if it weren't for you being willing to throw your body in the way to protect him, he could have been seriously injured or worse. I'm grateful you are his instructor," I tell her.

She tears up. "I hope you let him continue. The boys know that they aren't allowed to be on a tractor, mower, four-wheeler, or any other machine anywhere near the stables during my lesson hours ever again. It's important that he comes back, especially after a fall," she explains.

"He's already been on the back of a horse since we got home," I tell her.

Her eyes widen. "Really?"

"Yep. Myer insisted on taking him as soon as we got to his place from the hospital," I tell them.

"That was smart," Doreen says as she starts setting coffee cups around the table and pouring.

"That's what he said. I nearly threw up at the thought," I confess.

"I broke my arm after falling from Blackberry when I was little. Do you remember that?" Sophie asks me.

"I sure do," Ria answers before I can reply.

"Daddy made me get right back on her too."

We hear the front door swing open.

"Hello?" my mother's voice calls.

"In here, Dottie," Doreen answers.

She enters the kitchen, her arms loaded down with boxes. "I brought bagels, muffins, doughnuts, and a few fresh-baked loaves," she says and hands them off to Doreen.

"Thank you. I'll toast up some bagels now. You want a cup of coffee?" she offers.

"That would be lovely." She looks around the room. "Where's my grandson?"

"He's out, showing his cast off to the fellas," Doreen answers.

She sits down beside me. "And how are you holding up, sweetheart?"

"Hanging in there. I hope I never get another phone call like that though," I answer and lay my head on my momma's shoulder.

She reaches up and pats it. "Oh, honey. He's a boy. It's just the first of many, I'm afraid." She laughs.

Yes, laughs. Sometimes, I think she enjoys watching my perils in motherhood a little too much.

"He's going to fall from horses, trees, monkey bars, and he'll wreck bikes, four-wheelers, and motorcycles. Payne once flipped the riding lawn mower while racing one of his friends down the hill near the creek. I can't remember how old he was, maybe twelve or thirteen. He could have cut his foot off. That boy nearly drove me to drink."

"Are you trying to make me feel better? Because it's not working," I grumble.

"I'm just saying, as their mothers, we do the best we can to protect them and teach them to use good sense and act responsibly, but we can't control everything. When you had that fender-bender on the way to school the week you got your driver's license, my first instinct was to take that car away and never let you back behind the wheel again. Your father wouldn't let me. He said I couldn't let my fear keep you from living. Scared me to death every time you drove out of the driveway for months. He would have to hold my hand while I cried, watching you disappear through the gate."

"I don't even want to think about Beau driving a car. I might not survive the teen years."

"It doesn't get any easier once they are adults. You still want to protect them from pain, physical and emotional," Madeline adds.

"The emotional ones are the worst. Broken bones can be set, and you can give them medicine to ease the pain. But broken hearts? Those you have to watch them go through helplessly. As a momma, that's the worst," Momma says.

"I don't look forward to that either. I would hate to have to whoop some little girl's ass," I say.

Her eyes round at my statement.

Ria chuckles.

"You might have to stand in line behind his nana," Momma declares.

We all giggle.

"I need a couple of days, but I know you're right. I guess I'll let him go back to his riding lessons as soon as you're recovered and ready to return," I tell Madeline.

Momma looks at me thoughtfully. "You're a good mother, Dallas. Do you hear me?"

I look up at her. Tears start to well, and then my insecurities leak out and roll down my cheeks.

"You are a good mother. We all doubt ourselves and second-guess our decisions sometimes, but never, ever forget that."

Agreement rings out from all of them.

"I feel like I fail him constantly," I admit.

"Do you love him?" Momma asks.

"More than life itself."

"That's all he needs. That's all any child needs to thrive."

"It's what we all need," Sophie adds.

I look over at her. I catch what she's throwing.

"Yep," Momma agrees.

Guess she caught it too.

Thirty-Eight

MYER

It's branding day. I wake up, excited. It's practically a holiday on the ranch. Everyone looks forward to and anticipates it like it's Christmas.

I've been so busy the past few days that I haven't seen Dallas and Beau since they stayed over on Tuesday.

Waking up to them snuggled up in my living room was my favorite thing ever. I could wake up to that sight for the rest of my life.

I get dressed and head out to the corral. Braxton and Jefferson are already standing there with Pop.

"Hey. Man, you guys are early," I say as I slap Braxton's back.

"Nah, your lazy ass just slept in," he says with a grin.

"Whatever. Let's go pick the horses."

He follows me to the stables.

"I'll be on Bolt. Any of the others on this side would be great out there," I point out.

"Which one is the most temperamental?" he asks.

"The gray-and-white one. The damn thing is like riding a bull," I inform him.

He grins. "Walker can ride that one."

I shake my head. We are mean sons of bitches to each other.

"I really appreciate your help today," I tell him as we walk the horses to the corral.

"Happy to be here. Now, let's go round up some calves."

Walker and Emmett have arrived when we make it back up.

We mount and take off to the pasture.

By the time we return with them and get them sorted into the branding pens, the crowd is already assembling.

Payne and his pop are raising the tents for the food tables, and Reverend Burr and some of the men from the church are unloading and setting up folding tables and chairs.

Ladies are coming down the drive, carrying pots and ceramic dishes.

Children have gathered in the field beside the barn and are chasing each other.

I spot Momma fussing over tablecloths with Bells and Dallas by her side. Dallas is wearing a pale blue sundress with yellow-and-white flowers.

She takes my breath.

Braxton follows my gaze. "How's that going?"

"Your guess is as good as mine," I tell him.

"That well, huh?"

"Yeah," I admit.

"Sounds about right. Women have a way of keeping us on our toes."

As the words leave his lips, Sophie comes walking down the drive with Elle.

"But they're worth it," he says as he clasps my shoulder and walks off toward his bride-to-be.

Dallas breaks off from Momma and walks down to me.

"Hey." She smiles a blinding smile and walks into my side.

I wrap an arm around her and look down at her face. I've missed her the past few days.

"Is everything ready for the day?" she asks.

"Everything is perfect now," I tell her, and a blush hits her cheeks. "Where's Beau?" I ask.

"He's chasing the Andersons' twin girls with his Hulk arm." She rolls her eyes.

"Already a little Casanova," I muse.

"He'd better slow his roll, or he's going to be grounded till he's thirty," she says.

"He's a stud, and he has the same genes as Payne, so you're going to have to deal," I tease.

"Jesus, help me."

I chuckle and plant a brief kiss to her lips.

"Doc just arrived. The show's about to start."

"Good luck," she offers before taking off and joining Sophie and Elle on the hay-bale bleachers.

We spend the rest of the morning and into the early afternoon roping calves, and Pop and Jefferson freeze-brand them.

We have a robust and healthy herd this year.

There are few things I enjoy more than riding and roping. Braxton, Walker, and I are worn out by the time the last calf is branded and cut.

A cheer rings out across the crowd, and then Reverend Burr stands to pray the blessing over our ranch, the land, the cattle, and the hands that work it.

This is Pop and Momma's thirty-fifth branding as owners of Stoney Ridge. My grandfather passed it down to Pop and his brother before he died. Uncle Ray wasn't that interested in being a rancher, so Pop bought him out a few years later.

I watch as Pop proudly embraces her at the reverend's side.

He finds me standing to the side and beckons Bellamy and me to stand with them.

After the blessing, the reverend says grace, and everyone disperses to the backyard to start filling their stomachs with food.

Pop puts his arm around my shoulders as we watch everyone retreat. All of them chatting and laughing.

"This is what life is all about, son. Friends and family and honest work," he says with pride.

"It is," I agree.

"The work is over; now, let's go eat and celebrate," he prompts, and I follow behind him.

We're all seated with our plates piled high.

"Brandt! Over here," Dallas calls out.

I look up to see the new doctor crossing the lawn with a nicely dressed older lady.

"Guys, have you met the new vet?" she asks the table.

"He came by the ranch with Doc Sherrill last week," Braxton answers.

"Wait, that's the new doctor in town?" Elle asks as she watches him approach.

"Sure is, and he's single," Dallas singsongs.

"Really?" Elle's interest is obviously piqued.

"How old is he?" Braxton asks as he frowns in Brandt's direction.

"Twenty-six," Dallas answers immediately.

"I see you've done your research," Sophie adds.

"You bet. Plus, I was at Janelle's this week. Janelle knows all," Dallas replies.

They make it to the table, and she introduces them around.

Sophie forces Braxton to move down the table, so they can squeeze in seats, putting Brandt right next to Elle.

"Don't they look good together?" Dallas whispers in my direction once the doctor and Elle are caught up in conversation.

"I guess." I shrug.

"Braxton keeps giving him the stink eye," she continues to whisper conspiratorially.

"He's a big brother. It's our job to intimidate any man who sniffs around our little sister," I explain.

She huffs. "Payne never gave two cares who I was dating."

"Yes, he did. He and I got in more than one fight because of some jackass you were seeing in high school."

She blinks at me. "What?"

"When we were seniors and you were a sophomore. Every other weekend, he was dragging me with him to warn a guy off."

"You're joking."

"Nope."

"I had no idea."

Then, she looks back at me and narrows her eyes. "I guess you passed the test, huh?"

"Yep."

I grin at her, and she rolls her eyes.

Thirty-Nine

DALLAS

THE PARTY MOVES TO MYER'S CABIN AFTER THE PICNIC. Braxton and Walker build a fire out front and pull out the coolers they have stashed in the beds of their trucks.

The boys start a cutthroat game of horseshoes while the girls sip moonshine and dance in the yard to the radio.

Doc Sherrill gave Brandt's mother a ride home so he could join us.

He and Elle are currently up on the porch, chatting. Both Braxton's and Walker's attention have been focused in their direction all night.

They finish up their game, and we all sit around the fire. Myer finds me and settles on the step behind me. I lean back into his chest, and he wraps his arms around me.

"Sorry to break up the party, guys, but we're going to head home," Braxton says as he pulls Sophie up from her perch on a bale.

"Damn, son. It's only eight," Walker points out.

"Some of us have been up since five," Braxton retorts.

"You've gone soft, man," Walker says as he shakes his head.

"We working out at the house tomorrow?" Silas asks.

"I am, and I'll take any free hands you guys have to offer," Braxton answers as he slaps hands with Silas.

"I'll be there."

"I'm there too, man," Myer says. "Thanks again for today. We couldn't have done it without you, brother."

Braxton gives him a macho two-finger salute, and then calls to Elle, "You coming, sis?"

She looks up from her conversation with Brandt and frowns.

"I'll bring her home," Walker offers.

Braxton's forehead wrinkles.

Walker reassures him, "I've only had two beers, I swear, and I won't have another. Scout's honor."

"You weren't a Boy Scout, dumbass," Payne says.

"Still counts," Walker insists.

"What's up with you tonight?" Myer asks.

"I'm working with Jefferson in the morning to build the new troughs. I know better than to show up late or hungover. He'll create more work and do his best to make me puke," he says.

That makes complete sense, so Braxton relents.

"Fine, but not one more, and don't stay much longer. Jefferson is going to expect you at sunrise."

"I know," Walker moans.

Everyone clears out by ten. Including Brandt, who got Elle's number before Walker wrangled her into his truck.

"Do you have to be home?" Myer asks as he starts to back me up the porch steps.

I shake my head. "Beau's staying with Momma tonight, and I brought an overnight bag. It's in my truck," I inform him.

He sticks his hand out. "Key," he demands.

I pull the key from the pocket of my dress and place it in his hand, and he immediately turns and jogs out to retrieve my bag.

I go in and kick my shoes off. Then, I fish two more beers from the fridge and curl up on the couch.

He returns, drops my bag beside the door, and joins me.

He plops down heavily beside me. He looks beat.

I reach up and run my fingers through his hair, and he closes his eyes and hums in appreciation.

"How tired are you?" I ask.

"On a scale from one to ten? Twenty," he deadpans.

I let out a disappointed mewl.

Then, he cracks one eye open and focuses it on me. "What was that?"

I bear up and straddle him. His hands land on my hips as I settle against him.

"I think I can rally," he says as I bring my lips to his ear.

"I'll do all the work," I offer.

That's all it takes to convince him. He stands and carries me to the bedroom.

And I make good on my word.

I wake to the smell of sausage and coffee. I roll over and blink my eyes open. I'm in Myer's massive bed. I stretch and sink back into the pillows. I'm so comfortable that I don't want to budge, but the aroma of food is beckoning me.

I wrap myself in the top sheet and pad into the kitchen.

He is behind the island, stirring something on the stove. I come up behind him and kiss a trail across his bare back. I slide my hands around him and across his abs and lay my cheek against his skin.

"Mornin', sleepyhead," he greets.

I mumble something incoherent, and he chuckles.

"Are you hungry?"

I nod against his skin.

He turns and takes me in. I'm sure I look a mess. All tangled hair and tangled sheet.

He leads me to the island and sits me down. Then, he proceeds to make my plate. Homemade biscuits smothered in sausage gravy.

I quirk an eyebrow at him.

"Don't be too impressed. Momma made the biscuits. She makes a batch about once a week and stocks my freezer."

"Still impressed," I say as I take a bite.

It's fantastic, and he watches me as I devour the entire plate.

"What?" I say as I pop the last morsel into my mouth. "I worked up an appetite last night," I remind him.

His eyes go dark.

"Don't look at me like that. Finish your breakfast," I say as I grab my mug and shuffle into the living room.

He follows and sits beside me as I study the view.

"I'm going to build a deck out there this summer. One that spans the entire backside of the cabin with doors that open from here and the master bedroom."

"That would be amazing. Sitting out there, having breakfast, watching the sun rise over the mountains," I muse.

There is nothing more beautiful than our mountains.

I lie back into his arms as I sip my coffee.

"What time are you heading over to Braxton's?" I ask.

He sighs. "Soon. I know his ass is already up and over there."

Bummer. I could lie here in his arms all day.

He must sense my disappointment because he suddenly shifts us, and I'm on my back.

He peels back the sheet and runs his hand up my inner thigh.

My legs fall to the sides to give him access.

"He can wait a little while," he says against my mouth.

Forty

DALLAS

The next few weeks are a whirlwind of activity. Rustic Peak hosts its branding party, as do several other local ranches. We basically spend two solid weeks eating and drinking, and now, Poplar Falls is gearing up for the annual Memorial Day celebration.

It consists of more food, a parade, games, vendor booths, and a bluegrass concert downtown.

Today, after I drop Beau off at school, I'm helping Momma at the bakery to prepare for the influx of people in town.

"What day is today, Beau?"

"The best day ever!" he replies.

"Why is it the best day ever?"

"Because we woke up this morning," he answers.

"What are we gonna do today?" I ask.

"We are going to be kind and give everyone our brightest smile."

"What aren't we gonna do?"

"Let anyone steal our shine."

"How much do I love you?"

"All the way up to the moon and back."

"That's right, baby." I look at him through the rearview mirror and smile. "Your cast comes off next week. Are you excited?"

He nods. The novelty of the Hulk arm wore off a couple weeks ago, and now, he's begun to complain more and more about the itching and discomfort from chafing.

I drop him off and head to the shop.

Main Street is in full bloom. The gorgeous pink cherry trees line the streets, and all the flower beds are bursting with spring color.

I love this time of year.

I pull into the spot in front of the shop. I see Miss Elaine walking a little white poof on a leash and call her over.

"Good morning, Dallas," she greets as I bend to pet the poof.

"Good morning. Who do we have here?"

"This is Lou-Lou; she's a bichon frise," she says proudly.

"Aren't you just adorable, Miss Lou-Lou?" I coo as I scratch her head.

"Why don't you two come in and have a cup of coffee?" I invite.

She accepts my invitation, and we find Momma and Doreen inside, chatting over pastries.

"Hi, y'all. Remember Dr. Haralson's momma, Elaine?" I say as we make our way in.

"Yes, of course. Good morning, Elaine," Doreen says as she pats the chair beside her.

"And this is Miss Lou-Lou. I'll go grab us a cup of coffee and her a bowl of water."

The three of them are discussing the church's ladies' auxiliary when I return. Always recruiting, those two.

After a nice visit, Doreen offers to take Elaine and Lou-Lou and introduce them around to the other shop owners in town before her appointment with Janelle. Momma and I get to work on making all the red, white, and blue cupcakes for the church's table at the Memorial Day picnic as well as an assortment of brownies, lemon bars, cookies, chocolate croissants, and of course, her signature apple pies—made with apples from our orchard—to fill the bakery's display cases.

"I can't believe Sophie's wedding is in a couple of weeks. Spring sure flew by," I say as I load another batch of cupcakes into the oven.

"I know. I'll be starting on her cakes soon. I might need extra hands." She nudges me.

"You know all you have to do is ask, Momma."

"Actually, I've been wanting to talk to you about something. Patty wants to start keeping her new grandson when her daughter-in-law goes back to work, and I need to hire someone to replace her. Would you be interested?"

"I have two jobs, Momma," I remind her.

"Yes, but I'm not getting any younger, and now that your daddy is somewhat retired, I'd like to think about retiring myself in the next few years. I was thinking maybe you'd like to take over the bakery one day?"

I pause and turn to her.

"Hear me out. I can pay you what you're earning at Faye's. You can work for me, and I'll teach you everything from the baking itself to running the business. All the state health code rules and regulations, my wholesale partners, how I run the books. The entire business inside and out."

I look around the shop, a place where I spent most of my childhood under her feet. I can't imagine it without her behind the counter.

"Oh, stop it," she says. "I'm not going anywhere anytime soon, but I want to start preparing, and I'd love to see this place stay open and in the family. Your daddy was so proud to hand the farm and orchard over to Payne and know that the Henderson legacy would live on in Poplar Falls, and I feel the same about this bakery. Your grandmother helped me get it up and running, and I've poured everything I have into it for nearly forty years. The name Bountiful Harvest Bread Company means something to this town. But if it's not your dream, I understand."

I've never really had a dream. I've been so busy just trying to provide for my son and keep my head above water that I haven't had time for one. I love this bakery. I love that it's a vital part of this town. And I have been baking with my momma since I was a little girl. Most of her recipes are stored in my head.

"I think I'd like that," I tell her.

"Oh, wonderful!" she squeals as she pinches my cheeks like she did when I was small.

I'm excited as I leave the shop to pick up Beau. It feels like I have a plan for our future. I've honestly been adrift since I landed back here in Poplar Falls, doing whatever I need to do to keep us afloat, and I'm not complaining. I love the diner and Butch's Tavern and even working with Sophie at Rustic Peak, but all of those are the results of other people's dreams come to life. I can see myself with gray in my hair, opening the bakery every morning, my grandchildren underfoot.

Ha! Who am I kidding? As long as Janelle has breath, I'll never be gray.

Beau is a bundle of energy when I pick him up. His class made Memorial Day crafts for the celebration, and he has a handful of flags he made for us and Nana and Pop-Pop to wave during the parade.

"Matthew's pop-pop died in the war, and so we made the flowers with our handprints for the sign that he and his daddy are going to carry in the parade," he informs me with pride.

"That's awesome, baby. I'm sure his nana is going to be so proud."

He beams. "Momma, how come I don't have a daddy?"

I look at him in the mirror. He has asked this question before when one of his friends' fathers showed up for a school activity or at a birthday party. It's been a while since he asked. In the past, I evaded the question or changed the subject as quickly as possible, knowing he was too young to understand. This time, I decide to be as honest with him as I can.

"I told you I used to live in another city before you and I came to live with Nana and Pop-Pop, right?"

He nods.

"I was married to your daddy, and … well, he did some things he shouldn't have. He got into a lot of trouble, and the police took him to jail. You were still in my tummy, and that's when I came back home."

I see the wheels turning behind his eyes.

"So, my daddy is a bad guy?"

"Do you remember when you got in trouble for throwing that rock at McKenzie, and I had to punish you? We talked about making choices, and when you make the wrong one, you have to suffer the consequences," I ask.

"Yep. I couldn't go to Jeremie's birthday party."

"That's right, and you aren't a bad guy. It's like that. Your daddy made a mistake, and he has to suffer the consequences. He has to stay in jail, and he doesn't get to be my husband or your daddy anymore."

"Will we forgive him?"

Jesus, please help me here.

"Yes, baby, we will forgive him, but that doesn't mean he gets his privileges back."

"Do you think he misses me?"

"How could he not?"

He looks out the window. The conversation is over, and my heart is racing.

I say a quick prayer, *Lord, if you could help me to keep from scarring this child for life, I would greatly appreciate it.*

Forty-One

DALLAS

Sunday morning, we all attend church service, and Reverend Burr takes the rich opportunity to drive home the message that the church's pews should always be as full as they are on holiday weekends.

When you are the reverend of a church in a town predominately populated by men and women who operate ranches, which require seven-days-a-week care, it's hard to get everyone to Sunday service.

Not that I have that excuse. Late nights at Fast Breaks or around a bonfire, drinking moonshine, doesn't exactly compare in the reasoning department. I know I need to make it here more often. I'm going to make more of an effort.

Doreen side-eyes me and Sophie, saying as much.

After the service, we all head downtown for the parade and celebration.

Momma, Doreen, Ria, and Myer's momma, Beverly, sell cupcakes and potted tomato plants for the church's veterans assistance fund.

Sophie and I are at a booth, selling jewelry she created and donated, using red and blue stones—also for the church's fund.

Myer, Braxton, Walker, and Payne are helping with the parade floats while Daddy looks after Beau.

The day couldn't have turned out any better. The weather is perfect. Sixty-five degrees and not a cloud in the sky. All the shops along Main Street are open today even though most are closed on Sundays.

All donating a percentage of their sales to the veterans family assistance program in Poplar Falls.

Memorial Day is a big deal here, as is Veterans Day and Fourth of July. Poplar Falls is a town teeming with American pride and people who want to help their neighbors in mourning or in need. People come from miles away and several towns over for events like today's, and even folks who grew up here and moved away choose weekends like this to visit family and catch up with old friends.

I look out into the sea of faces and recognize some I haven't seen in years.

Braxton and Myer stop by to bring us lemonade and check and see if we need anything else.

"Looks like you're doing well," Braxton says as he sees how low we're getting on stock.

The jewelry has been a hit. All the ladies have had a fit over Sophie's creations.

"Yep. Looks like we're going to have to convert it into a kissing booth soon," I tease.

His eyes flick to me. "You'd better be the only one offering kisses."

"What? Sophie here will bring in a ton of cash. Don't you want the church to make lots of money? I bet, between the two of us, we could make at least two hundred dollars, selling kisses for five dollars a piece," I say.

Sonia's grandfather, Mr. Pickens, is at the next booth, purchasing a T-shirt, and he turns to us. "I'll give you ten dollars for a kiss," he says with a wink.

"See," I say with a giggle.

"I'll match whatever you make on the jewelry," Braxton offers.

"I'll do the same," Myer pitches in.

"Really?" Sophie squeals.

She wants to raise as much money as the aunts. They have some sort of competition going.

"Jeez, you two are no fun at all," I tell them.

Braxton cuts his eyes to me.

I throw my hands in the air. "I was just kidding. No kissing booth. Got it."

"You, I don't trust," Braxton accuses as he points to me. Then, he looks at Sophie. "And you, I don't trust not to let her talk you into it."

Sophie huffs.

Beau comes running up with his face painted to look like The Incredible Hulk. "Look, Mommy! They painted my face to match my arm!" he announces excitedly.

"Wow, you look just like the Hulk," I praise.

"Can I have ice cream? Pop-Pop said I could if you said it was okay."

"I think you need lunch first."

"Ah, man." He pouts.

"Braxton and I were just about to get cheeseburgers. You want to eat with us? I'll take you for ice cream afterward," Myer offers.

"Can I, Mommy?"

"*May I,*" I correct. "And, yes, you may, as long as you eat a burger first."

"Okay." He reaches for Myer's hand.

Braxton leans in and kisses Sophie, and the three of them take off in search of food.

We sell out within the next hour, so we close our booth and go to find the fellas before the parade starts.

I spot Beau playing the ring toss game with Daddy and head that way while Sophie looks for Braxton.

"Hey, guys. You about ready to watch the parade?" I ask when I reach them.

"In a minute. Look, Mommy, I won a prize." Beau points to the plastic bag in Daddy's hand.

"Is that a goldfish?" I ask, hoping he says it's not.

"Yep," Daddy says with a grin.

Fabulous.

"I'm going to run to the truck and grab the quilts and find us a spot near the gazebo. Come find us when you finish up here," I tell Daddy, and he nods.

I head toward the parking lot and spot Myer standing with a group that includes Morgan, Braxton's ex, and a few others in front of the hardware store. I cross the street to let him know where we're going to set up to watch the parade. When I get close, I overhear a snippet of the conversation.

"So, you're just working the ranch now?" asks one of the guys standing in the group.

"Yeah, I run it with Pop," Myer replies.

"Damn, man, that sucks. I hate that the ankle injury sidelined you. You would have made it to the pros for sure. You ever consider coaching?"

"Not really, no."

"I know the University of Colorado is looking for an assistant offensive coordinator. I bet they'd love to have you. I can get you a meeting with the head coach if you're interested."

Myer shifts, and I can see the owner of the voice is one of his old teammates from high school.

"Samantha is still in Boulder, and she's single again. She split from that banker she was engaged to last year. When I told her I was coming home for a visit this weekend, she asked me to say hello for her and to give you her new number."

"Is that right?" is all Myer says.

Samantha is the ex-girlfriend who dumped him the minute his football dreams died. I guess she wasn't able to find another player of his caliber to latch on to after all.

Sophie comes jogging up behind me. "Dallas?"

I turn to answer her.

"You find Myer? Oh, there he is. Where are the blankets?"

"I was on the way to the truck to get them," I say.

When I turn back around, the old teammate and Myer have their phones out, and Myer is typing something into his.

My heart sinks.

"Hey, Myer," Sophie calls to him, and he looks up and smiles at us. "The parade's about to start. We're gonna set up in front of the gazebo."

"I'll be right there," he says before turning back to the group.

Sophie loops her arm in mine, and the two of us walk to the parking lot.

"You okay? You look pale," she asks as we load our arms with blankets.

"Yeah. I don't think that hot dog we ate is agreeing with me though," I lie.

"It's the chili. It was delicious but greasy. I have Tums in my purse. I'll get you a couple."

We walk back and set up, and I plant a happy smile on my face for Beau when he bounces over with his new friend, Flipper the goldfish.

Forty-Two

MYER

DALLAS ACTED OUT OF SORTS AFTER THE PARADE. WHEN I ASKED what was wrong, she said she was just tired and something about greasy chili. I gave her some space, but she isn't getting away with that shit for long. The past few weeks have been so busy with the brandings and Memorial Day and moving the cattle to the new pastures that I've barely gotten to see her and Beau, and space is not gonna be an option for her tonight.

After the fireworks, everyone starts dispersing. I walk with her and Beau to her truck.

"I'll follow you guys," I say once I have Beau in his seat.

"I'm awfully beat tonight, Myer," she says as she turns the key.

"That's fine. We can just curl up in front of the television with popcorn," I suggest.

"Yeah, popcorn with extra butter," Beau approves.

She turns around and says to him, "Maybe another night, baby."

I fold my arms on the window of her truck. "What's wrong, Dallas?" I ask.

"Nothing. I'm just not in the mood to hang out tonight. I want to go to bed early, and I have to get all that paint scrubbed off Beau's face and figure out what to put a goldfish in," she starts listing off all her bogus excuses.

"Flipper lives in a bowl," Beau chirps from the backseat.

"I don't think I have a bowl big enough for Flipper. He'll have to go in a jar for now."

"I'll stop in the general store right quick before Peterson closes it up and grab a bowl and rocks and some fish food," I offer.

"Yeah, we have to feed him," Beau says.

Dallas sighs in defeat as Payne walks up beside me.

"Fine. Meet us at the house," she relents before throwing the truck in reverse.

"What was that all about?" Payne asks as she peels out of the parking lot.

"I have no idea, but I'm going to find out."

I pull up to her house forty-five minutes later, and she already has Beau clean and in his pajamas.

He and I set up the fish bowl while she picks up around the house, effectively avoiding me.

I carry the bowl into Beau's room. "Where do you want him, buddy?" I ask.

"Right here. He and Fritz can be friends, so they won't be lonely when I'm in school."

"We're gonna have to get you a dog or something. I don't think we can fit many more tanks in here," I tell him as I set the bowl down.

"Momma says I can't have a puppy until I'm big enough to walk him all by myself," he says.

"It's true, buddy. Dogs are a much bigger responsibility than a frog and fish. You have to feed them, give them baths, take them out to use the bathroom at all hours of the day and night, and clean up after them. They require a whole lot more work and time than these guys do," I explain.

"That's what Mommy says."

"Mommy's always right."

"Yeah," he agrees, "but when I get bigger, I can ask Santa for one."

After Flipper is all set up in his new home beside Fritz's aquarium on Beau's dresser, we join Dallas in the living room and settle in for popcorn and cartoons.

She sits on the other side of Beau and as far away from me as possible.

He doesn't notice the tension, but I can feel it thickening the air in the room.

Beau falls fast asleep before the first show is over. I pick him up and carry him to bed for her. She spends an unnecessary amount of time tucking him in before she joins me again in the living room.

"All right, I know something's bothering you. Now, talk," I demand.

"Can we not do this right now?" she asks brokenly.

"Jesus, Dal, what's wrong? You were fine this afternoon, and now, you're acting like you want to be anywhere but in a room with me. What's changed in the last four hours?"

"I'm not the one who wishes they were somewhere else," she says softly.

"What the hell does that mean?"

"How's Samantha doing these days?" she asks, her eyes never leaving the floor.

"Samantha?" I ask, confused.

Samantha was my high school girlfriend. We dated junior and senior year, and then we both went to the University of Colorado Boulder. When I left school after my injury, she stayed. She wanted to be an athlete's wife. It was her entire life plan, so when the possibility of going pro was gone for me, so was she. I never mourned the loss of that relationship because I knew the minute she decided to end it that I had dodged a bullet. I thank God every day that I saw her true colors before it was too late.

"Yes, Samantha. I overheard your conversation earlier today," she says, her jaw starting to tremble.

"What? Are you talking about what Paul said?"

She nods.

"What does that have to do with us right now?"

She's not making any sense.

"I don't want to be anyone's consolation prize. You don't belong in

Poplar Falls. He's right; you should be on a football field somewhere, like you always dreamed."

"Who said I want to leave Poplar Falls?"

"Look at me, Myer. I'm a single mother in debt up to her eyeballs, who works two jobs. I drive a truck that's basically held together with duct tape at this point and live in my parents' backyard. You deserve someone like Samantha, who probably has her life together. You should call her," she says as she folds her arms over her chest.

You have got to be kidding me.

"Is that what's in your head? Seriously, Dallas?"

"I know the thought crossed your mind. I saw you put her number in your phone," she accuses.

"Really?" I pull my phone from my pocket. "In this phone?"

She just stands there and doesn't answer.

"The only number I put in here today is Paul's, and that's only because I didn't want to seem like an asshole when he gave it to me," I roar.

She swallows back tears.

"Dammit, Dallas. I cannot believe this. Seriously? Have I ever given you a reason not to trust me?"

I head for the door, and she follows me out onto the porch.

"I—" she starts.

I cut her off, "I'm not a boy anymore, Dallas. I don't dream about winning MVP trophies and taking the head cheerleader to prom. I'm a man. A man who knows exactly what he wants, and that is you and Beau. Waking up to the two of you every day for the rest of my life. But I'm tired of trying to convince you to want the same thing. I give up. You call me when you figure out what the hell it is you want."

I give her the ultimatum before I climb in my truck, slam the door, and pull away, leaving her standing on her porch.

That woman drives me insane.

I must be nuts for loving her so damn much.

Forty-Three

DALLAS

Myer has stayed true to his word, and I haven't heard from him at all this week.

After four days of sulking, I finally confess to Sophie what happened as we work on Friday morning.

"Oh, Dallas, you didn't," Sophie says, her words dripping with sympathy.

"I did. I'd misunderstood the entire exchange between them, and instead of just asking him, I got in my own head and let my insecurities run away with me."

"Well, at least something good came from all of this," she deduces.

"What would that be?" I ask because I see no good at all.

"You know how you feel now," she points out.

It's true. I've been angry with myself and sick over the whole thing. I've missed him this week. And not just the way you miss a friend. When I gave my notice and worked my last day at Faye's, the first person I wanted to call when I got in my truck was Myer. And when we went to the bank and Momma put me down as a signer on all the bakery's accounts, he was the first one I wanted to share my exciting news with.

"Yeah, I think I'm in love with him," I confess.

She nods in agreement. "You need to call him. Braxton and I will keep Beau for you tomorrow night. Ask him to come over, or better yet, you go to him and apologize for jumping to conclusions and then tell him how you feel."

I take a few deep breaths.

"Don't hyperventilate on me," she warns. "I'm zero help in a crisis; ask Aunt Doreen. When Beau was bucked from that horse, I just froze and then freaked out. She and Aunt Ria were the cool heads who handled the injured child and Madeline like pros. My future children are clearly screwed," she says.

That makes me laugh.

"You'll be fine. It's different when it's your own kid. Your instincts take over, and you handle the crisis and then freak out later behind closed doors," I assure her.

"God, I hope that's true."

"Also, I'm not feeling so confident about your offer to keep Beau now either," I say as I side-eye her.

"Don't worry. Braxton never loses his cool. He'll keep Beau alive," she promises.

Good to know.

I pick Beau up from school, and we head home for the evening. My heart is lighter after my conversation with Sophie this morning, and he can tell.

For the last few days, he has been able to read my mood, and he in turn has been melancholy. He has also been sticking close to my side.

Today, he is talkative and excited for the weekend.

He gets his cast off on Tuesday, and he is so ready.

"Mommy, is Myer gonna come with us to the doctor when they take my green arm off?" he asks as we sit down for supper.

"I'm not sure, baby. I'll ask him though."

"Where is he?" he asks.

I know that he has felt Myer's absence this week, but he hasn't mentioned him until now.

"He's upset with Mommy right now."

"Why? What did you do?"

"Well, it's complicated, but basically, I said something stupid, and it hurt his feelings," I confess.

"Did you say you were sorry?" he asks.

"Not yet."

"You should say you're sorry. He'll forgive you. Nana says you always forgive people you love when they say they're sorry," he says as he takes a big bite of mac 'n' cheese.

"That's really good advice. When did you get to be so smart?" I ask.

He shrugs. "When I was four," he informs me.

I laugh. "Is that right?"

"Yep. I remember."

I make up my mind to call Myer after I put Beau to bed tonight and ask him to come over tomorrow night. I'll make supper, and we can sit down and talk. Hopefully, he'll be open to it.

I tell Beau that he'll be spending the night with Braxton and Sophie tomorrow, and he can barely contain his excitement. He asks me at least five times when I'm going to take him over there. He loves Sophie, but I'm sure his impatience has more to do with Hawkeye than it does the two humans. He lights up every time he sees that pup. I need to get him a puppy of his own. It's selfish for me to keep him from that joy because of the extra work it's going to cause me.

I make a mental note to start putting out puppy feelers for his birthday this year.

The phone rings as I'm clearing the dishes. It's Payne. Momma and Daddy left this afternoon for Arizona to visit Aunt Barb and Uncle Clyde for the weekend.

Payne is helping out at Braxton and Sophie's this evening, so he asks if I can run over to the farmhouse and take care of a few things for him.

"Beau, get your boots on. We're going to Nana's," I call to him.

Forty-Four

DALLAS

Beau and I go up to the main house to water Momma's potted plants and flower garden.

Before we walk up the drive to water the beds at the entrance gate as well, we go back to our house to grab an extra watering can.

I have a small one that is just Beau's size, which we bought from the hardware store in town last Christmas. It came with children's gardening gloves and tools. It is one of the best investments I have ever made because he uses the hell out of those tools, following his pop-pop around the farm.

We walk up our porch steps and into the house, Beau chattering away about his sleepover with Hawk tomorrow.

I click the light on and scream.

"Travis?"

My ex-husband is casually sitting on my couch in the dark. One of the beers from my refrigerator dangling from his fingers.

"Hello, wife," he snarls.

I halt a startled Beau and tuck him behind my legs.

"Mommy?" he says nervously.

"It's okay, baby. We have an unexpected guest, is all," I say calmly.

"Unexpected guest? Why, I'm your husband. Doesn't that make this my home too?" Travis asks with a grin.

"We're not married anymore," I remind him.

He looks up at me with rage in his eyes. He looks older than the last time I saw him. His hair is darker, and he has grown out his facial hair. He looks like he hasn't slept or showered in a long while.

"Well, now, I didn't agree to that," he says as he casually sits back and throws his arms over the back of the couch.

I start slowly backing up toward the door without taking my eyes from him.

"I didn't know you were out," I say as I reach behind me, trying to find the doorknob.

"Yep, for a couple weeks now. I was paroled and they let me out early for good behavior. Turns out, I'm a model inmate. Which you would know if you'd bothered to read any of my fucking letters," he spits.

Beau is wedged between me and the door. My hand finds the knob, and I start to turn it.

Travis bolts up and rushes toward us. I bend and hoist Beau up, and he immediately wraps his arms and legs around me. I throw a protective arm out, which Travis grabs and yanks forward, slinging us into the room.

He twists the dead bolt on the door and turns back to face us.

Beau is trembling, and he clings to me, crying harder now.

"Calm down, son. I'm not here to hurt you," Travis commands.

Beau's face is hidden in my hair, and he lifts his head and looks over at Travis. "Mr. Stanley?" he asks, confused.

"What was that, baby?" I look down at him in question.

"We're friends. Ain't that right, boy?" Travis says with a wiry grin.

Beau's arms around my neck tighten, and I recall him telling me a dad of one of the kids at school was visiting. My eyes snap back to Travis.

"You've been to his school?" I yell.

"Yeah, he's my kid. I wanted to get to know him. Didn't want him to be afraid when I picked him up," he explains.

"When you picked him up?"

"That's right. See, the plan was to pick him up one day before you did, and then the two of us would come home and surprise you." He looks down at Beau and smiles.

Oh my God, if he had gotten Beau in a car and taken off with him, there would be nothing I could do. He is his father. I have been trying for six years now to get his rights taken, and it has been nothing but red tape on top of red tape. Apparently, a felony drug conviction is not grounds to strip parental rights, and each time my attorney, who has cost me a fortune, approached Travis to just sign over all rights, he refused.

"You know the Feds railroaded me on bogus charges because they couldn't touch the real dealers. I should've never been sent up for the small amount of selling and laundering I dabbled in. I'm not a criminal."

They had an ironclad case against him. They showed me every piece of evidence they had, and it was damning. He was in deep with those real dealers. I was living in a minefield where dangerous men could have come after him at any time for doing something stupid, and I was clueless. No way is my son ever going anywhere with him.

He continues, "I want my family back. I was going to prove to you that I'd changed, and the three of us were going to move back to Denver and get the auto shop back on track. Start over and put this whole ugly mess behind us," he says in a quiet voice.

A chill runs up my spine at the thought of him getting so close to Beau. He was within grabbing distance of him on the playground.

How did I let this happen?

"That is, until I saw you with Wilson the other night."

Anger lights his eyes, and I know all too well what it looks like. He was filled with it the first time I left him.

"So, you've left me no choice; we're leaving now. Grab your shit, and let's go," he demands.

"We aren't going anywhere with you," I tell him.

He snaps and crashes the beer bottle against the stone end table by the couch. Beer and glass shards fly everywhere, making the floor slippery and dangerous. Beau jerks in my arms at the loud sound, and I cover his face to make sure nothing hits him.

Travis stands there with the broken bottle in his hand, waving it in my direction. He might have had his moments of angry outbursts when we were together, but he was never violent. Not with me. He's not the same man I was married to. I can see it in his eyes.

I have to get Beau away from him.

"Baby, I want you to go upstairs, okay?"

I try to set Beau on the floor, but refuses to release me.

"No, Mommy," he whimpers.

"He ain't going anywhere," Travis growls.

I look up and meet his gaze. I keep my voice calm and placating. "He's scared. If you want to talk, fine, we'll talk, but I want to do it alone. Let him go up to my room," I say as I try to untangle Beau's arms from me.

Travis looks up to the loft. "He can still hear and see us from up there."

"I have a walk-in closet. He likes to play in it," I tell him.

I have to get Beau up there, safely tucked into that closet. I can see the moment Travis relents.

"Fine. He can go while we gather your shit."

I set Beau on his feet, and he wraps his arms around my legs.

I bend down to look him in the eye. "It's okay. I want you to go to the Batcave and wait for me. Can you do that? Close the door and don't come out until I come and get you," I calmly say to him.

"I don't want to leave you," he whines, and his little fist wipes at his nose as tears stream under his glasses and down his red cheeks.

"I'll be okay. I promise. I need you to be a big boy and obey me right now though," I say a little more sternly.

He purses his quivering lips and tries to pull himself together.

"Okay, Mommy," he says, and he puts his arms around my neck and squeezes tightly before letting go and running toward the stairs.

I watch him go, and once he is out of sight and I hear the door close behind him, I turn to face Travis.

Forty-Five

DALLAS

"Come on," Travis commands as he grabs my arm and jerks me toward Beau's bedroom door. "Grab some of his stuff."

I dig my heels into the floor and try to yank my arm from his grasp.

"Fucking do what I ask, Dallas," he says, frustrated. "I don't want to hurt you."

It's a threat, and I know it.

"You've never hurt me before. This isn't you. Can't we just talk about this?" I try to reason with him.

"You're right; this ain't who I used to be. Prison changes a man."

He advances on me and gets me backed into the wall between Beau's bedroom and the stairs.

"You left me there to rot. You ungrateful bitch. Everything I did, I did for you. So you could have everything you ever wanted. And how did you repay me? By abandoning me," he spits angrily.

I have to stay calm. I keep telling myself to be smart and not panic.

"I was perfectly happy with our life, Travis. You didn't do it for me. You did it for you. You were the one who wasn't content and wanted to live a lifestyle we couldn't afford."

He sneers at me and grabs my chin. "I always did like that smart mouth of yours. Makes me hard, having you talk back to me again," he says as he rubs his erection against me to prove his words.

He tries to kiss me, and I turn my head. He pries my face back to him and presses his lips to mine. I keep my mouth tightly closed, and he takes two fingers and clamps them down on my throat.

I can't swallow. When I open my mouth to tell him to let go, he slides his tongue inside and starts to kiss me. He releases my throat, and I bite down hard on his tongue.

He jumps back and then backhands me powerfully across my right cheek. My head bounces against the wall.

"My tongue is bleeding, you stupid—" he starts when we hear a phone ringing upstairs.

My eyes dart to the steps, and I start to run.

"Oh no, you don't," he says as he grabs me and slings me back into the wall.

The phone stops ringing.

He brings the jagged end of the bottle up to my throat. "I'm giving you one last chance to pack a bag for you and the boy, or we're getting in the truck and leaving with nothing. The choice is yours."

I nod because I can't speak, and I feel the glass pierce my neck.

My phone starts to ring again.

It distracts him, and I take the opportunity to bring my knee up and crash it between his legs. He immediately drops the bottle, and it shatters further as his hands fly to his crotch.

I take off in the direction of the door to grab the lamp sitting on the table beside it. I need something to strike him with.

My feet hit the living room floor, and I slip through the beer and glass and land on my ass just short of the door. Travis recovers and grabs me by my hair before I can get back on my feet. He drags me back toward the stairs.

My hands fly to my hair. It feels like he's ripping it out from the roots. I hold in the scream caught in my throat. I can't make a peep. It will terrify Beau if he hears me cry out. Tears blur my vision.

"Time's up. We're getting the boy and leaving," he says as he tries to pull me up the stairs.

I grab the railing on both sides and throw all my weight in sitting on my ass. He keeps yanking at my hair, but my body isn't budging. He gets pissed and kicks me in the back, and I plant face-first onto the floor. I feel the blood ooze from my nose as I flip to my back and start to crab-walk backward.

He picks me up by my waist with my arms and feet flailing. He'll have to kill me to get up those stairs to Beau. He slams me back against the wall, and his forearm presses into my throat.

I struggle to pry his arm off, but it's no use. He's so much stronger than me. My vision starts to blur, and I know that I'm moments from passing out. I can't. I have to stay conscious.

"That's right, baby; stop fighting it. You're going to take a little nap, and when you wake up, we'll be home," he says.

I try to pick up my leg to kick his shin, but my whole body feels heavy.

Everything is starting to go black.

Forty-Six

MYER

I JUST FINISH THE EVENING PERIMETER RIDE WHEN I SEE PAYNE'S truck coming up the driveway. I dismount and walk Bolt over to him. Walker is in the passenger seat.

"Hey, man. We're heading over to Braxton's place. They got the floors in, and he wants to start painting this evening," he says as I approach his window.

"Sounds good. I need to put Bolt away, and I'll be ready. You want me to meet you there?" I ask as my phone chirps in my pocket, and I fish it out.

"Nah, we'll wait for you," he says and throws his truck in park.

I look down at the text I just received from Dallas's phone. It's a bunch of *H*s in a long row. I'm confused for a half a second, and then it hits me.

The Bat-Signal.

My eyes snap up to Payne. "Where're Dallas and Beau?"

He looks confused at my sudden alarm.

"At the house, I guess. They were eating supper when I talked to her. I was going to go over and water for Momma before Brax called. She said she and Beau would do it before she gave him a bath. Why?"

I dial her number and bring the phone to my ear. It rings until her voice mail picks up.

Shit.

"Something's wrong," I tell him.

I walk over and jump up onto Bolt's back. Dallas's family's orchard backs up to the ranch behind my house. I can get there faster on horseback than in a truck.

I look over, and Payne has his phone to his ear.

"She ain't answering. What the hell's going on?" he asks, panicked.

"I don't know, but I got a distress text from Beau from her phone ten seconds ago. I'm heading that way. Call the sheriff and meet me there," I say before I take Bolt's reins and turn him toward the hills and take off.

I run the horse as fast as his legs can take us. The route is tricky, full of thicket and steep hills. But he stays with me and flies through the brush like lightning.

I pass Payne's house, and Dallas's comes into sight. Her truck is out front. My racing heart starts to settle. Maybe the text was a mistake. I slow down and bring Bolt around to the front of the house. I dismount and leave him in the drive as I hop up onto the porch. I hear yelling inside. I try the door, and it's locked, so I move over to the window and look in. Some guy has Dallas pinned to the wall, and she's struggling.

I jump from the porch and run to the back door to see if it's locked. The window beside the door is smashed in. I grab the two-by-four that is propped against the house—it's probably what was used to break the glass—and I reach inside, twist the lock, and open the door.

Then, I explode into the living room.

Dallas's pleading eyes dart up to mine. Her face is turning blue, his arm against her throat blocking her airway. She has her fingers wrapped around it, trying to pry it free.

He sees her eyes and jerks around. Dallas slides to the floor, gasping for air, and I start swinging.

The sound of the board cracking against his jaw rings around the room. He stumbles forward, bringing his fists up in defense, and I swing again. This time, blood splatters across the room as I hit his face square on, and his nose shatters. Before he can take another step, his eyes roll back in his head, and he drops to the floor like a ton of bricks.

I hear Payne banging at the door and walk over to click the lock. He bolts inside with Walker on his heels. He looks at Dallas and then the man sprawled on the floor.

"Jesus, sis, are you okay?" he chokes out.

She's still on the floor, her back against the wall and her knees to her chest. Her eyes are trained on her attacker, and she's shaking.

I kneel in front of her. "Dal, baby, are you okay? Is anything hurt?"

Her eyes come up to me, and she shakes her head. "I'm okay," she manages to get out.

"Where's Beau?" I ask.

"Upstairs in my closet. I don't want him to see me like this," she says as she wipes under her eyes. She takes the hem of her shirt and starts scrubbing at the blood running down her chin.

"I'll go get him," I say. I look over at Payne. "Did you call the sheriff?"

"Yeah, he's on his way," he says.

"Can you come help Dallas get to the bathroom and cleaned up? Walker, can you handle him? I don't think he's gonna wake up anytime soon, but pull him out onto the porch, so he's not lying there. I'm going up to get Beau," I order as I help her to her feet.

She throws herself into my arms, wraps herself around me, and starts sobbing uncontrollably.

"It's okay. I got you," I say softly.

"Who the fuck is this son of a bitch?" Walker asks as he grabs the guy's arm and starts dragging him.

"Travis. It's Travis," her muffled answer comes. Her face is planted against my shirt.

"Travis?" Payne says as he charges toward him.

Walker rolls him over, and sure enough, it's him. Payne puts his boot in his side, and we hear ribs crack. Then, for good measure, he does it again. Travis grunts in pain.

Good thing he's not dead. Not that I'd care if he were.

Walker drags him out the door. Payne comes over, and I turn her into his arms. He steadies her and looks over her shoulder at me.

"I got her. Go get Beau," he says, and I dart to the stairs.

I knock at the door. I can hear soft whimpers on the other side, but he doesn't answer, so I crack the door and open it.

"No!" he cries.

He scurries toward the back of the closet on his hands and knees. He has been sitting in the dark, and he blinks rapidly to adjust to the light pouring into the closet when he stops against the wall.

"Beau, it's me, buddy, Myer," I say.

He stays where he is.

I bend to one knee and look him in the eye. "Hey, are you okay?"

He sniffles and nods.

"You want to come out now?" I ask softly.

"Mommy said not to come out until she comes to get me," he stutters, as he rocks.

"It's okay. She told me to come find you for her, I promise," I say calmly as I scoot toward him.

"Where is she? Why didn't she come get me? Is she okay?"

His watery eyes look up at me pleadingly. He thinks she's hurt, and that's why I came instead of her.

"She's okay, buddy, I promise. She's downstairs with Uncle Payne."

"Is the bad guy gone?" he asks.

"He is. Walker and Uncle Payne came with me to help, and Walker has him outside, waiting for the police to come and get him," I assure him.

His lips quiver as he sits there. I want to reach out and scoop him up, but I wait for him to come to me.

After a few more minutes, he leaps to me. I catch him with one arm and hold him tight as he sobs uncontrollably into my neck. His entire body convulsing.

"It's okay, buddy. I've got you," I console as I stand.

"You came," he says through his tears.

"I told you I would. I'm so proud of you for sending me the signal. You did a good job, protecting Mommy by sending for help," I tell him as we walk to the stairs.

I can see the lights of the sheriffs' cars through the window. They will want to talk to the both of them. So, I carry Beau down. Dallas and Payne emerge from the bathroom just as we reach the bottom, and as soon as he catches sight of her, he starts calling for her.

Dallas hurries over and takes him from my arms. "Hey now, it's all right. Everything is all right." She soothes as she rocks him.

Everything is not all right. I can see the marks on her neck and the place that's turning purple underneath her eye that she tried to hide with makeup. A blood vessel has burst in her right eye, and I'm pretty sure she'll be covered in bruises tomorrow, but she is whole and breathing and here.

Thank you, Lord.

Forty-Seven

DALLAS

I walk out onto the porch and catch Travis's eye just as they shove him, cuffed, into the back of the squad car.

Beau is in my arms. He refuses to let go of me.

Jonathon Trodden, a sheriff's deputy that I've known since high school, stands before me with a tablet in his hand. "Dallas, I hate to do this now, but I need to get a detailed statement from you."

I watch as the car pulls away with Travis.

I finally breathe a relieved breath.

"Can it wait until tomorrow?" I ask.

I don't want to recount what just happened with Beau in my arms.

He apologetically shakes his head. "We really need to do it now," he says.

I turn to Payne and nod down at Beau. "Can you?"

He steps forward and wraps his hands around Beau's waist.

"No!" Beau yells and starts to cling harder to me.

"Hey," I say soothingly, "calm down. Uncle Payne is going to hold you while I talk to the nice policeman."

He is hiccuping in my neck.

"Please, baby. Mommy has to talk to him right now. I promise I'm not going off the porch, and Myer and Walker are going to be right here with me the whole time."

He picks his head up and looks around at all the men he knows and trusts. He sniffles and nods his head in agreement, and Payne lifts him from my arms.

I gesture toward the door, and Payne takes the cue and walks him inside, closing it behind them.

I sit down in the chair beside the door, and Walker hands me a glass of water he must have brought out from the kitchen. I take it in my hand, and it shakes water onto the porch.

"I know this is hard, Dallas, but I need you to start from the beginning," Jonathon prompts.

I start from the time Beau and I walked in to find Travis on the couch and end with when Myer came through the back door.

Fury builds and rolls off Myer and Walker with every word.

Jonathon looks like he would like a few rounds in the cell with Travis himself.

"We've had reports of a man who fits his description loitering around town. No one recognized him though," he informs us.

"I think he might have been coming in the diner too. Kim said a man had been coming in, asking after me and my schedule, and he definitely has been at the schoolhouse. He talked to Beau on the playground," I tell him.

"How did you three know what was happening?" he asks Myer.

"I got a text from Beau," he says.

"What?" I ask him.

He pulls his phone from his pocket and holds it up.

The screen shows a text from me, which is just a bunch of *H*s in a row.

I look at him, confused.

"It's our Bat-Signal," he says and then proceeds to explain the conversation he and Beau had weeks ago. "I knew they were in trouble. So, I jumped on my horse and got here as fast as I could. The boys followed in the truck."

"And you incapacitated the suspect with that piece of wood?" Jonathon points down to the two-by-four propped against the house.

"Yeah. I found it sitting by the broken window by the back door. He must have used it to smash his way into the house." He looks over to me. "He was probably the one who came in the window a couple weeks ago too."

Shit. How long has he been tracking us?

"I'm going to take this," Jonathon says as he picks the two-by-four up with his gloved hand. "Dallas, are you sure you don't need me to take you to the hospital to get checked out?" he asks.

I shake my head. "I'm fine. A few cuts and bruises, that's all," I assure him.

"That eye is starting to swell. You're probably going to be in a lot of pain tomorrow. If nothing else, the doctor can give you something to ease that."

"No," I refuse. "I don't want to take painkillers while taking care of Beau."

"All right."

"I promise, if she starts hurting too bad or has any other issues, I'll take her straight to county," Myer tells him.

He nods. "I'm going to write in the report that Beau was too traumatized to give a statement. I think we have all we need to press charges. We'll charge him with breaking and entering, felony false imprisonment, attempted kidnapping, felony assault and battery, and felony domestic assault. His parole will be revoked immediately, and he'll be incarcerated while he awaits conviction on these charges."

He pauses and looks up at me and smiles. "You know what all of this means, right?"

I start to cry and nod. "It means I can finally have his parental rights revoked."

Jonathon tears up too. He was there every time I filed another motion, asking for termination of parental rights. He knows how hard I've fought the past six years. The drug charges weren't enough but a felony domestic charge is.

"Yes, ma'am. I'll be happy to contact your attorney myself as soon as I get back to the station and get that ball rolling for you," he offers.

"Thank you, Jonathon." I stand and hug him.

He gently hugs me back and then says his good-byes before taking the piece of wood and leaving.

Once his car is out of sight, my body starts shaking uncontrollably as the adrenaline leaves.

Myer picks me up and sits down in the chair while he holds me until I have control of myself again.

Walker walks inside with Beau and Payne to give us privacy.

"I'm sorry," I cry into his throat.

He strokes my hair. My scalp is tender, but I don't complain. I'm just thankful to have his touch.

"Sorry for what? None of this is your fault," he assures me, misunderstanding what I'm saying.

"No. I mean, for Sunday. I heard you guys talking, and I misread your actions; instead of talking to you, I got all insecure and stupid."

He sighs. "It's okay." He lets me off the hook.

"It's not. I'm crazy and impulsive, and I say things without thinking first," I admit.

"Yep," he agrees, and I snap my head up.

He smiles.

"I know all of that. I knew where your head was, and I knew there was no reasoning with you that night. That's why I left, but I would have been back. You can't run me off that easy, Dal. You think I deserve better? Better than you? Baby, it doesn't get any better than you," he says.

"I love you," I blurt out.

"I know."

"Why didn't you tell me?" I ask.

"Because you had to find your own way out of that darkness. I've always been the candle at the end, lighting your way."

He gently touches his lips to mine.

We hear Beau calling from inside, so Myer stands me on my feet, and we go in.

Payne and Walker stay until Beau falls asleep.

He told them that he'd found my phone in my purse on the closet floor when I sent him upstairs, and he sent the text to Myer's phone. When it started ringing in his hand, it scared him because he thought Travis would know he sent for help, so he'd slung it under the closet door.

It must have slid under my bed because that's where it's found, still showing the missed calls from Myer and Payne.

Payne tries to talk me into coming to his house or going to Myer's for the night, but I think it's important to stay here. I don't want Beau to be afraid of his own house. So, he and Walker go grab materials to board up the broken window.

Myer gets Beau changed into pajamas even though he is dead asleep.

I carefully change into a nightshirt. My right side is already stiff. Tomorrow is going to suck ass.

It takes me a while to get back down the stairs.

Myer comes back into the living room, carrying Beau in his arms.

"I couldn't leave him in there alone. Not tonight. I think we need to have one of our sleepovers in here," he says, cradling my son.

I love him. There is no denying it.

"The window is secure for tonight," Payne says as he and Walker walk back into the house. "I'll get new glass ordered for it tomorrow and replace it next week. Then, we're getting an alarm system set up in this place right away," he continues, in full overprotective big-brother mode.

"Thank you," I say as I settle in with pillows piled behind my back.

Payne stands there, wanting to say something else.

"I'm okay, Payne, I promise," I tell him.

He walks over and kisses the top of my head. "Momma and Daddy will be here by the time you wake up in the morning. They got in the truck the minute I called. And Sophie will probably come too. Braxton had to lock her down to keep her from getting here. Jonathon didn't want anyone else driving up while he was talking to you guys, so I asked him to have her wait to come. She was not happy."

"I can imagine," I say.

If it were her, they'd have to hog-tie me to keep me from getting to her.

"And me too. I'll be back first thing in the morning to see how y'all are," he keeps going.

"Okay," I agree.

"Okay, good night," he says and turns to leave.

"Good night, Dal," Walker says as he, too, presses a kiss to my forehead. "Still the most badass woman I've ever met," he says with a wink.

"Hey, Walk, Bolt's loose out there somewhere," Myer says.

"We got you. He headed toward the orchard. I'll get him and get him tied in Payne's barn for tonight."

"Thanks, man."

He gives him the bro salute and follows Payne out.

I lay my head against Myer's shoulder.

"Get some sleep, baby. Sounds like there's going to be a parade in your living room tomorrow morning."

Forty-Eight

DALLAS

I WAKE TO WHISPERS AND THE AROMA OF COFFEE AND PANCAKES.

I try to lift my head from the couch, and it feels like a lead weight is sitting on top of my neck.

"Mmm," I mumble as I struggle to open my eyes.

Momma rushes over to my side. "Here, sweetheart, let me help you," she says softly as she snakes her arm behind my back to help lift me to a sitting position.

"Good morning," I croak out.

"Oh." She covers her cry with her hand. "Good morning."

I turn slowly toward the kitchen island, and I see Sophie, Doreen, Ria, Beverly, and Bellamy.

"It's a full house, I see."

They all just stand there with tight smiles.

"Okay, how bad is it?" I ask.

"Not bad at all," Momma says as she brushes the hair from my eyes.

"I feel like I was hit by a truck; you can be honest with me," I tell her.

Sophie walks over and sits down beside me.

"You guys being so quiet is freaking me out. Quit it," I demand.

"Myer told us he'd throw us out if we riled you up. He made us all promise to be calm and quiet," Sophie confesses.

"Well, I don't like it. So, stop. Now, tell the truth."

She carefully looks me over. "You look like you fought with a gorilla last night and lost miserably," she says.

"That sounds about right." I look around. "Where's Beau?"

"He went to check on the flowers with your father," Momma tells me.

"Did he freak out when he saw me?" I ask as I reach up to my cheek. I can tell it's swollen.

"They both did. Your father had to take a walk before he put a fist through a wall," Momma says, and a sob escapes.

I put my hand over hers. "I'm okay, Momma. I'm sure it looks worse than it is."

"Are you hungry, Dallas? We made pancakes, and we're just about to start some bacon and eggs," Doreen asks.

"You need to eat something so you can take some ibuprofen," Momma encourages.

I smile up at Doreen and Ria. "I'll have some pancakes and bacon. Thank you."

"Coming right up," Ria says, and they set to doing what they do best—loving everyone by feeding them.

"Myer?" I ask Sophie.

"He ran to the pharmacy in town with Braxton to pick up some medicine for you. Aunt Doreen called Dr. Cohen's wife—she's in the ladies' auxiliary at the church—and explained what happened. Dr. Cohen called in some things to help you for a couple of days."

"Thank you," I tell Doreen.

As much as I didn't want to take anything, I think I might need something a bit stronger than ibuprofen.

"I'm so sorry we weren't here," Momma cries.

"Momma, don't. You couldn't have known. Besides, I'm pretty sure he has been watching us for a while. He waited until you guys were gone. And if it hadn't been this weekend, he would have grabbed Beau from school. I'm glad it happened the way it did."

She cries harder.

"I'm sorry," she says as she gets up and heads to the bathroom.

"Great," I say and close my eyes.

"She'll be fine. She's allowed her breakdown. She drove all night, knowing her baby girl had been attacked and she couldn't get to her. I can't imagine how excruciating that had to be. Then, to walk in and see you black-and-blue and barely able to move. I think she's holding up really well," Doreen defends.

She's right. I remember the wreck I was during the fifteen-minute drive to the hospital when Beau broke his arm. If it'd been an eight-hour drive, I'd have lost my mind.

Sophie carefully places her arm around my shoulders and leans her head against mine. "I'm sorry this happened to you."

"I'm sorry I'm going to look like I lost a fight with a gorilla in your wedding photos."

"Please. You have a couple weeks to heal, and Mom is bringing her hair and makeup team from New York. Those guys can make sixty-year-old socialites look like they're in their forties. A few bruises don't stand a chance against their skills."

"Thank goodness for Viv and her bougie cowgirl vision," I say.

"Damn straight."

The front door swings open, and Beau comes running in, carrying a huge bundle of flowers from Momma's garden.

"Mommy!" he calls as he barrels to me.

"Careful," Daddy's voice warns. "Remember what we talked about. You have to be gentle with your momma."

Beau stops short of jumping in my lap and stands in front of me.

He holds up the flowers. "Pop-Pop and I made you a bouquet to make you feel better," he says.

He very carefully lays them on my lap.

"Thank you, baby. They do make me feel better," I tell him as I lift them to my nose to smell them.

"Myer went to get you some medicine," he informs me.

"I know; I heard. Everyone is taking such good care of me."

Daddy walks over, leans down, and kisses my forehead for a long minute. "I love you, baby," he says hoarsely.

"I love you too, Daddy."

He backs up and calls to Beau, "Come on, Beau; let's go feed the chickens."

"I'll be right back, Mommy, okay? Pop-Pop needs my help, and then I'm coming to check on you," Beau says as he pats my knee.

"All right, baby," I agree, and he follows Daddy out the door.

"I hope he isn't traumatized for life," I whisper to the room at large.

"He'll have a rough go for a while, but you just be honest with him, and he'll process. Eventually, you'll both heal." Ria dispenses her wisdom as she flips pancakes.

What would I do without this gaggle of women in my life?

Forty-Nine

DALLAS

"It feels funny," Beau says as the nurse removes the cracked cast.

"It's because the air is hitting it for the first time in a long while. It'll feel normal by the time you get home," the nurse says.

"Why come it looks funny?"

"*Why does it look funny*. Not *why come*," I correct him. "Because, baby, it's been covered up, and it hasn't been getting air or sunshine. Mommy has some creams we're going to rub on it so it won't be so dry and chafed, and it'll look like your other arm again in no time," I tell him.

"Now, lift it up and wiggle those fingers for me," the nurse instructs.

"My fingers tingle," he says. Then, he picks up his arm and flings it around, and then he rapidly opens and closes his hand.

"I think you're all good." The nurse laughs as she backs out of the way.

We check out, and she leads us to the waiting room where Myer sits, thumbing through a magazine.

"Look, Myer," Beau calls as he races toward him.

Myer catches him before he collides with his knees.

"Doesn't it look gnarly?"

Gnarly—that's a new word.

"Ew, it sure does," Myer says as he wrinkles his nose in mock disgust.

Beau collapses into a fit of giggles.

Myer stands and takes his hand. "Come on. Let's take you and that gross arm of yours to breakfast before we drop you off at school."

I thank the nurse and follow my guys out of the office.

Myer drives me out to Rustic Peak after dropping Beau off at school. I shouldn't be driving while taking the medications the doctor prescribed, and he hasn't wanted to leave my side since Friday night.

He needs to get back to his normal routine, but when I bring up the subject, he shuts me down, saying that his dad, Truett, and Foster have everything covered for this week and that Walker and Payne offered to pitch in if needed.

I want to go into the bakery and start working with Momma, but I'm still having a hard time focusing. I can't stay cooped up in the house any longer though. I'm going stir-crazy.

When we pull in, Payne and Walker are by the barn with Braxton and Silas.

"Hey, what're you doing here?" I ask my brother as he opens my door and helps me out of the truck.

"Dropping off the auger Jefferson let Daddy and me borrow to dig postholes for the new fence behind the barn," he answers.

"Sophie inside?" I ask Braxton.

He inclines his head toward the gate. His truck is coming up the drive.

She stops in front of us. The passenger door flings open, and Charlotte leaps out.

A blur of blonde comes barreling toward me.

"I came as soon as I heard," she bellows as she embraces me.

I wince.

"Easy," Myer warns.

She pulls back. "Oh, sorry. God, you look awful!"

"Thanks," I deadpan.

She turns on her heels, marches over to Payne, rears back, and socks him in the gut.

"Ouch," he cries as he protectively covers his stomach. "What was that for?"

"Where were you when that happened to Dallas, huh?" She whirls to Walker and shoves a finger in his chest. "And you? Where were you, tough guy?"

Braxton chuckles, and she slides her accusing eyes to him. She cocks a hip and stares at him.

"Easy, Rocky," he says as he backs up.

She blinks. "What is your obsession with Rocky? Do you have a man-crush on Sylvester Stallone or something?"

He rolls his eyes.

"I'm just saying, it's odd how often you bring him up in conversation." She looks around at all of us. "Am I right?"

Braxton just grunts at her in answer.

"What're you doing here? You didn't have to come. I'm fine," I tell her.

She waves me off. "I was flying in Sunday anyway, so I just wrapped things up at the office and took an earlier flight. I can help with Beau, work, or wedding stuff. I just want to be here in case you need me."

I start leaking again. Jeez, it takes nothing to turn on the waterworks these days.

"Don't. You'll make me cry, and then Soph will cry because she's a big ole baby," she says as she bursts into tears, and Sophie follows.

"Jesus," Walker mumbles, "I need a beer." He walks off to the barn.

"I'll be needing one of those too," Payne calls after him.

Braxton and Myer just patiently watch our girl slobberfest.

"I can't believe your wedding is next weekend," I say as we settle in at Doreen and Ria's table.

"I know. It seemed like it was forever away, and now, it's coming so fast," Sophie agrees.

"Forever away? Girl, this time last year, you were living alone in New York with only a potted plant to talk to. I'd say this wedding day slid into home at warp speed," Charlotte points out.

Sophie sighs. "It's strange. I can't imagine living in that apartment anymore."

"Ha, and I can't imagine living anywhere else. Don't get me wrong. I love it here. It's fun to visit. I love you guys and all the woodsy bumpkin shit you make me do, but I need the smog, the noise, the lights, cocktail hour, SoulCycle, and cranky New Yorkers," Charlotte admits.

Her eyes light up. "We should do a girls' weekend in New York! Let me show you my city," Charlotte suggests.

"I've lived there my entire life, Char," Sophie reminds her.

"Yeah, but Dallas hasn't. We can give her the full New York experience."

"You could go up with me for the International Gem and Jewelry Show in December. We can stay at Mom and Stanhope's place on Central Park West. They'll be in the Bahamas," Sophie offers.

Charlotte claps her hands. "Oh, New York at Christmastime. There is nothing better. I swear you'll love it!"

I promised Beau I would take him to see where Miss Sophie lived and to catch fireflies in Central Park, but one quick trip alone to check out the city first with my friends would be amazing.

I accept their offer. "Sounds good, but if one of those cranky New Yorkers tries to mug me on the streets, I will put a Colorado boot in his ass. And I'm not wearing those torture devices you guys call shoes either. I almost lost a pinkie toe at the engagement party."

Charlotte looks at Sophie. "Oh, she's going to be lots of fun at the Rockefeller Center Christmas gala. I can't wait!"

I can't wait either. Life is opening up to so many new adventures this year.

Fifty

MYER

"You nervous, man?" I ask Braxton as we head out to stand with the reverend.

"Not the least bit," he says with a grin, awaiting his bride.

We file out and stand before the seated guests. Most faces I recognize, but some I don't. A host of people flew in with Vivian from New York to be a part of Sophie's big day.

Both Vivian and Madeline, seated up front with their husbands, burst into tears as soon as we are all standing in front of the altar.

The harpist starts strumming a melody, and Elle appears at the end of the aisle. Braxton's smile widens as his baby sister walks up and kisses his cheek before standing opposite us. Then, Charlotte appears and walks to Elle. Next is Dallas. She takes my breath away. Vivian's makeup people did an excellent job, hiding the fading bruising under her eye and at her throat. She left her hair loose and wild. Everything is gorgeous—the dress, the boots, the woman. Her eyes shine as they find me while she slowly makes her way to stand with us.

Beau comes next, skipping down the aisle faster than the music's tempo, with Hawkeye at his heels. The damn dog has on a vest and bow tie that matches his. It's the cutest thing I've ever seen, and the sound of, "Aw," that rolls through the tent says the crowd agrees.

He bounds over to me, and I tuck him in front against my legs. Hawk follows and sits at my feet.

"Good job, buddy," I whisper as he bends his head back to look up at me.

The music pauses for a moment, and then a violinist joins the harp. Sophie walks through the entrance on Jefferson's arm.

The guttural sound that escapes Braxton says it all. She is a vision. A tear rolls down his cheek, and it's the first time I've ever seen him emotional.

She practically floats down the aisle to him. Happy tears welling in her eyes. Their love is so big that it fills this tent, and every person sitting here can feel the power of it surrounding them.

The reverend asks who is giving this woman away, and Jefferson answers and kisses her cheek before placing her hand into Braxton's.

We face the altar, and much of the rest of the ceremony is a blur to me because my attention is focused on Dallas. Her face is alight as she watches her friends commit themselves to each other, and all I can think is that I want to stand before our friends and family and make the same promises to her.

"Do you, Sophia Doreen Lancaster, take this man to be your lawfully wedded husband?" Reverend Burr asks.

"I do," Sophie cries.

"And do you, Braxton Ty Young, take this woman to be your lawfully wedded wife?"

"I do," Braxton chokes out.

Beau looks at me because he knows his cue is coming, and when the reverend asks for the rings, I nudge him forward.

He proudly raises the pillow, and Braxton unties the rings and mouths, *Thank you.*

Once they are pronounced man and wife, Braxton grabs her face and kisses her breathless.

Beau gets excited and starts jumping up and down, cheering, which riles Hawk up, and he starts yapping and jumping at Brax's and Sophie's feet.

The audience starts cracking up and the newlyweds burst into laughter.

After the ceremony, Walker, Payne, Silas, and I sneak out to decorate the happy couple's ride. We pull the John Deere tractor to the front of the reception tent and string it with tiny heart garden lights and tie a couple dozen beer cans to the back. We strap a wooden sign to the front that reads *She Thinks My Tractor's Sexy* and one in the rear that reads *Just Hitched* with the date. We figure it's the perfect vehicle for Braxton to drive off with his new bride for their first night in their new home.

Once we're finished, I walk into the reception to join Dallas and Beau, and supper is served.

"Beau's getting restless. I think I'm going to take him for a walk outside while we wait for the cake to be cut," I whisper into Dallas's ear as she chats with the other guests seated at our table.

"Okay," she says distractedly as I pluck him from his seat beside me.

We exit the tent, and I take him by the hand and lead him out into the meadow. Hawk leaps from his perch on the ground and runs after us.

"I want to ask you a question, man to man," I start.

He looks up at me.

"What do you think about me asking your momma to marry me like Miss Sophie married Braxton today?"

"So, you can kiss her all the time?" he asks, a huge grin planted on his face.

I chuckle. "Yes, and because I love her, and I want you guys to come live with me in my house, so we can be a family," I tell him.

"Okay," he says.

After a few moments, he stops walking and asks, "Are you gonna be my daddy?"

"Yes, sir. I'd like to be. If that's what you want."

"Even though you didn't put me in Mommy's tummy?"

I stop and bend on one knee so I'm looking at him, eye to eye. "The way I see it, all you need to be a daddy is love, and I sure love you, Beau Stovall."

"Will I get to call you Daddy?" he asks.

"You can call me anything you want to call me."

"Can I change my name like Mommy will?"

I get choked up at his question. "I'll work on that, buddy, and if it's okay with your mommy, as soon as we are able, I'd be proud to give you my name."

His eyes well with tears, and he leaps up into my arms. I stand, and he lays his head on my shoulder as I walk us back to the party.

We return in time for the cutting of the cake and champagne. Beau is grinning from ear to ear at Dallas as we approach the table. She gives us both a curious look. He's gonna spill the beans. Looks like I'd better talk to Dallas's daddy real quick.

The toasts begin, and to everyone's surprise, the first one to stand is Jefferson.

He clears his throat. "I'm a man of few words. My pop taught me a long time ago that people should know a man by the life he lives, not by the talk he talks."

He looks to Braxton and Sophie. "I think you get that from me, son."

Laughter bubbles up from all around.

"I didn't have to be told that you loved my girl. Contrary to what my daughter thought, you weren't fooling anybody. I saw it in the way you treated her, even when you thought you didn't like her. In the ways you protected her, your worry over her comfort, and simply in the way you looked at her. You tried to fight it, but it was a losing battle from the beginning. I knew before either of you two knew because I recognized the actions of a man falling in love."

He lifts his glass. "I'm so proud of the man you have become. And, my sweet Sophia, baby girl, a father couldn't ask for a more loving and forgiving daughter. I can't wait to watch you two build a beautiful life together. I love you."

He takes a sip of the champagne as the clinking of crystal sounds around the tent.

A beautiful life—that's what it all boils down to. The good times and the bad times, they all swirl together, and in the end, you get beauty.

Fifty-One

MYER

I climb the steps to Dallas's parents' home. I've known them since I was a boy. I spent a huge amount of my childhood playing in their fields and racing four-wheelers through the paths in their orchard. Mr. Henderson helped Payne and me build that old tree house out back when we were in fifth grade. They are like my second family.

Beau is in school today, and I knew Dallas would be at the bakery, so it's the perfect time to catch Marvin without her spying on me. I knock at the door and wait.

"Hello, Myer." Dallas's mom's voice drifts through the screen door. "Come on in."

I walk in to find them seated at the kitchen table.

"I'm sorry to interrupt," I start.

"Oh, please. You aren't interrupting anything. I just ran some sandwiches over for a quick lunch before I head back to the shop. Are you hungry?" she asks.

"No, ma'am. I just wanted to speak to Mr. Henderson for a minute, but since you're here, I can talk to you both," I say as I take a seat at the table across from Marvin.

"Oh, really? What's on your mind?" Dottie asks, her voice pitching a little higher than normal as she glances at her husband and smiles.

I think she's onto me.

I clear my throat. "Well, sir, I already had a man-to-man talk with Beau, and he gave his permission, but I need your blessing too. I'd like to ask Dallas to marry me," I spew out, all in one breath.

That was easier to get out than I'd thought.

Dottie brings the back of her right hand to her mouth and covers a small sob. Marvin fixes his eyes on me as he reaches across and takes his wife's other hand.

He doesn't say anything for a long time, and I start to get nervous.

"Nothing would make me prouder than to give her hand to you, son. I trust her and Beau to you. I know you'll love and protect them the way I would love and protect them. That's all a man can ask for in a husband for his daughter."

The weight on my shoulders rolls off.

"Thank you, sir. I promise, as long as I have breath in my body, I'll do just that."

I stand to shake his hand, and Dottie embraces me.

"I have been praying for you. Since the day she came back home. I didn't know you were the one until sometime later, but I knew God had a plan for my baby girl."

"They're the answer to my prayers too," I choke out.

"Beau, hurry up and get your boots on. Braxton and Sophie are going to be here any minute," Dallas calls.

Braxton and Sophie agreed to keep Beau tonight so that I could get Dallas alone. She has no idea that once we leave, they are coming back and helping Momma and Dottie set up a little get-together in the backyard.

Our mothers have been in cahoots for weeks now, planning. Dallas thinks her folks have gone to her dad's hunting cabin for the weekend. As soon as I text the all-clear, they will get everything set up.

We hear a knock at the door, and Sophie opens it and walks in.

"Where's my movie partner?" she calls into the house.

Dallas's head peeks over the loft. "He's getting his boots on. He's so excited to be staying with y'all tonight. He's been bouncing off the walls all day."

Sophie gives me a secret smile. We both know he's been excited for totally different reasons. I'm shocked the kid hasn't exploded from keeping the secret bottled up.

Beau comes bounding into the living room. "I'm ready. Let's go," he says as he grabs Sophie's hand and starts tugging her toward the door.

Dallas comes running down the stairs. "Wait," she cries. "First of all, don't pull on Miss Sophie. Second of all, where is your overnight bag?" she asks.

He huffs and scurries back off to his room.

"And you can't leave without giving your momma a good-bye kiss!" she calls after him. "Should I be offended that he seems like he can't get away from me fast enough?" she asks.

"Nah. He's just a kid looking forward to a sleepover. You remember what that was like when we were kids," I reassure her.

"I guess." She accepts my explanation.

"Ready!" he announces as he runs back in the room, toting his bag, and skids to a stop at her feet.

She leans down and hugs him tight before kissing him. "You be good tonight and listen to Braxton and Miss Sophie, okay?" she commands.

"Yes, ma'am," he says quickly before turning to Sophie and taking her hand again.

"I guess that's my cue. You guys have fun tonight," Sophie says as she lets Beau lead her out the door.

"So, what's the plan?" Dallas asks me as she waves good-bye and then shuts the door behind them.

I walk over to her and wrap my arms around her middle. "I'm taking you horseback riding," I say before I place a kiss on her lips.

She wrinkles her nose. "I'm not a strong rider. I haven't been on a horse in forever," she protests.

"That's okay. I'll be on the horse with you," I say.

She relents. "Oh. I thought you were wanting to put me on my own horse."

I brought Bolt over earlier, and he's tied in Payne's barn. Once she's ready, I fetch the animal and pick her up at the door.

"My chariot," she breathes as I help her up to sit in front of me.

It's a beautiful evening. There's not a cloud in the sky, and moonlight is bathing the path as we ride out into the meadow.

She leans back into me. "This is nice. I've never had a boy take me riding on a date before. Are we going to find a spot where we can make out in the woods like teenagers?" she asks as she presses her backside into me.

I groan and scoot back. "Maybe later. Now, behave," I whisper into her ear.

"You're no fun," she says as she giggles.

We ride out to the campsite clearing out by the river. Chairs and food are already set up, courtesy of Walker and Payne.

"Are we camping?" she asks when it comes into sight.

"Not tonight. I just thought it'd be nice to have a picnic out here," I inform her.

I wanted to bring her here because this is where it all began. A night cuddled up in a tent changed everything.

Thank you, Payne and Charlotte.

We stop, and I dismount and help her down. I pull what I need from the saddlebag, and we take a seat in the chairs sitting by the firepit. I reach in the cooler and grab a beer. I open it and hand it to her.

"Wow, you went out of your way. You know you don't have to work this hard to impress me. I'm a sure thing. All you have to do is feed me takeout on the couch, and I'm happy," she says as she grins at me.

"I'm kind of fond of this spot," I tell her.

She smiles and looks around. "Yeah, me too."

We enjoy the next hour, eating and drinking. Momma packed us a meal fit for a king. Dallas tells me all about her week at the bakery and about Beau's report card. Once we finish, I ask if she's ready to head back.

"How are we getting all this back?" she asks as she stands.

"Don't worry about that. I'll take care of it," I say as I take her hand and lead her over to the spot where our tent was set up.

I stop and turn her toward the water.

"What're you doing?" she asks, confused.

I palm the box in my pocket and begin, "This spot right here, this is where everything changed. I felt it that night as I held you and you snuggled in close and let me. The next morning, I knew I was done waiting for you to heal. So, it just feels right to be here when I tell you that, again, I'm done waiting."

I pull the box out, open it, and lower to one knee.

She gasps.

"Dallas Stovall, I don't want to waste any more time. I'm ready to build a life with you and Beau. I'm ready to be the husband and father you both deserve because I love you more than I ever thought possible. Will you marry me?"

She just stands there, staring at the ring. Minutes tick by.

"Dal?"

She lifts her tear-filled eyes to me and bites down on her bottom lip. Then, she hiccups and nods.

"Is that a yes?" I ask.

"Yes!" she cries before leaping into my arms.

Whew, thank God.

On the ride back to the house, she's bouncing with excitement. She can't wait to get back and call her mom and Sophie.

When we come out of the woods and hit the clearing behind her parents' house, she hears the music and sees the lights. I hear her breath catch.

"What's this?" she asks.

"Good thing you said yes, or this would have been awkward," I say into her hair.

When the gathering comes into sight, we see Beau standing in front of Sophie, and he breaks away and runs toward us. I bring Bolt to a stop and swing her down just as he makes it to us.

"Did you say yes?" he calls as he barrels into her.

She catches and swings him up into her arms.

"I did." She shows him the ring on her finger.

"I helped pick it out," he proudly tells her.

"You did?" she asks as she looks over his shoulder to me.

"Yep. It was the prettiest one in the store. Just like you," he says as he plants a kiss on her cheek.

Catcalls and whistles start sounding, and we hear Walker yell, "Get your asses up here, and let's celebrate!"

Fifty-Two

DALLAS
One Month Later.

I LOOK OUT THE WINDOW OF THE BAKERY TO THE SMALL STANDING crowd that has gathered at the gazebo.

I only wanted our close friends and family here. Nothing fancy or expensive.

Momma is busy fussing over my hair and lacing flowers through the braid. I'm wearing the simple antique white cap-sleeved gown that she wore the day she married Daddy. It's retro-cool and Sonia's mom altered it to fit me perfectly and brought the hem up to hit just above my knee.

Sophie, Bells, and Charlotte are wearing cornflower blue sundresses. The boys and Beau are all in khakis and blue linen shirts.

The bell chimes above the door as it swings open.

"It's time," Daddy says as he peeks his head in.

I take a deep calming breath and nod.

The girls all hurry out ahead of us and take their places beside the men in the gazebo.

Daddy sticks his elbow out for me, and I place my arm in his.

"Ready to do this again, Daddy?" I ask.

"I never truly gave you away the last time, but now"—he looks down at me—"I'm ready to give you to a man who deserves you. You should have the best life, baby girl, and I know in my heart Myer will make sure you have it."

He leads me out and across the street. Everyone I love is there. Momma, Doreen, Ria, and Beverly are already sobbing.

I try not to look at them because I don't want to start crying yet.

We make it to the steps of the gazebo and there they are—my boys. Beau is standing at Myer's side with his hand in his. He breaks away and runs to me.

"You look so pretty, Mommy."

"Thank you, baby," I whisper.

He takes my free hand, and Daddy walks us both to Myer.

Reverend Burr looks down for a moment, and then he begins.

"The Bible says in Deuteronomy 30:3: 'God, your God, will restore everything you lost; he'll have compassion on you; he'll come back and pick up the pieces from all the places you were scattered.'"

He looks down at Beau and smiles.

"Never have I seen greater evidence of this promise than I do standing before me today. A family is being created, and everything lost restored except better and stronger as God is known to do."

Daddy kisses my cheek and places my hand in Myer's, and Beau scoots close to me and wraps an arm around my leg.

I say my vows for the second time in my life, but I know in my heart that this time those vows mean something different to both of us and neither of us will break them.

"I now introduce to you, Mr. and Mrs. Myer Wilson."

"And me!" Beau calls.

"And their son, Beau," he corrects.

Myer lifts Beau in his arms and takes my hand and walks us out to greet our loved ones. It was a perfect ceremony. In the ideal place in the center of our hometown and now we will celebrate with fried chicken at Momma's house and then dancing and drinks with our friends at Butch's Tavern.

A truly authentic rustic chic wedding.

Epilogue

DALLAS
October

It's Beau's seventh birthday, and we're having a big party this weekend for his friends and classmates, but Myer and I decided to have a small private family celebration tonight and give him our gift. The puppy has been hidden at Myer's parents' house for the last week. I can't wait to see Beau's face when he lays eyes on the Lab pup. I wanted a smaller dog, like Miss Elaine's Lou-Lou, but Myer insisted that a boy needs a big dog, not a tiny, prissy furball. I look forward to the day I have a little girl, so I can veto his macho tastes for daintier choices.

I stop by my attorney's office on the way home from the bakery. I stare at the papers in disbelief. I've waited so long and fought so hard for this day, and the timing couldn't be more perfect.

I decide to surprise both my boys.

Momma's picking Beau up from school and dropping him off for me. I prepare his favorite meal of chicken fingers and mac 'n' cheese and bake a German chocolate birthday cake for dessert. Myer ran by his parents' to pick up the puppy earlier, and it's currently sleeping in our closet.

"You ready for the big surprise?" he asks as he wraps his arms around my waist and plants a kiss on my neck while I stir the cheese into the noodles.

"Yes. He's going to be so excited. It's been hard, keeping it from him." We get the table set and blow up a few balloons. Just as I get the candles on his cake, the front door swings open, and Beau flies into the kitchen. I swear the boy has one speed, and it's turbo.

"Mommy, guess what! Mrs. Martin bought us all Popsicles for recess because it's my birthday. The whole entire class!" he bellows as he drops his book bag by the door and kicks his shoes off.

"Wow, that was nice of her," I say as I bend to give him a kiss.

"Are you hungry?" Myer asks.

"Yep. Nana wouldn't let me have a snack. She said it would ruin my birthday supper," he informs us as he hops up into a chair.

We eat while Beau regales us with all the news from his day at school. His teacher always makes the kids feel extra special on their big day. After we finish and clear the table, I light the candles, and Myer carries the cake to the table and places it in front of Beau while we sing "Happy Birthday."

"Blow out your candles, baby, and don't forget to make a wish," I remind him.

He closes his eyes tight, takes a moment to make a silent wish, and then blows them out in one big huff. I cut the cake, and we each eat our slice. Beau is doing well. I know he's trembling with anticipation, waiting for his birthday present, but he doesn't rush us.

"Okay, little man, go have a seat on the couch," Myer instructs as I put away the remainder of the cake.

Beau runs to the couch, and Myer goes to our room to get the box. I placed the puppy with a blanket in a large cardboard box I wrapped in paper. It has a lid, and Myer places a huge red bow on top just before he walks it in and sets it on the floor in front of the couch. The puppy must still be sleeping because he doesn't make a peep. I join them.

"Happy birthday, baby. Go ahead and open it." I give him permission, and he jumps down and tears into the box.

He squeals in delight when he catches sight of the dark brown bundle. The puppy stirs as Beau reaches in and picks him up. Once he is fully awake, he starts squirming and licking Beau's cake-smeared face with vigor, and Beau can barely hold on to him as he giggles.

"What's his name?" Beau asks as he sits down with the pup in his lap.

"He doesn't have one yet. He's your dog. You get to name him," Myer answers.

He thinks for a minute, and then his face lights up.

"Cowboy. His name is Cowboy!" he exclaims.

The puppy starts yapping.

"I think he likes that," Myer agrees with the choice.

I walk over to my purse and pull out the envelope, and I stand in front of them both.

"I have something else for you," I announce, and Myer gives me a quizzical look.

"Oh boy! Another surprise?" Beau says.

I slide the paperwork out of the envelope and hand it to Myer. He briefly looks it over before his eyes come back to mine, watery.

"What is it?" Beau asks as he scoots closer to Myer to look at the papers.

"It's adoption papers, buddy," Myer chokes out as he wraps an arm around Beau's shoulders.

Beau brings his big brown eyes to me for an explanation.

"We're going to fill those out tonight. Then, in a couple weeks, we'll go before the judge down at the courthouse, and when he signs them, you'll officially be Myer's son," I tell him as I hold back tears.

He lets the news sink in, and he looks at Myer. "You'll be my daddy for real?"

"Yes, sir. I'll legally be your daddy," Myer confirms.

"And my name will change to yours and Mommy's name?" he asks.

"Yes, baby. I'm petitioning for the name change at the same time as the adoption," I inform them both.

"Mommy, it worked! My birthday wish came true!" he squeals in delight.

The puppy slides off his lap and onto the cushion as Beau leaps up into Myer's lap and wraps his arms around his neck.

"I knew God accidentally gave me the wrong daddy the first time. We just had to find you," Beau cries into Myer's throat.

I watch my husband hold our son through tears. Then, I unleash the last surprise.

"I have one more present, and this one is for both of you," I say.

They turn to me, and Myer's eyebrows rise in confusion.

I pull the test from the envelope and hand it to Myer. Beau looks down at his hand and wrinkles his forehead.

"Are you ready to give your last name to two?" I ask Myer as he stares at the stick.

"Are you serious?" he asks in amazement.

I nod and bite my lip.

"What is it?" Beau asks as he watches Myer's reaction.

"Mommy is making you a big brother for your birthday," Myer says as he squeezes Beau tight.

I join them on the couch, and Myer wraps us both in his arms.

"Are you happy?" I ask him.

"So damn happy," he answers.

"Yeah, so happy! It's the best birthday ever!" Beau pronounces, and Cowboy barks his agreement.

It sure is.

The End

Who says you can't teach an old dog new tricks?

He's too old for her.

She's innocent.

He's wild.

And her brother will kill them both.

Wicked Hearts

Poplar Falls, Book 3

April 2020

Preview of *Rustic Hearts*

Rustic HEARTS

Prologue

SOPHIE
Twelve Years Old

"WHY DO WE HAVE TO LEAVE NOW?" I ASK DROWSILY as Momma frantically throws my belongings into my pink suitcase at the edge of my bed.

"Because we need to be gone before your father gets home tomorrow. I already explained this to you."

"I still don't understand. What did he do that was so bad?"

"You're too young for all the details, Sophia. I will tell you one day, but for now, we have to get our things and get out of here if we're going to catch our flight to New York. You've always wanted to go to New York, right? That's why I chose it."

I have always wanted to go to New York City. Ever since I became obsessed with *Big City Girl*, which was a television program that came on Friday nights and followed the lives of a glamorous group of friends living in the Big Apple. They were all beautiful, wealthy, in college, and having the time of their lives. I wanted to be Sinclair Alcott one day. I didn't think that day would be today.

"When are we coming back? School starts in two weeks, and Blackberry's foal is due anytime now. I have to be back in time to help. She's my horse."

Momma stops her progress and finally looks at me. The manic excitement is draining from her face.

"I'm not sure when we will be back," she says a little more calmly. "You might be going to school in New York for a while."

What? I might want to visit New York one day, but this is home. The ranch, my horse, Daddy, and all my friends are here.

"I don't want to go to school there. I want to go to school here in Poplar Falls."

Her face falls at my declaration. "We can discuss this later. Here, get up and get your coat and shoes on. *Now*, young lady."

I begrudgingly do as I was told. I know my mother well enough to know that arguing with her when she is in this state is futile. I'll just have to call Daddy as soon as I'm able and get him to calm her down. He's the only one who has ever been able to talk her down, and he'll convince her to come back home.

"Stop sulking, Sophia," she says as she wraps her arm around me in the back of the taxi as we drive away from our farmhouse. "You're going to love this new adventure of ours. I promise."

I turn and look out the back windshield at the barn as we drive down the long driveway. I sure hope Blackberry holds on a little longer. I don't want her to wonder where I am when her baby is born. She'll think I abandoned her. I would never leave her or my daddy and my best friend, Dallas. They're my absolute favorite people. Technically, Blackberry is not a person, but she loves like one.

I do my best to hold back tears as the barn fades off into the distance.

Momma continues to try to convince me of the fun we're going to have.

"We will find an apartment in the city, close to Central Park. There are lots of animals in the park and horse-drawn carriages. You'll be able to see horses every day. I'll get a job and work during the day, we'll enroll you in a fabulous school, and in the evenings, I can audition for Broadway. It might take me a little while to get back into performance shape, but I will, and you can take ballet classes and voice lessons. It's going to be an amazing adventure. You'll see."

Excitement oozes from her pores as she squeezes me into her side.

There is no use in trying to reason with her when she gets like this, so I nod and play along for now.

"Sure, Momma, it'll be amazing."

I hope Daddy sees my note soon.

One

SOPHIE

"STALL THEM UNTIL I GET THERE. OFFER THEM COFFEE AND doughnuts or a margarita or ten. Whatever it takes to keep their asses in those seats," I instruct my assistant, Charlotte, as I frantically try to hail a cab.

The electricity to my building was cut while I was in the middle of washing my hair this morning. A construction worker on the building site at the corner had dug in an area that he wasn't supposed to and cut our main power line. I got out of the shower, tried to get myself dressed appropriately in the dark, and towel-dried my long blonde hair as best I could. Then, I threw it up in an unflattering top knot and ran out the door, only to find the elevator was in slow motion, running on the backup generator. This left me with the option of waiting a long while for an elevator packed full of frustrated occupants or to take the stairs down the ten flights to the lobby. I opted for the stairs—bad choice. Ten flights down on my sky-high Manolos was a dangerous undertaking, and it took forever, so now, I'm facing rush-hour traffic in Midtown Manhattan on an unusually warm September day, heading to meet with what will undoubtedly be some pretty put-out business associates when I finally make it in.

I arrive at my office off 36th Street and run as fast as I can to the conference room with Charlotte on my heels.

Charlotte and I have been friends since we were in middle school. She was the first person I met when Mom and I arrived in New York over twenty years ago. Why my mother placed me in a private Catholic school is beyond me—I had been raised Baptist—but I'm so glad she did. I would have been lost without Charlotte and her blonde pixie cut and no-nonsense attitude.

Right now, however, she is a tad frantic. Like a little fairy flitting around me.

"The gentleman's name is Marcus Stedman. He's the general manager of the Park Avenue store, and the lady's name is …"

"Gail Caldwell, the head buyer for all of the Maple and Park department stores. I know who she is." I snatch the folders she just dug from her briefcase and pass her my coat and bag as we hurry down the hall.

"They've had coffee and doughnuts, and I entertained them with stories from my SoulCycle class. Thank God you're here because I don't think they want to hear about last night's disaster of a date, and I'm running out of interesting material."

Dear Lord. If I'm able to save this deal, it will be a miracle.

I stop in the hallway leading to the conference room and take a moment to compose myself. "How do I look?"

"Like a wet puppy who ran all the way here from Chelsea."

"Perfect, just the look I was going for. How do I smell?"

Charlotte leans in and wrinkles her nose in disgust. "Like an old gym bag."

Awesome.

She reaches in her briefcase, grabs a bottle, and liberally spritzes me.

"Ugh, what was that?"

"Perfume. It'll help."

"Perfect. Now, I smell like a sweaty flower."

"There's nothing you can do about it. They aren't here to sniff you anyway. Go." She shoves me toward the door. "They're here to pitch to you, not the other way around."

I turn back to her and say in a small voice, "Tell me we deserve this."

"You deserve this, Sophie," she confirms.

"We," I correct her. "We deserve this."

She smiles a pleased smile. "We deserve this. Now, go get 'em."

I smooth the front of my dress and take a deep, calming breath before I open the door and walk in.

All eyes turn to me as I make my way to the head of the conference table and introduce myself. "Hello, Gail, Marcus. I'm Sophia Lancaster." I clear my throat and continue, "But you can call me Sophie. Please accept my sincere apology for keeping you waiting. There was an unavoidable hiccup at my building this morning that delayed me."

Marcus shifts to extend his hand to me. Annoyance clear in his expression.

Gail offers her hand next with a genuine smile. "It happens. I'm afraid we're going to have to jump right into business though. We have another meeting in an hour."

"Of course."

She taps on the laptop in front of her, and the screen of the television on the opposite wall illuminates with a PowerPoint presentation.

"As you know, Maple and Park is interested in a partnership. We would like for you to design a few exclusive pieces to be sold only in our stores and online through our website."

A small thrill shoots through me at the thought of my jewelry designs being sold in one of Park Avenue's trendiest department stores.

"When you say exclusive pieces, that means, we can't sell other designs to other partners or on our website, correct?"

She looks up and smiles warmly. I'm obviously new to all of this.

"No, you are only obligated to keep the pieces we approve exclusive to Maple and Park. You can continue to design and sell anything else privately or through any other retail outlets."

I give her an appreciative nod as Marcus takes over.

"We want new designs. Something no one else has seen or worn before. We've outlined what we're looking for to help you. Simple.

Elegant. We'll start small with a few pendants, rings, and bracelets. Test the market. If those do well, we can revisit our contract and extend to earrings and brooches. We want to launch the line before the holiday season, so that gives you a couple of weeks to get with our art department and get samples in."

"Okay, I can get some sketches together fairly quickly. Do you have projected sales? As of now, our newly purchased warehouse is being renovated and equipped to begin assembly, and I think we'll be up and running within the month. My staff is still minimal, but we're interviewing. Depending on the volume—"

He puts his hand in the air to halt my rambling. "We realize you're a start-up. We're buying the designs, and the customers will know and appreciate they are custom pieces. So, at first, we'll need a small amount for display and for purchase at our two locations. Online orders can be made to order."

Relief replaces the tension that was strumming through my body.

I started designing quirky jewelry pieces while I was a student at New York School of Design. I would sketch out each unique piece, then buy the materials, and make them by hand in my apartment at night. I sold a few of them at the Williamsburg open market in Brooklyn on weekends, and that led to me opening an online Etsy shop. It was a way to make easy money while finishing my degree. Sales were steady enough, and I was pleased to be creating something. Then, one day this past June, my world exploded when *the* Judy Winston wore one of my brooches to the Tony Awards. She won for Best Actress in a Musical and was photographed with her award, wearing my piece front and center on her gown. She later that night told an E! News interviewer that she had purchased it from my online site. The next day, orders started pouring in—hundreds and hundreds of orders. There was no way I could fulfill the volume from my living room. That was when Stanhope stepped in. Stanhope Marshall is one of the most successful businessmen in Manhattan, and he just so happens to be married to my mother, Vivian. He came to me with a proposition, and just like that, I had my first investor in Sophia Doreen Designs, LLC.

It's been a whirlwind ever since. Now, I have a sleek office in an uptown building owned by Stanhope; twelve full-time employees, including Charlotte; and a warehouse in the Fashion District that is being converted into a workshop as we speak. I'm about to close my first major deal to have my line in a real-life brick-and-mortar store. Exciting doesn't begin to describe this feeling.

After we hash out costs and crunch numbers, they stand to leave with a signed contract in hand.

"Thank you for your time, Sophie. I think this is going to be a profitable relationship for both our companies. I love your designs and think they will fit perfectly with the Maple and Park brand." Gail squeezes my hand before they enter the elevator.

Marcus gives me a quick wink as the doors slide shut, and I release the breath I've been holding since I walked into the meeting.

Charlotte comes bounding out from behind her desk and skids to a halt in front of me. "Well?" Her eyes, full of nervous anticipation, expectantly stare into mine.

"We did it," I whisper through a huge grin.

"Oh my," she squeals as we both start jumping up and down. "I knew you would nail it. In spite of the wet doughnut on your head and your sweaty pits."

"Thanks. We need to celebrate."

"Okay, I'll call and get us a table at Marea for seven p.m. Just us?"

"And my parents. I'm going to call Stanhope now and tell him the good news. I know Mom will want to rush right over."

Other Books

Cross My Heart Duet

Both of Me

Both of Us

Poplar Falls

Rustic Hearts

Stone Hearts

First, I want to thank every single reader, blogger, and fellow author who took a chance on this series. Each message, text, e-mail, share, giveaway, and review has meant the world to me. Poplar Falls and the people that inhabit it, although fictional, have earned a place in my heart. I wish I could pack a bag and join them for a summer.

To my friends and family who not only encouraged me to chase my dream, but also supported me every step of the way—I love you all with my whole heart. Your enthusiasm and excitement with each release brings me so much joy. I love peppering the books with our memories and history.

To the gracious and amusing members of the Stockman Message Board who patiently answered a million questions about cattle ranching the past few months—I thank you from the bottom of my heart. Seriously, I know enough about branding and calving seasons now to purchase and run my own ranch.

Amanda White and Gloria Green, as always, thank you for your encouragement and honest feedback. You're both priceless.

Autumn Gantz, you are an amazing and hard-working publicist, but most of all, you are a fabulous friend. I cannot imagine being on this journey without you.

Jovana Shirley, you are invaluable. Thank you for making me look good. If the world saw the hot-mess first draft of these books, they would know how true that statement is. You are an angel, and commas are still the devil.

Judy Zweifel, Stacey Blake, Sommer Stein, and Michaela Mangum, thank you for your contributions to this book. You are all incredible at what you do, and I'm truly blessed to have you all be a part of my team.

Kyla Linde and Corinne Michaels, thank you, thank you, thank you for taking my pitiful attempts and helping me transform them into articulate and interest-inspiring blurbs. I would rather write an entire novel than a blurb. Fact.

Last but not least, David Miller, you are the unicorn husband. Never a complaint when you have to pick dinner up night after night or answer your own questions or remind me to eat and bathe when I am engrossed in yet another make-believe world. I love you.

About the Author

Amber Kelly is a romance author that calls North Carolina home. She has been a avid reader from a young age and you could always find her with her nose in a book completely enthralled in an adventure. With the support of her husband and family, in 2018, she decided to finally give a voice to the stories in her head and her debut novel, Both of Me was born. You can connect with Amber on Facebook at facebook.com/AuthorAmberKelly, on IG @authoramberkelly, on twitter @AuthorAmberKel1 or via her website www.authoramberkelly.com.

Made in the USA
Middletown, DE
15 July 2022